Another WHOLE NOTHER STORY

Dr. Cuthbert Soup

illustrations by

Jeffrey Stewart Timmins

BLOOMSBURY

NEW YORK BERLIN LONDON SYDNEY

First published in the United States of America in December 2010
by Bloomsbury Books for Young Readers
www.bloomsburykids.com

For information about permission to reproduce selections from this book, write to
Permissions, Bloomsbury BFYR, 175 Fifth Avenue, New York, New York 10010

Library of Congress Cataloging-in-Publication Data
Soup, Cuthbert.
Another whole nother story / Dr. Cuthbert Soup ; [illustrations by
Jeffrey Stewart Timmins]. — 1st U.S. ed.
p.   cm.
Sequel to: A whole nother story.
Summary: Ethan Cheeseman takes his children, ages eight, twelve, and
fourteen, and Captain Jibby and crew, to the year 1668 to end an ancient family
curse and save the children's mother, but damage to the time machine and the
arrival of Mr. 5 complicate their return.
ISBN 978-1-59990-436-8
[1. Time travel—Fiction.   2. Inventions—Fiction.   3. Family life—
Fiction.   4. North America—History—Colonial period, ca. 1600–1775—
Fiction.   5. Denmark—History—17th century—Fiction.   6. Humorous
stories.]   I. Timmins, Jeffrey Stewart, ill.   II. Title.
PZ7.S7249Ano 2010   [Fic]—dc22   2010025634

Book design by Donna Mark
Typeset by Westchester Book Composition
Printed in the U.S.A. by Quad/Graphics, Fairfield, Pennsylvania
2 4 6 8 10 9 7 5 3 1

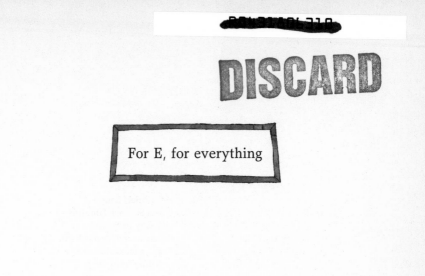

For E, for everything

THIS BOOK IS PART OF A COMPLETE BREAKFAST
AND STAYS CRUNCHY EVEN IN MILK.*

* Warning: Do not immerse in milk.

"You can lead a horse to water,
but you can't make him participate
in synchronized diving."

DR. CUTHBERT SOUP, ADVISOR TO THE ILL-ADVISED

A LITTLE ADVICE

Greetings, everyone. I'm Dr. Cuthbert Soup with a startling announcement. Time travel is now a reality. I repeat: I'm Dr. Cuthbert Soup, founder, president, and vice president of the National Center for Unsolicited Advice.

The question I'm asked most frequently—besides "Who are you and what are you doing here?"— is "Why on earth would you, the multimillionaire owner of a huge corporation, take time out from your busy schedule to write a book?"

Well, for one thing I have always enjoyed telling stories. Living in Vienna at the height of the Great Sausage Famine, my family had very little money for books. But every Friday night we would all sit around the fire and tell stories, which was very exciting because we did not have a fireplace. So, as you might imagine, most of the stories were about how to escape from a burning building.

But my real inspiration for writing a book came to me not long ago while strolling through my friendly neighborhood bookstore, where I spied, high upon one of the many shelves, a very conspicuous empty slot. Needless to say, I was appalled. It occurred to me rather immediately that someone needed to write something in order to fill that awful black hole of booklessness right between *War and Peace* and *Wig Making for Dummies.*

I now had the motivation to write a book but still lacked a good story to tell. That would change sooner than I expected. I returned home to my luxurious mansion and opened my equally luxurious mailbox (it has its own bowling alley) to find a postcard from my good friend and former classmate from Southwestern North Dakota State University, Ethan Cheeseman.

The news, as it turns out, was not good. I was shocked to learn that Ethan's lovely wife, Olivia, had been poisoned by evil villains (for my money, the worst kind of villains), forcing Ethan and his three smart, witty, attractive, polite, and relatively odor-free children to go on the run. In case something happened to Ethan or the children, he wanted to make sure that his story was told—and he had chosen me to be the one to tell it.

I started receiving postcards on a regular basis, sometimes as many as four or five per week, each one relaying Ethan's desperate attempt to stay one step ahead of an ever-growing number of pursuers while he worked to perfect his greatest invention: a time machine, which he hoped could be used to save the life of the woman he and his children loved so dearly.

I began the task of turning these postcards into the story of Ethan's desperate plight, though my progress was slow. You see, unlike most writers today, I do not use a computer. I write the old-fashioned way: on the walls of caves. (Unlike computers, they rarely crash.) With a blend of seven different berries smooshed together, the end result is perhaps the only book you will ever read that is made with ten percent real fruit juice. But please don't eat it. Instead, I strongly advise you to read it because, in addition to being rich in vitamins A and C, it is also chock-full of excitement, intrigue, adventure, misadventure, pirates, castles, consonants, vowels (including the controversial "sometimes Y" vowel), and scads of unsolicited advice.

And, if all that weren't enough, it also includes documentation of mankind's first attempt to travel through time, as Ethan and his children embark upon this historic journey in an effort to save the life of Olivia, their beloved wife and mother, and to break the curse of the White Gold Chalice.

CHAPTER 1

Everyone knows that time flies when you're having fun. What many don't realize is that time also flies when you're having: breakfast, lunch, a bad hair day, people over for dinner, difficulty with math, your cake and eating it too, second thoughts, a nervous breakdown, trouble breathing, a baby, or a cow.

In other words, no matter what you may be having at any given moment, time is always flying. Thus, in order to travel into the past, one must fly even faster than time itself. This can make for a very bumpy and a very long ride.

"Dad, are we there yet?" groaned Gerard, his skinny, eight-year-old legs fidgeting in perfect rhythm with his reckless gum chewing. The gum was Gerard's last piece and, since he and his family were racing along the Time Arc to a year long before bubble gum had been invented, he knew the flavorless wad of pink goo might have to last him quite a long time.

"I told you to go to the bathroom before we left the twenty-first century," said Gerard's father, who was perhaps the greatest scientist and inventor of all time. Mr. Cheeseman kept his eyes on the control panel, expertly working the many knobs and dials, fighting to keep the time machine, known simply as the LVR, on course for the year 1668. I should mention, by the way, that LVR stands for Luminal Velocity Regulator. I suppose it could also stand for Large Venezuelan Rats, but in this case it does not.

"Sorry, Gerard, you'll have to wait a few minutes yet," Mr. Cheeseman continued.

In the rush to stay one step ahead of the many government agents, international superspies, and corporate villains all trying to get their hands on the LVR, he did not have time to hook up the plumbing system on his mirrored, egg-shaped, disco ball–like time machine before he and his three children—along with Captain Jibby and his band of misfit circus performers—piled in, buckled up, and slipped into the past.

"But I really have to go," Gerard insisted.

"We should be there soon," assured Mr. Cheeseman. "Unless we run into some unexpected disturbulence."

Disturbulence is the term used to describe any small fissures or static along the Time Arc that can result in a time traveler being bounced off course and ending up in the wrong time, the wrong place, or, in the most unfortunate of cases, several times and places at once, a phenomenon known in the scientific community as Some Times, which is not at all where Mr. Cheeseman and his passengers wanted to end up.

He wiped a bead of sweat from his forehead, then turned to Jough, his fourteen-year-old son and copilot, sitting at the controls next to him. "It's awfully hot in here. What's the reading on that refractometer, Jough?"

"Forty-two hundred and climbing," said Jough, his voice alternating between man and boy.

"Are you sure?"

"I'm sure. Why?"

"The refractor shields . . . they're only good to forty-five hundred." Mr. Cheeseman looked worried, and this worried Jough. It didn't help matters that Pinky, the family's hairless fox terrier, was sitting at Mr. Cheeseman's feet, growling steadily. You see, Pinky had psychic abilities and almost never growled unless she sensed danger.

"So what happens if it hits forty-five hundred?" Jough asked, though he was pretty sure he knew the answer. After all, there was a reason the LVR had no windows. The light along the Time Arc was so intense and produced such extreme heat that, if the refractor shields failed to hold, the LVR and everyone in it would be instantly reduced to cinders.

"It'll be okay," said Mr. Cheeseman, not entirely convinced of this but not wanting to alarm the children.

"Forty-three hundred," announced Jough from the side of his mouth, his eyes refusing to leave the refractometer as the needle continued to inch into the red zone. Pinky's growling grew louder.

"Dad?" said Maggie, Mr. Cheeseman's twelve-year-old

daughter and the spitting image of his auburn-haired wife, Olivia. "What's going on? Why is Pinky growling?"

"It's nothing. Everything's fine." Mr. Cheeseman threw the words quickly over his shoulder, then returned his focus to the control panel. "We'll be there soon. Why don't you make the announcement?"

A veritable genius, Maggie was smart enough to realize that her father was only attempting to take her mind off the danger growing with every upward tick of that temperature gauge. Still, she did as he wished. Without hesitation, she unbuckled her seat belt, stood up, and turned to face her audience. In addition to her little brother, there were the six members of Captain Jibby's Traveling Circus Sideshow, all sitting in the cramped confines of the LVR's interior, constructed mainly of parts from a used motor home.

"Ladies and gentlemen, may I have your attention please," began Maggie. "We are approaching the year 1668. At this time, make sure your seat belts are securely fastened and your seat backs have been returned to their full upright and locked position. In the unlikely event of a water landing, your seat cushion may be used as a flotation device."

"My seat doesn't have a cushion," said Gerard. He demonstrated by slapping the hard wooden surface of the chair with his open palm.

"Then you'll have to swim. And please put your seat back forward."

"But I don't get it," said Gerard. "Do you want me to put my seat back or forward?"

Maggie stepped behind Gerard's chair and shoved it forward, putting an immediate end to any confusion.

"Forty-four fifty," said Jough. Sweat now poured from beneath the thick black curls that adorned his head and gathered among the wiry fibers of his patchy teenage mustache.

There was no question that the interior of the LVR was heating up. Jough removed his navy blue baseball cap, stitched with a white letter P, and ran his forearm across his sweaty brow.

Suddenly, a very large and very loud bump rocked the LVR. Maggie quickly returned to her seat and buckled up. "Forty-four seventy-five," said Jough.

"Come on," said Mr. Cheeseman, begging the machine to hold together. "Come on!"

Gerard looked up at his big sister sitting next to him. "Is it okay? Are we going to die?" Maggie said nothing, unwilling to make a promise she might not be able to keep. Instead, she reached out and took Gerard's hand in hers and squeezed tightly. If this was meant to reassure Gerard, it did not.

At that moment, he realized just how much he missed Steve, his beloved sock puppet, knitted with love by his late mother just days before she was killed by corporate thugs. For two years Steve had been Gerard's constant sidekick, providing him with companionship, words of encouragement, and a wicked tan line. But now, like Gerard's beloved mother, Steve the sock puppet was gone.

"Twenty seconds to landing," said Mr. Cheeseman.

"Four-four eighty-five," said Jough, biting his lip.

"It's going to be close," said Mr. Cheeseman.

There was another bump, this one louder and stronger than the last. Maggie looked at the ceiling, which vibrated mightily. It appeared as though it could be torn away at any second, exposing them all to the deadly light just on the other side of the four-inch-thick protective shell of the LVR.

"Forty-four ninety!" Jough struggled to remain calm but he could feel his sense of reason slipping away.

"Fifteen seconds!" Mr. Cheeseman had to shout to be heard over the deafening rattle as the LVR fought to remain joined at the seams. He began counting down the seconds. And as he counted down, Jough counted up.

"Ten! Nine! Eight!"

"Forty-four ninety-five!"

"Seven! Six!"

"Forty-four ninety-seven!"

"Five! Four!"

"Forty-four ninety-nine!"

"Three! Two!"

"Forty-five hund—"

Before Jough could push the words from his mouth, a chunk of ceiling the size of a beach towel peeled away with the sickening sound of rent metal. Blinding light poured into the LVR. Gerard screamed. Maggie screamed. Pinky yowled. The chunk peeled back farther yet until it tore off completely from the rest of the LVR, and more light poured in, followed by more screams and a deafening crash.

And then, just like that, there was nothing.

ADVICE FOR EXPLORERS EVERYWHERE

When one thinks of great explorers, certain names come to mind right away: Cortés, Ponce de León (literally: Leon's Pants), and Magellan, to list but a few. Perhaps the most famous explorer of all time is Christopher Columbus, who discovered America. And he found it right where it had been sitting all those years.

Of course some people claim that Leif Eriksson discovered North America in the year 1000. Well, if he did, he forgot to tell anyone, which is why today all the cities, rivers, universities, and savings and loans are named after Columbus. Nothing is named after Leif Eriksson—not even leaves, which are named after someone else.

Advice to explorers everywhere: if you would like to receive due credit for your discoveries, keep a detailed account of your journeys as Columbus did. On September 28, 1492, after four weeks at sea, he writes: "Dear diary . . . I mean journal. Yes, dear journal. That's what I meant to say. Whew. Anyway, we have yet to discover America, and the crew has become increasingly rebellious. I have decided to turn back if we have not spotted it by Columbus Day. Will write again later if not killed by crew. P.S. Last night's buffet was fabulous, the ice sculptures magnificent."

Columbus's crew was understandably spooked because in those days it was believed that the Earth was flat, and if you sailed too far, you could fall off the edge. Today we know that the Earth is not flat but rather quite bumpy, particularly if you are driving in the downtown area. The point is that whether you are sailing through uncharted waters or across the mysterious Time Arc, there will always be unforeseen dangers and I advise you to prepare yourself for the absolute worst.

CHAPTER 2

Many who have had near-death experiences have reported leaving their bodies and drifting toward a warm, bright light. These people assume they are on their way to heaven, never stopping to consider that a warm, bright light might also be fire.

The warm, bright light that Maggie saw when she opened her eyes was neither the welcoming gleam of paradise nor the flaming bonfire of the netherworld. It was, quite simply, sunshine. It punched its way through a canopy of trees above, filtered through a thin screen of smoke, streamed in through the massive gash in the LVR's ceiling, and came to rest gently upon her furrowed brow.

"Maggie? Maggie, are you okay?"

Maggie looked around to see concerned faces peering back at her. "I'm fine," she whispered. "At least, I think I am."

"You must have passed out from the heat," said Mr. Cheeseman as Pinky trotted over and gave her hand an affectionate lick. When Maggie lifted her head to look down at the dog, a dull pain raced across the back of her neck.

"Ahhh," she said, pressing her hand to the afflicted area.

"Don't move," said Mr. Cheeseman. "Let's take a look at that." He reached into his pocket and removed a black plastic box no larger than a deck of cards. There were several knobs on the box and two long wires extending outward, each with a small suction cup at the end. He flipped on the power switch, which sent a wave of lime-green light flickering across the tiny screen. He then placed one of the suction cups on his right temple and the other on the back of Maggie's neck.

"Is that where it hurts?" he asked.

"A little to the left," said Maggie. Mr. Cheeseman adjusted the suction cup accordingly, then winced and grabbed the back of his own neck.

"You're right. That does hurt."

"What in the name of Neptune's whiskers is that thing?" asked Captain Jibby through his bushy red beard while his crew looked on, always amazed by Mr. Cheeseman's inventions.

"It's a little device I like to call the Empathizer," said Mr. Cheeseman, peeling the suction cups from his temple and from Maggie's neck. "I developed it as a means of helping doctors diagnose their patients. Instead of a patient having to describe a pain or sensation, a doctor can simply hook up the Empathizer and feel exactly what the patient feels."

"It's a great invention," said Jough. "Unless you're trying

to get out of taking a math test by pretending to have a stomachache."

"Or if you say you have a sore throat just so you can eat more ice cream," said Gerard.

"Well, I'm no doctor," said Mr. Cheeseman to Maggie. "But I'd say you've got a mild case of whiplash. Be careful not to move your head any more than you have to."

Just then Jibby let out a crisp, hacking cough. By way of height, he was closest to the hazy cloud that hung overhead.

"I don't like the looks of that smoke," said Mr. Cheeseman. "We'd better get out of here and assess the situation." But when he unlocked the pod door and turned the handle, it would not open. He put his shoulder into it but still the door would not budge.

"If you don't mind," said Jibby. This was his way of suggesting that he might have better luck.

"Be my guest," said Mr. Cheeseman, stepping aside for the much larger man. Captain Jibby looked at the door, clenched his teeth, and worked his face into a scowl so fierce you would think the door had insulted his mother— which, for the record, it had not.

With a two-step approach, he thrust his shoulder against the hatch with far more force than Mr. Cheeseman had but with an equal degree of futility. The only thing that moved was Jibby's face, which transformed from angry scowl to painful scowl. "It's stuck," he said. Never in the history of humankind had the obvious been so clearly stated.

Gerard smacked his gum and calmly looked overhead.

"Well, good thing there's a hole in the ceiling," he said. Mr. Cheeseman knew Gerard had a very good point. That terrible unintended opening, the one that nearly resulted in their untimely deaths, now seemed to be their only means of escape.

"You're right, Gerard," said Mr. Cheeseman.

"I know," said Gerard, matter-of-factly and without the slightest trace of arrogance.

"I'll go first," said Mr. Cheeseman, "to make sure it's safe out there. When I give the word, the rest of you may follow."

"Aye, aye," said Captain Jibby, with a quick salute of his right hand. (Or perhaps I should say the Swiss Army knife that stood in place of his hand ever since it was bitten off years ago by one of his circus tigers.)

Mr. Cheeseman climbed onto the chair that Maggie had been sitting on, his head disappearing into the wafting smoke. "Be careful, Dad," said Jough.

"Don't worry, Jough. I will." With a quick hoist, the children watched as Mr. Cheeseman ascended into the mist. When he swung his legs onto the roof of the LVR and stood up, it became apparent to him why the door would not open. The LVR had come to rest next to a very large sycamore, the tree's sturdy trunk rising up precisely where the LVR's door was meant to open. *A design flaw*, was Mr. Cheeseman's first thought. The door should have been made to open inward.

His second thought was, *Where the heck are we?* For in every direction, all he could see were trees. Well, that's not entirely true. He could also see plants, shrubs, grass, weeds, dirt, flowers, and a young chipmunk named Phillip. In other words, a forest. And on that forest floor, a good ten feet away, was the LVR's smoldering ceiling panel, just lying there like the lid of a sardine can that had been eagerly and violently torn away by someone who very much loved sardines.

A quick glance at the LVR's exterior gave rise to more concern. The source of the smoke was the LVR itself. Its outer shell had partially melted on one side, the crystals having dissolved and re-hardened into one smoldering mass. It should go without saying that this was not good. Ethan's plan had been a simple one. He and his children would travel back to 1668, stopping just long enough to drop off Jibby and his crew so that they might return the White Gold Chalice to its rightful owner, thus putting an end to the curse that had plagued the family bloodline for centuries. Ethan would then fire up the LVR and reverse course, heading back to the time just before Mrs. Cheeseman was murdered by the corporate villain known as Mr. 5, and save the day.

As a man of science, Mr. Cheeseman took many laws into account when formulating his plan. He did not, however, take into account Murphy's Law, which states that anything that can go wrong will go wrong. And, true to form, everything had gone wrong.

He drew in a deep breath, as if he might need additional oxygen for the lie he was about to tell. "Okay," he shouted down to the others. "Everything looks good here."

"All right then," said Jibby, assuming the role of second in command, which Jough did not necessarily appreciate. Though he was a teenager, grown-ups still insisted on treating him like a child most of the time. "Let's go now. Women and children first."

Pinky let out a yip and leaped into Gerard's arms. "What about dogs?" Gerard asked.

"And dogs," Jibby agreed.

Though Pinky had no hair and was, as a result, quite pink in color, I should point out that this is not how she came by her name. You see, long before Mr. Cheeseman and his children were forced to go on the run to protect the LVR from corporate villains, government agents, and international superspies, they lived a perfectly normal existence, complete with friends and neighbors. One day, one of those neighbors had puppies. Actually, it was their dog that had the puppies. For the neighbors themselves to have puppies would really be a newsworthy event.

There were five puppies in the litter, and the children chose the one they deemed to be the cutest and, coincidentally, the smallest of the bunch. If the puppies were fingers, that puppy would certainly have been the pinky and that's how Pinky got her name. If the children had not found her so adorable, I might very well be telling you the story of a short, plump dog named Thumb.

Jibby took Pinky from Gerard and passed her up to Mr. Cheeseman, who set her on the ground. Jibby then turned to Gerard and said, "Ready?"

Gerard nodded and Jibby took him beneath the arms

and hefted him up through the opening, where his father took him and lowered him to the ground next to Pinky. Maggie struggled out next, refusing any help from Captain Jibby or anyone else, despite the tightness in her neck. Then, one by one, the rest of the passengers emerged until they had all gathered around the egg-shaped disco ball known as the Large Venezuelan Rat. Sorry. Luminal Velocity Regulator.

Jibby and his crew, exhausted from the ordeal, took a seat on a fallen log covered with moss and spongy wild mushrooms. His crew consisted of: Three-Eyed Jake, Jibby's best friend and right-hand man; Sammy, a strong man with both the might of two and a half men and a back injury; Aristotle, a psychic with short-term memory loss; Dizzy, a tightrope walker who suffers from an inner-ear imbalance; and Juanita, Jibby's lovely wife, with a soft smile and coffee-colored eyes.

"Wow," said Gerard, though he had seen plenty of forests before. "Where are we?"

"Well, just before we lost power, the chronometer read October 2, 1668," said Mr. Cheeseman.

"Actually," said Gerard, "my question was *where* are we. Not *when* are we."

"The last information I have is that we're somewhere near the eastern seaboard of North America," said Mr. Cheeseman.

The rest of the group just stood there, staring at the damaged time machine, afraid to say what they were thinking, hesitant to think the very worst. Finally, Gerard—who could always be relied upon to say what everyone else wanted to say but would never think of doing out of sheer politeness—spoke up. "So does this mean we're stuck in this time forever?"

"Don't be ridiculous," said Jough. "Of course we're not stuck here forever. Are we, Dad?"

"Relax, everyone," said Mr. Cheeseman in the most reassuring voice he could muster. "We're not stuck here forever. But I'm afraid we're definitely stuck here until I can make the necessary repairs to the LVR, which may take a while since I left all of my tools back at the house."

Captain Jibby cleared his throat and proudly displayed his Swiss Army hand. "At your service, sir."

"I appreciate that, Jibby," said Mr. Cheeseman. "But this is going to take more than a can opener and a hole punch. I don't suppose you have a blowtorch on that thing?"

Jibby looked at his knife-hand (or hand-knife, if you prefer). " 'Fraid not," he said.

"Where you gonna get a blowtorch in 1668, Dad?" asked Jough.

"I guess I'm going to make one," said Mr. Cheeseman without hesitation. "By borrowing parts from the LVR and fuel from its hydrogen thrusters. I'll still need some metals for welding. If we can find a blacksmith, we should be able to get some suitable materials for solder. Of course, in order to find a blacksmith we first need to find our way out of this forest."

"No problem there," said Jibby. He turned to Three-Eyed

Jake and slapped him affectionately on the shoulder. The slap came with such force that it disrupted Jake's eye patch and sent his glasses askew. "As a seafaring man and a first-class navigator, Three-Eyed Jake here can tell direction by the position of the stars in the night sky."

Long before they were circus performers, Jibby and his crew were pirates, reckless plunderers of the high seas. That all ended one day in 1668 when they found themselves in the thick of a powerful electrical storm that zapped them into the twenty-first century, which is where they happened upon the Cheesemans.

"Though I'm sure Jake is very good at navigating by starlight," said Jough, "that doesn't really do us a lot of good right now."

"I suppose you're right," Jibby agreed.

"That's okay," said Gerard, staring skyward. "I can tell direction by the position of the sun."

"Is that so?" Maggie challenged. "Then which way is west?"

Gerard studied the sun, then looked back into the trees. He licked his finger and raised it into the air. "Actually," he said, "I remember now that I can only tell which direction is up."

"Well, that's helpful. Why don't we all just go up then?" said Maggie.

"Actually, that's not a bad idea," said Mr. Cheeseman, which pleased Gerard to no end. "If someone could climb to the top of one of these trees, perhaps they might be able to spot some sign of civilization."

"I'll do it," Gerard quickly volunteered. "I'm an excellent tree climber."

"I know you are," said Mr. Cheeseman. "But these trees are a little out of your league." Ethan was right. Most of the trees were at least a hundred feet tall and some as much as a hundred and fifty. "I'm sorry, Gerard, but I think you're too small for this mission."

Gerard was convinced that being small was never a good idea.

After much discussion, it was decided that Dizzy would be the one to climb the tree. Once grounded by a severe case of vertigo, Dizzy was a climbing machine again, thanks to earmuffs invented by Mr. Cheeseman as a means of restoring inner-ear balance.

Dizzy rubbed his hands together and surveyed the area, looking for the tallest climbable tree. When he had settled on one, an enormous cottonwood, he took a running start across the lumpy ground and leaped into the air. Like an Olympic gymnast (or a spider monkey, your choice) Dizzy grabbed a branch with both hands and swung his feet up onto another, landing with precision and perfect balance.

A small round of applause rang out from all but Gerard as Dizzy acknowledged the praise with the exaggerated bow of a born showman. He then began the long climb to the top as the others watched.

"I hope he can get us out of here," said Jough.

Mr. Cheeseman agreed with a nod. "Still, even if he is able to see something in the distance, it would be almost impossible to find our way out of these woods without a compass," he said, thinking of the one on the LVR's control panel. "Jibby? I'll take you up on that offer for tools now if you don't mind."

Jibby twisted the Swiss Army knife in a counter-clockwise direction until it was free of its mount, then tossed it to Ethan. "The corkscrew is a little bent," he said. "One too many bottles of rum, I suspect."

"Screwdriver should do the trick," Ethan said before climbing up the side of the LVR by wedging himself between it and the sycamore tree.

"Hey, *todos. Mire esto,*" said Juanita, standing at the front of the LVR. Though no one else but Jibby spoke a word of Spanish, it was obvious by her hand gestures that she was saying "Hey, everyone. Look at this." When the others joined her, they were treated to a rather odd sight. Draped across the nose of the LVR was a thin rope, and attached to that rope, by way of clothespins, were two tie-dyed T-shirts; a pair of bell-bottom jeans; a red, white, and blue bandanna; and a pair of long white tube socks.

"Those are some awfully strange-looking clothes," said Aristotle, his woolly eyebrows scrunched together.

"Aye," agreed Sammy. "But what are they doing there?"

"Based on pictures and movies I've seen, I'd say we picked them up on our way through the 1960s," said Jough.

Gerard reached up and pulled one of the socks from the clothesline. "What are you doing?" said Maggie. "You have no idea where that's been."

"I know it's been through the wash," said Gerard,

sliding the sock over his left hand. "Look, it's my new sock puppet." Gerard was a child of boundless imagination who could carry on a conversation with just about any inanimate object. He had once named the family toaster Ethyl and would routinely discuss with her exactly how he preferred his toast. (Lightish brown, for anyone interested.)

"That's not a sock puppet," said Maggie. "It's a sock. To be a puppet it at least has to have some sort of face."

Gerard reached into his mouth and stretched out the bubble gum until a small piece of it snapped off between his fingers, the remainder retreating back into his mouth. He quickly rolled the small bit into a marble-sized ball and ground it into the cotton sock until it stuck. He repeated the procedure twice more to create a second eye and a large pink nose. He then held up the sock as if to show off his handiwork. "There," he said. "Now he has a face."

Maggie sized up the sock with its two misshapen bright pink eyes and blobbish pink nose. "He looks like a lab rat."

"He's not a lab rat," snapped Gerard. "He's a sock puppet. And his name is . . . Roy. Rat-Face Roy."

Everyone greeted the newest member of the group with warm regards, making Rat-Face Roy feel right at home; everyone, that is, but Maggie, who folded her arms across her chest and angled her eyes upward.

"Hey, speaking of names," said Jough, "we should probably pick new ones for ourselves."

"Yes," said Gerard excitedly. "I'll go first."

The only upside to being on the run from dangerous criminals, government agents, and international superspies, all falling over themselves to get their hands on the LVR, was that each time over the past two years that Mr. Cheese-man and his family had moved to a new location, he insisted that the children completely change their identities. This was done for their own protection.

"Are you sure?" said Maggie. "I mean, do you really think it's necessary in this situation? After all, it's not like we moved across the country. I doubt anyone will be after us in 1668."

"I don't know," said Jough. "You can never be too careful. I vote that we change our names to be on the safe side."

"I second it," said Gerard.

"I third it," said Rat-Face Roy.

ADVICE BY ANY OTHER NAME

The great William Shakespeare said, "What's in a name?" He also said, "Call me Billy one more time and I will stab you with this ink quill."

Unlike Jough, Maggie, and Gerard, most people will go through life without ever changing their names. It is far more common to have other people change your name for you. Back in my college days at good old Southwestern North Dakota State University, most everyone was given a nickname: "Lefty" Dufrain because he was left-handed; "Stretch" Tolliver because he was six-foot-four; and "Rusty" Malone because he had a metal plate in his head, and not a very good one I might add.

My school chums called me Bertie, which displeased my parents to no end, as they had given much thought and consideration to naming me Cuthbert, which means "clever and famous" or, in the language of the Lakota tribe, "cannot dance with wolves because I am watching my friend's purse."

When it comes to naming children, people look to many places for inspiration, including actual places. These days, names like Dakota, Montana, India, and Chad are all the rage. Of course, some places make better names than others, which is why you will meet very few people named West Virginia, Kennebunkport, or Swaziland.

So when naming someone else, I advise you to take great care to bestow upon that person a moniker befitting his or her character, as I did with my two pet snails, Gooey and Squishy. And when it comes to naming yourself, I strongly advise that you be careful not to choose one that might alert evil villains to your true identity.

CHAPTER 3

Before Gerard could announce his new name to the world, Mr. Cheeseman emerged from the LVR with the freshly extracted dashboard compass in hand. "Got it," he said, the autumn leaves crunching beneath his feet as he dropped to the ground. He handed Jibby his Swiss Army knife and Jibby expertly screwed it back on. "How's Dizzy making out?"

Like a slow, smooth elevator, all eyes moved up the giant cottonwood looking for Dizzy, who could be heard scrambling from branch to branch about three-quarters of the way up the tree. "Well, he hasn't fallen yet," said Jibby, leaning back against the LVR. "That's a good sign."

"It sure is," said Rat-Face Roy.

Mr. Cheeseman gasped and recoiled at the first sight of Gerard's new friend. "Ahh! Get that thing away from me," he said, jumping behind his twelve-year-old daughter. This resulted in much chuckling from the group, especially from Juanita, who, for an otherwise quiet woman, had a very hearty laugh, accompanied by wheezing, snorting, and some very enthusiastic knee slapping.

"Relax, Dad," said Jough. "It's just Gerard's new sock puppet."

"Oh," said Ethan, panting heavily and feeling rather foolish. "For a second there I thought it was a rat." Though you would think, as a scientist, he would be used to working with rats, Mr. Cheeseman was deathly afraid of them and thus was happy to learn that the creature before him was merely an old sock with pink bubble-gum eyes.

"So what's your friend's name, Gerard?" asked Mr. Cheeseman, trying to regain both his composure and his dignity.

"His name's Rat-Face Roy. But my name's not Gerard anymore."

"It's not?" said Mr. Cheeseman. "Did I miss something?"

"We've decided it's time to change our names," said Jough.

"Oh?" Mr. Cheeseman seemed somewhat surprised, even though the whole name-changing thing had been his idea to begin with. "So you really think it's necessary this time, considering the circumstances?"

"That's what I said," Maggie agreed. "But I was outvoted."

"Democracy in action," said Mr. Cheeseman. "That's what made this country great."

"Well," said Jough, "if it really is 1668, America doesn't exist as a country yet."

"True enough, Jough."

"Actually, my new name is Chip. Chip Krypton," said Chip, who had previously gone by such names as Don Von St. John, Rory McJagger, Gary Indiana, and, of course, Jough Psmythe.

"Chip Krypton," Mr. Cheeseman repeated. "Has a nice ring to it."

"Thanks."

"How about you, Maggie?" asked Mr. Cheeseman. "What should I call you from this moment forward?"

"Well, I've narrowed it down to two but I think I'm going with Penelope Nickelton. You can call me Penny for short," said Penny, who in the past had answered to various aliases including Shari Chablis, Brooke Babblestone, Calliope Plume, and most recently Magenta-Jean Jurgenson, or Maggie for short.

Mr. Cheeseman thought for a moment, running the name over and over in his head. "Penny Nickelton. It's both complimentary and contradictory, depending on how you look at it."

"Exactly," said Penny with a satisfied smile.

Gerard had originally wanted to go first but now was happy that, in his opinion anyway, the best had been saved for last.

"My new name is the bestest of all," said Gerard proudly.

"It's the *best* of all," said Penny.

"But you haven't even heard it yet," said Gerard, who had given himself such names as Luke Tuna, Po Ming, Chance Showers, and just a couple of weeks ago, Gerard LaFontaine. "My new name is . . ."

Gerard paused, as he always did, for dramatic effect.

". . . Captain Fabulous!" Gerard extended his arms out in front of him and performed a quick fly-around, complete with Mach 5 sound effects, before coming in for a forceful landing as if he were about to face off against an army of renegade robots.

Captain Jibby laughed and shook his head in disbelief. Juanita snorted and slapped her knee. Three-Eyed Jake treated Gerard to an exaggerated salute. Gerard saluted right back, then took flight once more while declaring loudly, "Captain Fabulous and his trusty sidekick, Rat-Face Roy, will save the world from evil villains everywhere."

"Uh, I don't think so," said Penny.

"What do you mean?" asked the confused superhero when he had touched down again.

"What I mean is, there is absolutely no way on earth I am going to refer to you as Captain Fabulous."

"Why not?"

"Yeah, why not?" said Rat-Face Roy.

"For the same reason you wouldn't want to call me Queen of the Universe."

"Well," Mr. Cheeseman interjected. "Perhaps there's an easy solution to this. Maybe Captain Fabulous has an alter ego."

"What's an alter ego?" asked Gerard.

"It's a superhero's true but secret identity," said Chip. "You know, the way that Superman is really Clark Kent."

"Superman is really Clark Kent?"

"It's pretty obvious," said Penny. "To everyone but you and Lois Lane."

"Okay," Gerard conceded. "Captain Fabulous's alter ego will be . . . Teddy Roosevelt."

Penny scoffed so hard she almost lost her balance. Sometimes she wondered if her little brother did things with the express purpose of annoying her. "What? You can't name yourself after one of our most famous presidents. People will think you're crazy."

"Not people in 1668," said Teddy. "In 1668, he hasn't even been borned yet. Has he, Dad?"

"Uh, no," said Mr. Cheeseman. "He hasn't been . . . borned."

"Someday, when he is, people will think he was named after me," said Teddy.

"I think it's disrespectful and in poor taste," said Penny.

"I don't know," said Chip. "Somehow I think the other Teddy Roosevelt would have approved."

A shrill sound interrupted the controversy and all eyes shot to the sky, where Dizzy was standing near the very top of the cottonwood tree, waving his arm wildly and whistling loudly.

"Smoke!" yelled Dizzy. "I see smoke!"

Off in the distance, a good five miles away, a single pillar of thin gray smoke was angling into the breezy, pale blue October sky.

"There, that should do it," said Mr. Cheeseman as he, Jibby, and Sammy lowered the ceiling panel back onto the LVR. "As long as it doesn't rain, we should be okay." For the next thirty minutes or so, everyone was put to work gathering leaves and branches, which were used to completely cover the LVR until it looked like nothing more than a large, egg-shaped mound of brush.

Mr. Cheeseman hid the fear and uncertainty in his heart by decorating his face with a confident smile. Would he be able to repair a very modern machine with only spare parts from 1668? Had he doomed them all to spend the rest of their lives in a time without electricity, indoor plumbing, bubble gum, and doughnuts? Would his children once more be able to hug the mother they loved so dearly?

Manning the compass, the doubtful, smiling scientist led the group through the dense forest in the direction Dizzy had pointed. Along the way, he jotted down notes on their exact position so that once they were able to secure the materials they would need to fix the LVR they would actually have a way to find it again.

"Are you sure this is the past?" asked Teddy. "It doesn't look very old-timey around here. It just looks sharp and stickery."

Several hundred years later, the land beneath their feet would be home to a large housing development, two car dealerships, and an enormous supermall featuring no fewer than three coffee shops and a place that sells deep-fried cheese. But for now, the ground on which they traveled had perhaps never before been trodden upon by human beings and the going was not easy.

"Are we almost there?" Teddy whined. "I'm hungry. And my feet hurt."

"Well, maybe you should turn into Captain Fabulous," said Penny. "Then you could fly to the nearest town and get something to eat."

"Hey, could you bring me back a burger and fries, Captain Fabulous?" said Chip.

"And a strawberry shake, if you don't mind." Penny laughed.

"Stop making fun of me," Teddy insisted.

With a sigh, Mr. Cheeseman stopped and turned toward the squabble. "Chip. Penny. That's not helpful right now."

"Okay."

Sammy took a knee next to Teddy. "Would you like a ride?" he asked.

"What about your bad back, Sammy?" Penny asked the strong man.

"Ah, it's all right. How much could he weigh? He's not the size of tuppence." Sammy hoisted Teddy onto his shoulders and then, with a plaintive wail, stood up, causing Teddy's head to smack into a low-hanging branch.

"Ow!"

"Sorry," said Sammy, stepping aside. "How's that?"

"Well, my feet don't hurt anymore," said Teddy, rubbing his head.

"It's the blasted curse," said Jake, narrowing his one remaining eye.

"Or it could have been a simple accident," Mr. Cheeseman suggested.

Aristotle stepped forward, his eyes dancing wildly beneath the shadow of his bushy eyebrows. "There are no such things as accidents," he said in a dramatic, whispery voice. "Everything happens for a reason."

"I don't understand this curse business," said Chip. "I mean, how did it all get started anyway?"

Jibby stroked his beard and drew in a deep breath. "Well," he said. "If you really want to know . . ." He reached into a small leather pouch attached to his belt and retrieved a shiny trophy-shaped cup, its base ringed with strange symbols. "Are you familiar with Odin?" he asked.

"I went to kindergarten with a kid named Odin," said Teddy.

"That was Aidan," said Penny.

"Yes, but his last name was Odin."

"His name was Aidan Odin?" said Chip.

Jibby let out a sigh of mild frustration. "I'm talking about Odin, the god of Norse mythology. It is said that this chalice was passed directly from his hand to the great king of Denmark, Harald Wartooth."

"Wartooth. Now *that's* a funny name," said Rat-Face Roy.

Jibby ignored the sock puppet interruption and continued with the story. "The cup was to be used by Harald and his descendants after every battle to offer a toast to those who had died. It gave those brave warriors a proper sendoff to the Viking heaven known as Valhalla, ensuring their entry.

"For centuries, the cup was passed down through Harald's children and grandchildren and great-grandchildren and—"

"Okay, we get the idea," Penny interrupted.

"Yes, right. Until it ended up in the hands of Horwendill, the ruler of Jutland, a region of Denmark. But on the very night that Horwendill was murdered by his own brother, the cup went missing. Since that day, he who wrongfully possesses the White Gold Chalice is subject to the dreadful curse, brought upon, they say, by all those lost souls stranded at Valhalla's gate." Jibby returned the cup to its pouch and tied the drawstring tightly. "And that," he said, "is the story of the curse."

"Well, that should be easy to fix," said Teddy. "Why don't you just let someone steal it from you and then the curse will be on them? One time I left my lunch box on the bus and the next day it was gone. I think Robbie Bentler took it but I could never prove it so I didn't put a curse on him or anything. Anyway, you should try it with that white gold thingy. Just go into a store or a restaurant, set it down for a minute, and someone will take it."

"Won't work," said Jibby. "The curse is nontransferable, I'm afraid. Were someone to steal the chalice from me, they'd become every bit as cursed as we are, but we'd remain so as well. So we must take very good care of this cup until we're able to place it in the hands of its rightful owner, the Duke of Jutland, Horwendill's natural heir."

"There's still one thing I don't get," said Penny. "Why would you want to steal something that had a curse on it?"

"Didn't want to," said Jibby. "But another pirate, one I mistakenly thought to be my friend, had robbed us blind the week before and left us penniless and hungry. A man can lose all sense of reason when he's hungry. But I learned my lesson, I assure you. That's why I've vowed to put my thievin' days behind me."

Chip suddenly stopped, spun around, and scanned the woods behind them. "Did you hear that?"

"I didn't hear anything," said Penny.

"Something's out there." Chip was right, because whatever that something was moved again, rustling leaves and crackling twigs as it went.

"Nothing to worry about," said Jibby, his eyes darting from tree to tree. He casually popped open the blade of his Swiss Army hand. Though he had been a fierce pirate in his day and feared no man on earth, his sailor's superstition could easily get the better of him.

"Probably just a deer," said Penny.

"Or it could have been a bird," said Sammy, turning a slow, cautious circle.

"Or a squirrel," said Dizzy hopefully.

"Or a savage, red-eyed half man, half lizard, slithering

through the forest in search of human blood," said Aristotle with an ominous stare.

While Penny and Chip stood there, deciding whether or not to run ahead and catch up with their father, Jibby grabbed Juanita by the hand and took off, his face white as rice beneath his thick orange beard. Dizzy, Aristotle, Jake, and Sammy, with Teddy bouncing along atop his shoulders, took off running too, leaving Chip and Penny to deal with any red-eyed lizard men on their own.

"What happened to women and children first?" said Chip. Penny shrugged and she and Chip hurried along. They quickly caught up to the others, who had stopped dead in their tracks at the edge of the forest, where they gazed upon a lush meadow, resplendent with flowers of yellow, white, and rich vermillion. Teddy, who had an almost obsessive need to grade sights, tastes, textures, and smells on a ten-point scale, rated this particular meadow a solid nine-point-six.

"No. Nine-point-seven," he corrected himself.

Before anyone could comment further, something suddenly appeared above the tree line at the other end of the meadow. Something that caused eyes to widen and mouths to gape. It was a small, searing ball of white light arcing from one end of the sky to the other at an incredible speed. They watched in silence as the blob of light disappeared below the horizon.

"Wow," said Chip. "Did you see that, Dad?"

"I sure did," said Mr. Cheeseman.

"What do you think it was?" asked Teddy.

"Could have been a comet," said Mr. Cheeseman.

"Or a meteor," said Penny.

"Or a flying saucer," said Rat-Face Roy.

"Full of red-eyed lizard men," said Aristotle.

"Grrrr," said Pinky.

SOME UNIDENTIFIED FLYING ADVICE

Since the beginning of recorded history, people have been encountering strange objects in the sky. Thankfully, most of these sightings can be explained away as: satellites, weather balloons, comets, meteors, military aircraft, flying squirrels, flying fish, flying monkeys, or my uncle Gordie, who accidentally built his outhouse directly over a geyser.

Those reports that are not explained by natural phenomena or exploding outhouses are known as UFOs, which is the official abbreviation for Unidentified Flying Objects. I suppose it could also stand for Uncommonly Fat Orangutans, but in this case it does not.

It seems that these so-called UFOs are always reported as being silver in color and saucer shaped, which makes you think that if these aliens are so advanced, why is it they can only come up with one model of spaceship? You would assume such intelligent creatures could, once in a while, put out something in a nice powder blue and shaped like a footstool or maybe like France.

Still, none of these flying discs has ever been proven to be an alien spacecraft. There is absolutely no evidence that we have been visited by creatures from other planets, despite an exhaustive investigation by the governments of the United States, Canada, Russia, China, France, Great Britain, and Mars.

So if you do happen to look up one day and see a strange light racing across the sky, rest assured that it's probably nothing to worry about. If, however, your psychic fox terrier growls at that mysterious light, you had best run for the hills or, at the very least, hide behind some uncommonly fat orangutans.

CHAPTER 4

As Mr. Cheeseman and the others neared the other side of the meadow, Chip, Penny, Teddy, Pinky, and Rat-Face Roy lagged behind, enjoying a slow stroll through a quiet and beautiful place. "I still say it was a comet," said Chip, brushing his hand across the tall grass and flowers.

"I'll bet it was aliens coming to take over the world," said Teddy, those same flowers slapping him in the face as they sprang back from Chip's caress.

"If aliens took over the world in 1668, I think I would have learned about it in history class," said Penny.

"Maybe you were absent that day," said Rat-Face Roy, which prompted Penny to reach out and flick the makeshift sock puppet on the head.

Chip stopped abruptly in his tracks and cocked his ear toward the forest on their left. "There it is again," he whispered. "The noise. It came from over there." But to the naked eye there was nothing but trees and bushes, and to the naked ear there was only the soft breeze jostling the brittle autumn leaves.

Chip's eyes moved from the forest to the ground at his feet, searching for something. He stooped over and dug out a small gray rock, half embedded in the ground and about the size of a cherry tomato. He rolled it between his fingers a couple of times to remove the dirt.

Penny knew what he was thinking. "Are you sure about this?" she asked.

"Don't tell me you believe in red-eyed lizard men," said Chip.

"Stand back," said Teddy, arms akimbo. "If a red-eyed lizard man attacks, Captain Fabulous will protect us."

"Captain Fabulous will cry and wet his pants," said Penny. "Besides, Pinky hasn't growled in a while, so it's probably nothing to worry about." It was true that Pinky had not growled since first seeing that coruscating ball of light racing across the sky nearly half an hour before.

Chip adjusted his baseball cap and inhaled deeply, then went into his pitcher's windup, extending his arms above his head and kicking his left leg high into the air before stepping in and hurling the rock in the direction of the noise that only he had heard. The rock sped silently above the weeds and flowers and disappeared into the trees with a *ploomph*. For a moment, they half expected a giant two-legged lizard to come charging from the underbrush. But instead, nothing happened.

"Whatever it was, I must have scared it away," said Captain Fabulous with a triumphant pump of his fist.

"Yes," said Penny. "I'm sure that's what happened." So Chip, Penny, their superhero protector, and his pink-eyed sidekick ran ahead to catch up to the group, where Mr. Cheeseman and Jibby were busy talking strategy.

"I absolutely insist," said Ethan. "Once we get to a town or settlement, you, Juanita, and your men should make your way to the nearest seaport and get on your way to Denmark. There's not much you can do for us now. It's going to be up to me to get the LVR running again." Jibby nodded. He hated to leave his friends in such a desperate situation but he knew that returning the White Gold Chalice to the Duke of Jutland, thus putting an end to the horrible curse, was most important.

By and by, they happened upon a wide path that ran along the edge of the meadow and split off into the trees in two different directions. A discussion soon began as to which of those directions might be more likely to take them to civilization. There were footprints on the paths leading both ways. But which footprints were coming and which were going? And where were they going to or coming from? Three-Eyed Jake knelt down next to a deep footprint and scooped up a portion of the mud with his fingers. "Tracks. And they're still fresh," he said through a mouthful of dirt.

"For the love of Persephone, what are you doing?" asked Jibby.

"Why, testing the tracks for freshness," said Jake.

"That's not how you do it."

Jake spat out the mud and wiped his mouth with his sleeve. "Well, how am I supposed to know? I'm a seafarin' man, not a landlubber."

Mr. Cheeseman checked the compass reading and ran his hand across the back of his neck. "I'm not sure, but I think we should take the path on the left."

"Don't say left," cautioned Jibby. "Left is bad luck. It's port or starboard but never left. Besides, the path on the right looks more promising to me."

"Ow!" said Chip, adding nothing to the discussion of which way to go. Something, it seemed, had hit him on the side of the neck. He looked down to see a gray stone about the size of a cherry tomato resting at his feet. In fact, upon further inspection, it was the exact same rock he had thrown into the woods just moments ago. He picked it up and rolled it between his fingers. "I think someone threw a rock at me."

"Who would do such a thing?" said Penny.

"Maybe it was her," said Teddy.

Standing just a few feet away, at the edge of the forest, was a dark-skinned girl of about fifteen. From beneath a floppy brown hat her jet-black hair hung in two long braids, tied off with bright red and light blue beads. Her shirt and pants were made of sienna-colored buckskin. She was well armed with a bow and a quiver of arrows slung across her back and a ten-inch hunting knife on her beaded belt. Next to her moccasin-covered feet stood a small brown fox. Both the girl and the fox seemed entirely unfazed when Pinky trotted over to give them an inquisitive sniff.

"Who are you?" asked Chip. The girl just stared and said nothing, most likely because she was busy sizing up the odd-looking group before her. Beyond their peculiar style of dress there was Jibby's Swiss Army hand, Dizzy's metallic earmuffs, and Teddy's strange pink-eyed sock pal. She must have thought she had come across an entirely new civilization. The fox crooked its head to the side, perhaps thinking the very same thing.

"She probably doesn't speak English," whispered Penny.

"Do you speak English?" Teddy blurted out before anyone could stop him.

The girl raised an eyebrow. "Indubitably," she said.

"Nope," said Teddy. "She doesn't speak English."

"That is English," said Penny. "In fact, it's very good English. What's your name?" she asked the girl.

"Well, if you insist upon knowing, my name is The Big Little, but most people just call me Big," said the smallish girl in the most perfect English.

"Is that fox your pet?" asked Teddy.

Big looked at the fox. The fox looked up at Big, who had never before been asked that question and thus had to think about it for a moment. "No," she said finally. "Digs isn't really my pet. I don't own him. I take care of him and he takes care of me. He's more of a traveling companion, I imagine."

"Do you call him Digs because he likes to dig holes?" asked Teddy.

"I don't know if he likes to," said Big, "but he's quite good at it." She clapped her hands sharply and pointed to the ground near her feet. "Digs, right here." Without hesitation Dig took to the dirt, and in no time flat he carved a hole about six inches deep and four inches a‿‿‿ and kept digging until Big said, "That's enough now."

Digs emerged from the hole with a swagger.

"There," said Big. "What do you think of that?"

"I think you look like Honkapotus," said Rat-Face Roy.

"I beg your pardon. What, exactly, is a Honkapotus?" said Big, surprised to find herself talking directly to a sock with bright pink eyes.

"I think he means Pocahontas," said Chip, puffing out his chest without realizing it. "Sorry about that. He doesn't mean to be rude. He's just a sock. So why were you following us anyway?"

"You dropped your rock. I desired to return it," said Big with the slightest of smiles. Chip smiled too, marking the first time he had ever smiled at someone who had just hit him with a rock. He slipped the small stone into his pocket for safekeeping.

"Your little group appears to be lost," said Big.

"We are a bit," said Mr. Cheeseman. "Would you happen to know the way to the nearest town or settlement? One that might have a blacksmith?"

"And to the nearest seaport," Jibby added.

"I would," said Big, folding her arms across her chest and leaning back against a tree. The fox sat down and appeared disinterested. Mr. Cheeseman and the others waited for more but that was all Big had to say.

This seemed to annoy Three-Eyed Jake, who stepped

toward the girl. "Now listen here, missy," he said with a wag of his finger. And then, in an instant, the smallish girl named Big and the little brown fox named Digs turned and vanished silently into the woods.

"Now look what you did," said Jibby. "You chased her off. What in the name of Pete's peg leg were you thinking?" Jake shrugged sheepishly and mumbled something about trying to control his temper in the future. "Now how are we gonna find our way out of here?"

"You could always hire me to guide you." The voice came from behind them. The group spun around to find Big standing on the limb of a tree on the opposite side of the path. Somehow she'd been able to slip across undetected and climb deftly into the tree in mere seconds without the slightest sound. "It'll cost you, though." She jumped from the tree, her soft leather moccasins landing silently in the dirt. Digs trotted out from behind the tree to rejoin his traveling companion. "I'm the best guide money can buy, so it won't be cheap."

Instinctively, Mr. Cheeseman pulled out his wallet but soon realized that all he had was a small assortment of paper money from the twenty-first century, hardly of any use in 1668.

"Don't worry," said Jibby. "I'll get it." He removed the leather pouch from his belt and, hooking the drawstring on the can opener of his Swiss Army knife, shoved his remaining hand inside. He pulled out a small sampling of gold and silver coins.

"Wow," said Teddy. "Pirate money."

Jibby shook the coins in his hand like a pair of dice. "You say you're the best guide money can buy, but how do we know that? After all, you're just a wee girl."

Big seemed about to speak when suddenly she pulled the knife from her belt, turned quickly to her left, and threw the weapon, end over end, burying the blade a good two inches in the trunk of a tree some twenty feet away. "Mosquito," she explained as she walked over and wiggled the knife from the tree. She wiped the blade on her pant leg and slid it back into its leather scabbard. "I hate mosquitoes."

Penny was impressed. Teddy was in awe. Chip was in love.

"Here," said Jibby, gladly offering the coins to Big. "I trust that will do." She took the coins and inspected each one closely from every angle.

"Not bad," she said. "Okay. It's this way to Shattuckton." To the chagrin of Jibby and his equally superstitious crew, she took the path to the left. Without further discussion everyone followed. She walked quickly, and Penny and Chip struggled to keep pace with her. Penny was dying to talk to her about archery, and Chip was dying to talk to her about, well, anything. Teddy and his short legs gave up and lagged behind, walking next to Juanita, of whom Teddy had grown immensely fond. Not only was she kind and pretty but, as Teddy had recently learned, she and Captain Jibby were his great-great-great-great-great-grandparents, which made him love Juanita all the more.

Juanita was equally fond of young Teddy and took the opportunity to teach him and his sock puppet sidekick some phrases in Spanish. The first words she taught him were *perro* and *zorro*—dog and fox—as Pinky and Digs each seemed happy to have a traveling companion of comparable height and species.

While *el perro* and *el zorro* became acquainted, Chip and Penny learned that Big's mother was Mohawk, her father English. She had even lived in London for a brief time, which probably accounted for her impeccable diction. Chip and Penny were delighted to discover that Big's father, like their own, was a man of science, an explorer, and a cartographer, a maker of maps.

The rest of her story, however, was not delightful in the least. When Big was only twelve, her father mounted an expedition and headed out west. Three years later, he still had not returned and was presumed to be dead.

To make matters worse, Big's mother had died of influenza the following winter, leaving the girl to fend for herself. She began working as a guide throughout the backwoods of a land still largely unexplored by the newcomers.

"I can't imagine what it's like to have no parents," said Penny. "Our mother was killed, but we're very lucky to still have our father."

"My father will return one day," said Big. "I'm sure of it."

At first Chip and Penny said nothing, though they were

both thinking the same thing. After three years, it seemed unlikely that Big's father was still alive. But she was entitled to her wishful thinking, just as they were entitled to theirs.

"So where do you live now?" asked Chip.

"I live everywhere," said Big. "Everywhere and nowhere. And you? Most certainly you're not from around here. 'Tis obvious by your clothing. And most assuredly you're not from England, yet you speak English. So from whence do you hail?"

Chip looked at Penny. One of them had better think of something pretty quickly. "We're from the future," Chip said.

Penny nearly fell over. What was he thinking? Or was he so enamored of Big that he simply wasn't thinking at all?

Big laughed and walked ahead. "The future! That is quite funny." Chip and Penny looked at each other, shrugged, and pressed onward.

With every step the path seemed to grow wider and wider until it could be said that it had become a dirt road. The trees became fewer in number and then disappeared altogether as the group happened upon large farms with houses of weathered gray wood, white plaster stucco, or impenetrable stone.

There were pastures as well, with grazing sheep and lazing cows. Young Teddy couldn't resist cupping his hands around his mouth and calling out, "Moooo!" but the cows said nothing in return.

"Maybe they don't speak English," he rationalized. He turned to Juanita. "How do you say 'moo' in Spanish?"

"Moooo!" said Juanita. In the distance, a cow mooed back.

"I knew it," said Teddy, and he rated the sound of the mooing cow at a very respectable eight-point-two.

Eventually the sound of rushing water made its way to their ears; the road took a sharp turn and crossed a river by way of a bridge made of thick wooden planks. Big stopped, turned, and spoke directly to Jibby.

"Sir," she said. "Shattuckton is nigh and but a short walk down this road. But if it's the nearest seaport you seek, this river will take you all the way to Boston Harbor. The distance could be walked in a day or two, but I'd take a boat. About a mile down the river, you'll discover a small cottage owned by a woman named Crazy Nellie. She can sell you a boat for a very good price."

"You want us to buy a boat from a woman named Crazy Nellie?" said Jake with an incredulous snort.

"Or you could walk," said Big. "It's your choice."

So this was it then. With no time to prepare emotionally, the moment had come when Mr. Cheeseman and his three polite, attractive, and relatively odor-free children would have to bid good-bye to their pirate friends. For the past two years, since they had first found it necessary to go on the run, the children had grown accustomed to making friends only to leave them behind a short time later. It's one thing to become accustomed to something. It's quite another to be okay with it.

"No," Teddy protested. "You can't leave."

"Teddy," said Mr. Cheeseman both firmly and gently. "It's already been decided."

Tears crept into Teddy's eyes until there was room for no more and a half dozen or so scrambled down his cheeks. Penny, with tears of her own, put her arm around her little brother and gave his shoulder an affectionate squeeze.

Big decided to give her clients some privacy while they said their farewells. She and Digs walked ahead and sat on the bridge, watching the water scuttle over the rocks below.

"You'll be needin' some proper money," said Jibby to Mr. Cheeseman. "Okay, men. Dig deep."

Jibby's crew reached into their pockets, each removing a variety of crudely minted gold and silver coins and dropping them into Jibby's hand as he walked the ranks. Jibby inspected the coins and did not seem impressed. "Deeper," he said. The men returned to their pockets and drew forth more coins. "That's better," said Jibby. He handed the coins over to Mr. Cheeseman. "This should last you at least a month, I would think."

"Well, I hope it's just a day or two before we're on our way back home," said Mr. Cheeseman. After a brief, awkward silence, Jibby snapped his Swiss Army hand to his forehead. "It's been an honor to serve with you," he said, his voice cracking ever so slightly.

"The privilege has been all mine," said Mr. Cheeseman, saluting back. "And I hope we meet again someday."

"I hope we don't," said Jibby.

"Yes," agreed Mr. Cheeseman. "I suppose you're right."

One by one, the rest of Jibby's crew stepped forward and shook Mr. Cheeseman's hand and gave him a spirited salute or, in the case of Juanita, a warm hug. Jibby turned his attention to the children. "Chip," he said. "You're a brave and honorable sort and I'd welcome a man of your caliber aboard me ship anytime."

"Thanks, Jibby," said Chip, happy to be seen as a man in Jibby's eyes. "We're sure gonna miss you."

"Penny," said Jibby, brushing the auburn hair from her eyes, "I've no doubt you will do great things in the future. I know this because you've done great things in the past."

Penny stood on her tiptoes and gave her great-great-great-great-great-grandfather a kiss on his fuzzy cheek. "Good luck, Jibby. We'll never forget you."

"As for you, Captain Fabulous," said Jibby, turning to Teddy, "you are an awfully entertaining young lad. You make me laugh like no other." Jibby roughed up Teddy's spiky hair and then reached into his pocket and removed a cell phone. "It's no good to me here. Perhaps you'd like to have it. You can use it when you get back to your own time."

Teddy cradled the phone in his hands as if it were the Holy Grail or the world's largest wad of bubble gum. "Wow. I've always wanted my own cell phone. Thanks, Jibby."

"You're welcome, lad." He then turned to face his crew. "All right, this is it. Let's move out." With one last glance

and a warm smile, Jibby led his crew down the path along
the river.

"Good-bye," shouted Chip.

"Take care," said Penny.

"*Adios*," said Rat-Face Roy.

CHAPTER 5

At first glance you might think it was the LVR sitting there silently in the middle of the forest. It looked very similar, though this machine was bigger, sleeker, and shaped more like a football. Its outer surface, rather than an array of individual prisms and mirrors, was a solid piece of reflective material that made it almost invisible. Also unlike the LVR, this machine did not have a beach towel-sized hole in its roof. This machine was perfectly intact.

With the slightest squeak, the pod door opened—inward—and out stepped two strange-looking men. They might have been George Washington and Thomas Jefferson by the way they were dressed. Atop their heads were white powdered wigs. Their frilly shirts were partly covered by long vests and longer coats with cuffed sleeves, each adorned with a row of brass buttons. Their pants ended at the knee and gave way to long white stockings and black buckled shoes.

Beyond their questionable fashion choices, they bore

little resemblance to our founding fathers. The first man out the door was plump and doughy with the scarcest of chins, his murky eyes constantly darting back and forth beneath his thick glasses in wonder, fear, and suspicion. The man's name was Professor Acorn Boxley.

The second man to emerge from the LVR-ZX was tall and slim, with a bony face and cheeks as hollow as punch bowls. A graying goatee covered his pointy chin. Beneath his white powdered wig was a black toupee. Beneath that, his bald head was moist with sweat. This second man was known to Professor Boxley as Gateman Nametag, but to others he was known differently. To his mother he was known as Milton Cornelius Flowers, to the United States penal system he was known as prisoner #4398789, and to Ethan Cheeseman and his three children he was known as the pernicious Mr. 5, the man responsible for the death of their much-loved wife and mother.

So how did this man of many names end up here, in 1668, hot on the Cheesemans' trail and bound for revenge? After all, the last time they had seen Mr. 5, he was tied up in the back of an old school bus with the police on their way to arrest him. As the Cheeseman family was speeding along the Time Arc, Mr. 5 was being hauled off to jail, where he would stand trial for the murder of Olivia Cheeseman. So what went wrong?

Well, you see, the story goes a little bit like this.

From the very beginning of his murder trial, Mr. 5's attorney used every bit of legal wrangling at his disposal. He first argued that Mr. 5 should not be tried as an adult because he still lived with his mother and wore Spider-Man underwear. When the judge denied the motion, he attempted to persuade the jury that his client was certifiably insane, thus not legally responsible for the murder. He did this by having Mr. 5 show up to court each day with a turtle on his head.

"Ladies and gentlemen of the jury," he said during his closing remarks. "It's quite obvious that my client is totally insane. If there is any doubt, one has only to notice that he's wearing a turtle on his head and a maroon jacket. You'd have to be insane to try and match a green turtle with a maroon jacket. Certainly a sane person would opt for a navy blue, an aquamarine, or a nice beige."

But the judge was having none of it. He instructed the jury to disregard the statement and not to feed the turtle. Even without testimony from the Cheeseman family, after just sixty-one minutes of deliberation—which included a one-hour lunch break—the jury found Mr. 5 "unbelievably guilty." When the verdict was read, Mr. 5 showed no emotion (though he would later admit being jealous of the court reporter's thick and manageable hair).

As cameras flashed, he was led away in handcuffs and a sporty maroon jacket to a jail cell where he and his turtle would await sentencing. When that day came, the judge declared that Mr. 5 would go to prison for the rest of his natural life. And though the judge made it clear that he would never be eligible for parole, this did not seem to bother Mr. Milton Cornelius Flowers. He seemed to know that one day a person as devilishly clever as himself would be eligible for something much better—escape.

It would take twelve years for Mr. 5 to think of the perfect plan, which involved saving up broccoli from the prison cafeteria and using it to disguise himself as a bush so he could sneak out.

When his absence was detected by the prison guards, they turned the dogs loose to sniff him out. However, because there hadn't been an escape from the prison in many years, the dogs were very much out of practice and simply began sniffing one another.

"I think I know where he's hiding," said one of the least intelligent of the guards.

But Mr. Milton Cornelius Flowers had vanished, and no one knew where he was hiding because, as it turns out, he was very good at doing just that. He changed his name, altered his appearance with a fashionable goatee and a convincing toupee, then slipped into a state of extreme disappearedness.

It was not long after that fate intervened when the criminal formerly known as Mr. 5 had a chance meeting with a brilliant scientist and former faculty member at Southwestern North Dakota State University by the name of Professor Acorn Boxley. As luck would have it (bad luck for Ethan Cheeseman), the professor just happened to be in need of an assistant to aid him in his work on a most important device based on the theories and early designs of another scientist and former student. A device the professor called the LVR-ZX and that Gateman called a perfect opportunity for revenge.

Now, you might think it a terrible coincidence that

these two should meet up at a group therapy session for people who bite their toenails. I couldn't agree more. Yet there are those who will tell you that there is no such thing as coincidence and that everything happens for a reason. What these people don't tell you is that it's not always for a good reason. Sometimes things happen for a bad reason, and in this case, for a very bad one indeed.

Professor Boxley looked around the thick forest, nervously biting his fingernails. Gateman Nametag, a.k.a. Mr. 5, drew in a deep breath and promptly emitted a loud, wet sneeze.

"Please cover your mouth," said Professor Boxley, placing his hand over his own mouth to keep out any airborne germs.

"I can't help it," said Gateman, trying very hard to sneeze again but finding himself stuck halfway between sneezing and not sneezing. When someone sneezes, it is common practice for people to say "God bless you," "Gesundheit," or "For heaven's sake, cover your mouth." However, when a person is stuck in the awful in-between of having to sneeze but not being able to, people say nothing. They just stare at you with annoyance, as Professor Boxley was now staring at Gateman Nametag.

"I seem to be allergic to whatever that terrible smell is," said Gateman when the urge to sneeze had finally subsided.

"What terrible smell?"

"The air," said Gateman. "It smells . . . different."

"That's called oxygen," said Professor Boxley. "Fresh air. No cars, no buses, no factories; just pure, clean oxygen."

"Well, I like my oxygen with a little smog mixed in." Gateman sneezed again, this time remembering to cover his mouth. Instinctively, he wiped his runny nose with the sleeve of his jacket and was immediately reminded that it was lined with brass buttons, making the experience a bit like driving his face over a series of speed bumps.

"Ouch! Blasted buttons. And these shoes are absolutely killing my feet," he said. "Why on earth do we have to dress like this anyway? We look ridiculous."

"I told you, it's important that we blend in with the people of the time so as not arouse suspicion. Now quit being such a ninny."

"Okay, fine," said Gateman. "So what do we do now?"

"What do we do?" said Professor Boxley. "Why, we find the Cheesemans, of course. We find them and rescue them as planned."

"And how do we find them?"

"By taking whatever means necessary." Professor Boxley reached beneath his jacket and removed an old rolled-up magazine and unfurled it. The magazine was called *Science Today* and its cover featured a picture of a young, smiling Ethan Cheeseman taken during his college days at Southwestern North Dakota State University, where he was given the coveted Scientist of Tomorrow award for creating a fertilizer that made brussels sprouts grow to the size of cabbages and cherry tomatoes grow to the size of regular tomatoes. Professor Boxley gazed upon the photo with admiration.

"It is my duty to the scientific community and to mankind in general to rescue one of the greatest minds of all time," he said. "Not to mention the best student I ever had. And, as my trusted assistant, it is your job to do whatever I command. As men of destiny, we will succeed in executing the greatest rescue attempt of all time."

Gateman thought for a moment, then turned to Professor Boxley. "Your wig is crooked," he said.

Meanwhile, Big was proving to be not only the best guide money could buy but an excellent traveling companion as well, able to regale the children with many stories of her adventures in the backcountry of this untamed land.

"And this one is from a black bear," she said, pushing her sleeve up to show off a long pink scar.

"A bear attacked you?" Teddy gasped.

"No," said Big. "We attacked him. Digs and I. He was trying to steal our food, so we really had no choice." Pinky looked at Digs, trotting alongside her, with a new sense of admiration. Digs tried his best to look nonchalant, as if fighting off animals twenty times his size were an everyday occurrence.

Chip and Penny would certainly have been skeptical of such a story if it had been told by anyone else. But there was something about Big that made them trust her, something that assured them that everything she spoke was the truth, no matter how outrageous it may have sounded. Chip wished he could impress Big with his own stories just as she had impressed him. But how could he possibly tell her of his prowess as a baseball player when baseball didn't yet exist? And how could he relay to her the story of the time he rescued his father and little brother from corporate villains by using his expert skill behind the wheel of an automobile? If he had any hope at all of impressing her, he would have to do it with deeds, not words.

"So are you as good with that bow as you are with a knife?" asked Chip.

"I guess so," said Big with a shrug. "Good enough that we never go hungry."

"I've been taking archery lessons for three years now," said Penny. "Off and on. That's a beautiful bow, by the way."

Big stopped and lifted her bow over her head, slid it off her shoulder, and handed it to Penny. "Would you like to try it? My grandfather made it."

Penny took the bow as if it were a priceless Stradivarius. "It's so perfect," she said. "Is it okay, Dad?"

"Sure, but be quick," said Mr. Cheeseman. "It's going to be dark in a few hours."

"You needn't worry," said Big. "We're nearly there." She pulled an arrow from the quiver and handed it to Penny, who placed it on the bowstring and then looked around for a suitable target. With all the trees having been cleared, there wasn't much in the way of things to shoot at. She settled on a fence post and began to draw the bow back when

Big said, "No. Too easy." She removed her hat. "Here," she said. "Before it hits the ground."

"You want me to shoot your hat?" asked Penny.

"It wouldn't be the first time it's been shot. See this hole here?" She put her hand into the hat and stuck a finger through a finger-sized opening. "That's from a farmer who thought I was out to poach his cattle."

"Ready," said Penny, drawing back the bow and pointing it toward the sky.

With a flick of her wrist, Big flung the floppy brown hat high into the air. Penny followed it as it floated along on the breeze like an Uncommonly Fat Orangutan. She released the arrow and the bow propelled it straight and true, plucking the hat out of the air in mid-flight and carrying it onward toward a farmhouse in the distance, where it eventually stuck in the roof of an outhouse.

Before Penny could celebrate her excellent shot, the door to the outhouse flew open and out ran a man who was swearing and buttoning up his pants. The angry, foulmouthed man grabbed a rifle that had been leaning against the outhouse and swore some more.

"Uh-oh," said Big. "I think that's the same farmer who took a shot at me. We'd better run. Come on!"

Big sprinted down the road and Mr. Cheeseman and the children followed. A shot rang out in the distance, then another. When they could run no more, they stopped and tried to catch their breath, which was not easy because, in addition to having just run a half a mile, they were also giggling uncontrollably.

"I can't believe I shot an outhouse," said Penny, doubled over in a painful fit of laughter.

"I can't believe you shot an occupied outhouse," said Big, wiping a tear from her eye.

"You probably scared the daylights out of him," said Mr. Cheeseman.

"Probably scared something else out of him, too," said Chip.

"At least he got a free hat," said Teddy.

Mr. Cheeseman smiled. It was good to see his children laugh after all they'd been through. Even Pinky seemed to be laughing, or, at the very least, smiling, as she and Digs chased each other, playfully running between the children's legs.

"I'm sure glad we ran into you, Big," said Penny.

"Yes," Chip agreed. "That sure was lucky."

Big shook her head. "I don't believe in luck," she said. "Your friend was right when he said everything happens for a reason."

Mr. Cheeseman grew suddenly alarmed. He tried to recall just where they were when Aristotle uttered those very same words. "Big?" he said. "When exactly did you start following us?"

"I don't remember," said Big.

"When?" Mr. Cheeseman persisted.

"Ever since you left your strange shiny house. The one you covered with sticks and leaves." Big walked ahead. Penny and Chip turned to their father, who wore a look of panic. Chip broke into a jog and moved into Big's path, stopping her in her tracks. "Big, please. You have to promise not to say anything to anyone about our . . . strange house. If anyone were to find out, we might never be able to go home again."

"To the future?" said Big.

Chip laughed. "That's quite funny."

Big did not laugh. "Don't worry," she said. "Something has brought us together. Something great. I will do nothing to harm you. And I shall protect the secret of the house that will take you home."

"Thanks."

"May we one day meet again." She extended her hand, and Chip took it reluctantly. It was then that he and the others realized Big was saying good-bye. In all the excitement of running from the angry farmer, they'd failed to notice that the dirt road beneath their feet was now a cobblestone street and they were standing on the edge of the quiet little village known as Shattuckton. "This is as far as I go."

"You're not coming into town with us?" asked Penny.

"I don't much care for towns, I'm afraid. I get along much better with trees than with most people."

"You get along with us," said Teddy.

"Yes," Big agreed. "I do get along with you."

It didn't seem fair. Just moments before they'd said good-bye to Jibby and his wonderful crew of misfits. Now they would have to bid so long to Big as well. Chip was especially disappointed. At fourteen, he'd certainly had his share of crushes on girls, but his connection to Big felt different.

Their eyes met. Chip felt his palms moisten.

"I apologize for hitting you in the neck with a rock," said Big with a slight smile. "I meant to hit you in the arm."

"It's okay," said Chip, instinctively bringing his hand to the side of his neck. "Didn't hurt. Besides, I threw it at you first." Chip removed the rock from his pocket and tossed it from one hand to the other.

"Yes, you did," Big teased.

Chip smiled and pulled his baseball cap from his head, handing it to Big. "Here. You've gotta have a hat. It's got holes in it but they're supposed to be there. For ventilation."

"Thank you," said Big, inspecting the cap with admiration. "It's a beautiful hat."

"It might be too big, but it's adjustable." Chip showed Big how the size of the hat could be changed using the plastic band in the back.

"And the letter *P*?" said Big.

"It stands for Pals," said Chip.

Big twisted the hat onto her head. "What do you think?" she asked.

Chip reached out and straightened the bill slightly. "It's never looked better."

With great effort, Big pulled her gaze from Chip and spoke to Mr. Cheeseman. "The blacksmith is a good man. Not nearly as mean as he looks. His name is Lumley. He'll help you if he can."

"Thanks, Big," said Mr. Cheeseman.

"I wish you good luck and a safe journey."

"Hey, Big," said Teddy as she turned to go. "Roy wants to know how to say 'good-bye' in Mohawk."

"O-nen," said Big. "O-nen to all of you."

Big walked backward for just a few steps before turning and running silently down the road, away from the town and toward the trees, her braided ponytails surfing behind her on the breeze. Digs hesitated a moment and Pinky took the opportunity to give the side of his face an affectionate lick. Then he turned and ran to catch up to his traveling companion.

"O-nen," said Rat-Face Roy.

"O-nen," said Penny.

Chip said nothing. He just stood and watched, rolling the gray, cherry tomato–sized rock between his fingers.

ADVICE FOR THE LOVELORN

I believe it was the Beatles who said, "The love you take is equal to the love you make, which is equal to the square of the hypotenuse."

Musicians have always had a better understanding of love than the rest of us. Over the years they have told us that love: is like a rock, is like oxygen, is a battlefield, is here to stay, is all you need, will find a way, will keep us together, will tear us apart, stinks.

Regardless of which is true, most of us will never forget our first love, and I certainly haven't forgotten mine. The object of my affections was Betty from the long-running *Archie* comic strip. Though my heart would swoon each time I laid eyes on her, the relationship was doomed to failure because of our many differences—me being a mere ten years old, she being a cartoon character made up of hundreds of tiny colored dots.

Still, when it comes to affairs of the heart, my advice to you is that it is better to have loved and lost than never to have loved at all. Because even though love is a battlefield and may occasionally stink, sometimes it's like a rock—a rock that hits you in the side of the neck and leaves a mark that lasts forever.

CHAPTER 6

When no one answered the door of the small weathered shack, Jibby knocked again, this time harder, so as to be heard over the rush of the river but not so hard as to knock the loose, lazy door from its rusted hinges. Strewn about the shaggy grounds of the rickety shack were a multitude of items in a similar state of disrepair. There was a shovel with no handle, a handle with no shovel, a plow with a bent-up blade, a tin washtub with a hole rusted through its bottom, and a wagon wheel with half its spokes missing. There were also many smaller objects, broken or poorly patched, lined up on a long wobbly table.

Between two trees a rope had been strung, and hanging from that rope was a black wool jacket with one sleeve missing, along with a set of white frilly ladies' long underwear featuring a bright red patch on the seat. Tied to a larger tree and bobbing in the current of the river were three rowboats of questionable buoyancy. There was one blue, one gray, and one red.

"Looks like no one's home," said Sammy.

"We could just steal one of them boats," said Dizzy.

Jibby's face turned instantly dark and serious. "You're about this close to having your speaking privileges revoked." He held his thumb and his index finger so close together Dizzy could scarcely see daylight between them. "Our stealing days are over. Anything we need, we buy or make ourselves."

"What about borrowing?" asked Jake. "Nothing wrong with borrowing things as long as you give them back."

"Or winning them," said Aristotle. "Nothing wrong with winning things either. I once knew a man who won two chickens in a hog-calling contest. Or was it two hogs in a chicken-calling contest?"

"You can't call chickens," said Sammy. "Well, you can but they won't come. They're always too busy."

Before Jibby could revoke the speaking privileges of his entire crew, the door to the shack swung open with a sour, rusty groan and out stepped a small woman, her stringy brown hair partially covering her soot-streaked face. Her jaw was as loose and as lazy as her front door, and her mouth hung constantly open, giving her the look of a simpleton. "Yes?" said the woman. "What can I do for you?" Her slack-jawed expression revealed two gold teeth, two silver teeth, and one copper.

"We're looking for Crazy Nellie," said Jibby, as if there were even the slightest chance that the woman standing before them could be anyone but.

"Indeed you found her," said Nellie. She cackled loudly and her heavily metaled mouth looked like the tip jar at a coffeehouse. "I've got everything you might need right here in one location." Nellie pushed her way past Jibby and into the overgrown yard. "Everything you see is for sale—and all of it made or fixed by myself. Need an ax?"

Crazy Nellie grabbed an ax that had been leaning against a fallen tree. "Sharpened it myself. It's like a razor." She apparently felt a demonstration was in order and quickly raised the ax with both hands, which caused the rusty iron head to fly off the handle and soar through the air behind her. Aristotle ducked just in time as the blade passed over his head, stopping only when it sliced deep into the wall of Nellie's ramshackle house with a decisive crack.

"See? Told you so," said Nellie. "Like a razor." She offered the ax handle to Dizzy. "Can I interest you in a club? Never been used."

"No thanks," said Dizzy.

"Well, how about a coat?" Nellie tossed the ax handle aside and pulled the jacket from the clothesline. She held it up to Sammy's chest. "Looks about your size, I'd say."

"It's missing an arm," said Sammy.

"Vest. Sorry, I meant to say vest. And, if you act now, I'll throw in one bonus sleeve free of charge as well as these lovely knickers for the lady." Nellie snatched the long underwear from the line and thrust them toward Juanita, who responded with a polite but firm, "No, *gracias*."

"Listen," said Jibby. "All we need is a boat to take us down the river to Boston Harbor."

"Well, then you've come to the right place," said Nellie. She walked down to the waterline where the boats awaited, gently thumping up against one another like the sound of drums, muffled and distant. Jibby and the others followed. "I've got three and they're all priced right."

"Yes," said Jibby, sizing up the selection. "But are they seaworthy?"

"Well, you never said anything about the sea. You said you needed a boat to get you down the river."

"Fine," said Jibby, his patience all but expired. "Are they river worthy?"

"Absolutely," said Nellie. "They're all one hundred percent airtight. If any of them sink, I'll gladly refund your money . . . if you survive, of course. Except for the blue one. I make no guarantees on that one. But I'll gladly throw in this free baler." She bent forward and pulled a small cast-iron pot from the weeds, its wooden handle missing.

"How much for the gray one?" asked Jibby. It appeared to be the least patched and the one most likely to take them directly to Boston Harbor without an unscheduled stopover at the bottom of the river.

Crazy Nellie thought this over. She rubbed her chin and turned her head side to side, her loose, open jaw waggling freely. "Well, let's see. I can give it to you for one pound fifty or one Spanish dollar."

"Fine," said Jibby, digging into his pocket.

"Now, will you be needing any extra oars?" asked Nellie.

"And why would we need more than two oars?" inquired Jibby.

"Well, this boat only comes with one. But for an additional fee of twenty pence, you get two oars and this free doorknob." Nellie grabbed a rusted iron doorknob from the junk-laden table.

"Why in the name of Godfried's sword would we need a doorknob?" barked Jibby.

"Good point," said Nellie. "So just the oar then."

She outfitted Jibby and his crew with two oars and, after one last attempt to sell them a broken saw blade for half price, she sent them on their way down the river with a wave and a grin so full of metal that it must have been almost impossible for her to face in any direction other than magnetic north.

For Mr. Cheeseman and his children, strolling through the tiny town of Shattuckton, with its cobblestone streets and colonial buildings, was like going back in time. Wait a minute. That's right, they *were* back in time. Hmm. Well, regardless, just because they actually were back in time doesn't mean it couldn't also feel like going back in time. Right?

Anyway, young Teddy Roosevelt agreed. "Wow," he said. "Look at all the brand-new old-fashioned buildings." There were indeed brand-new old-fashioned buildings all around, though, unlike our downtowns of today, there was far more space between the buildings. There was a customs house made of stone, a large town meeting hall, a small inn called an ordinary, a church all in white, and several houses of varying sizes.

"So this is the main drag," said Mr. Cheeseman. "Quite a bit different than what we're used to. No fast-food restaurants, no coffee shops."

"Hey, Dad," said Penny. "Why do they call the main street of a town the main drag, anyway?"

"Good question. I'm not sure."

"I know why," said Teddy. "Before they invented the wheel, they had to drag everything down the street."

"You mean all those streets they built in anticipation of the wheel being invented?" said Penny.

"Exactly," said Teddy.

"Interesting theory," said Mr. Cheeseman with a wink toward Penny. Chip had missed out on the entire conversation. He was somewhere else entirely, lost in thought.

"Chip?" asked Mr. Cheeseman. "You okay?"

"Hmm?"

Mr. Cheeseman smiled and placed his hand on Chip's shoulder. "She's a very nice girl."

"Yeah," said Chip, partially snapping out of his love-induced haze.

"I'll never forget the day I met your mom," said Ethan, suddenly lost in thoughts of his own. "It was my junior year at Southwestern North Dakota State. There was a dance at the Student Union. She was sitting all alone. I wondered how someone so incredibly attractive could be sitting by herself." Mr. Cheeseman's eyes became increasingly sparkly as he related the story. "So I approached her table and asked her to dance. And, of course, she said no."

"She said no?" Teddy gasped.

"She said she couldn't dance because she was watching her friend's purse. So you know what I did?"

"What?" asked Penny.

"I grabbed that purse and ran out of the building."

The children squealed in disbelief. They could never in a million years have imagined their straightlaced father doing something so lawless and reckless. After all, this was a man who stopped at yellow lights just to be safe— unless, of course, he was being pursued by evil villains.

"You stole the purse?" said Chip. "What did Mom do?"

"She yelled, 'Stop, thief!' Then she followed me outside, just as I'd hoped she would. I told her I'd give her the purse back if she'd agree to go out with me."

"I bet I know what happened next," said Teddy. "She said yes."

"Actually, what happened next was that I was wrestled to the ground by campus security. When they finally took their knees off my chest and let me up, then she said yes. We were married nine months later."

"Wow," said Penny. "What a beautiful story."

"Yeah," Teddy agreed. "Tell us again how they tackled you."

Mr. Cheeseman retold the story as they continued down the main drag, where, thanks to the invention of the wheel, nothing had been dragged for years. Teddy decided that this might be a good time to explore the many features of his new cell phone. He tested the ring tone, assuming that Jibby would have it set to "Yo-Ho-Ho and a Bottle of Rum" or "What Can We Do with a Drunken Sailor?" Pressing the appropriate button, he was slightly disappointed when the phone played Jibby's favorite song, "The Girl from Ipanema."

Next he tried the memo feature, hitting the record button and speaking into the phone. "Greetings, people of Earth," he said in an authoritative, robotic tone. "This is Captain Fabulous. Fear not, for I am here to protect you." He hit the button again and played back the message, obviously quite pleased with the results.

"I know it's fun to play with, Teddy," said Mr. Cheeseman, "but it's probably best to keep that thing hidden while we're here. You'll have plenty of time to use it tomorrow while I repair the LVR." He spoke quietly, from the side of his mouth, the way someone is liable to speak when he knows he is being watched.

Standing beneath the eaves of a large brick house were two plump, red-cheeked women clad in long black dresses and black waistcoats. I must admit their names escape me, so I will refer to them as Appalling and Outrageous, being that those seemed to be their favorite words. Before they caught sight of Mr. Cheeseman and the children they had been deeply immersed in an absolutely riveting conversation about sewing.

"Just look at that," sneered Appalling, peering over her glasses at Mr. Cheeseman and his children. "Their style of dress. They're quite obviously not from around here. Appalling."

"Outrageous."

As they passed by the women, Teddy chose that very moment to blow a very large pink bubble. He sucked the flavorless gum back into his mouth with a pop, sending the ladies into a veritable tizzy.

"Did you see that? Some type of evil spirit lurched forward from that boy's mouth! Appalling!"

"Outrageous."

"And what manner of beast is that?" said Appalling, having never before seen a hairless fox terrier. "Looks like a jackal direct from the depths of Hades."

Mr. Cheeseman turned and waved to the women and offered a pleasant hello. The children smiled and waved and Rat-Face Roy said, *"Hola, señoritas."*

The señoritas were not amused. In fact, as you might have guessed, they were appalled and outraged. "My word," muttered Appalling, gently petting her hair to see that it remained in place after all the outrage. "That thing on the child's hand looks like the devil himself. Just look at those bright pink eyes. And he speaks in some strange tongue. No, those people are definitely not from around here."

"I think we should send for Mr. Bon Mot immediately," said Outrageous.

"I couldn't agree more," said Appalling. "Jacques Bon Mot will take care of this situation quite nicely, I believe."

The cold stares from the women did not go unnoticed

by Mr. Cheeseman. "Teddy," he said, when they were beyond earshot. "Let's keep the bubble blowing to a minimum while we're here, shall we? And maybe Rat-Face Roy could take a vow of silence . . . for a couple of days."

"But he's just being friendly," Teddy protested.

"Which is more than I can say for some people," said Chip.

"I can see now why Big doesn't care much for towns," said Penny, "if all of them are this unfriendly."

Before they could see the blacksmith's shop they could hear it, iron clanking against iron in rhythmic strokes. The doors, the size of those found on a barn, were wide open, inviting in the afternoon sun. Standing in the center of the dirt floor in front of a charcoal-burning furnace was a man in a sweat- and dirt-soaked white shirt, sleeves rolled to the elbow. His weathered face featured a horrible scowl and a dark brown beard shaped like a hammock, the same as many of the men they had passed along the way. Hammock-shaped beards appeared to be the style of the day.

Mr. Cheeseman and his children stood in the doorway for a moment, just watching as the man used a small sledgehammer to pound flat a sheet of heated metal against an anvil. In the corner was a wooden bin full of the blacksmith's raw materials: long rods, about four feet long, made of iron, bronze, and copper, waiting to be heated, pounded, and reshaped into household goods and farming implements or small hooks for saddles and clothing.

"He doesn't look very friendly," said Teddy.

"Big did say he's not as mean as he looks," said Chip.

"I would hope not," said Penny.

Only when the man stopped to wipe the perspiration from his forehead did he notice that he had visitors. He said nothing but nodded, perhaps unsure if they were customers or merely onlookers. It wasn't uncommon for young children to stand and watch the blacksmith work while their parents visited with friends or tended to business in town.

"Hello, Mr. Lumley?" said Mr. Cheeseman, walking slowly toward the scowly faced man.

"Yes," said Mr. Lumley. "What can I do for you?" He set down the hammer, then took a dirty cloth from a nearby table and wiped his face dry.

"I'm looking to buy some bronze," said Mr. Cheeseman, figuring it would be the metal best suited for reattaching the roof of the LVR.

Mr. Lumley's ordinary scowl became a confused scowl. Normally people came to him with items to repair or with requests for specific objects like a new garden hoe, a set of horseshoes, or an iron skillet. No one ever came in looking for raw materials. "Some bronze what?" he asked.

Ethan realized his request must seem odd to Mr. Lumley. Torch welding had not yet been invented and the need for solder would not be something familiar to a seventeenth-century blacksmith. Still, he hoped Mr. Lumley was not necessarily the suspicious or inquisitive type.

81

"Just the rods," said Mr. Cheeseman. "About four of them should do the trick."

Mr. Lumley nodded slowly, then looked at the bin and seemed to be counting the rods. "I can sell you some, but you'll have to wait a fortnight until the ship from England arrives with more. Right now all I have is spoken for. The governor is building a big fancy house and I've been charged with making the hinges and the knobs for all the doors."

This was not what Mr. Cheeseman and his children wanted to hear. The thought of having to hang out in this town for two weeks or more while they waited for repair parts for the LVR was in no way appealing. Their second option would be to journey to Boston and hope to find a blacksmith with a larger cache of metals, but Mr. Cheeseman did not want to leave so much distance between themselves and their only means of getting home. Mr. Lumley grabbed his hammer and prepared to resume his pounding when he noticed that Mr. Cheeseman and the children had not moved. "Was there something else?" he asked.

"No," said Mr. Cheeseman. "Well, yes, actually. You see, we were hoping . . . what I mean is, we really need those rods. We'd be happy to pay you more than they're worth. Double, let's say." Mr. Cheeseman removed a handful of coins from his pocket.

"Double?" said Mr. Lumley, eyeing the money.

"It's just that it's rather urgent. A matter of life and death, you might say."

Mr. Lumley sized up his customers. He couldn't imagine how a few bronze rods might figure into a life and death situation, but Mr. Cheeseman seemed an honest man. "You know," he said, "it just occurred to me that it might do the governor some good to have to wait for something for a change. I'll sell you the rods, but on one condition."

"Sure," said Mr. Cheeseman. "What's that?"

"You pay me what they're worth and not one penny more."

Mr. Cheeseman smiled. The children smiled. Even Rat-Face Roy smiled and successfully fought off the urge to chime in with an enthusiastic "*Muchas gracias.*"

"Big was right," said Teddy. "You're not nearly as mean as you look." Penny was quick but Teddy was quicker and deftly stepped aside, narrowly avoiding a backhand to the chest. He could not, however, escape her look of disgust.

"I'm sorry, Mr. Lumley," said Chip. "You'll have to excuse our little brother. He tends to speak without thinking."

"No harm done," said the blacksmith, though it was clear by the slight change in the scowl on his face that at least a little harm had been done. "Big said I looked mean, did she?"

"Well," said Penny, choosing her words carefully. "You do tend to—how should I put this?—frown a lot." Mr. Lumley considered this for a moment.

"Yes," he agreed. "I suppose that's true. I just can't help

it, though. It's this blasted headache." He gave his forehead a good squeeze as if hoping to force out the pain. "I've had it so long now I can't remember what it's like not to have it. If only I knew what the problem was."

"Have you been to a doctor?" asked Ethan.

"Nearest doctor's in Boston," said Mr. Lumley. "Doctor Dignan. Went to see him once and he suggested drilling holes in my skull."

"He wanted to drill holes in your skull?" gasped Penny.

"To ease the pressure. Anyway I told him I needed holes in my skull like I need a hole in the head."

Mr. Cheeseman and the children laughed. This turned Mr. Lumley's ordinary scowl into a slightly smiley one. Chip leaned close to his father. "Dad," he whispered. "What about the Empathizer?"

Though Mr. Cheeseman was no doctor, he was a brilliant twenty-first-century scientist and probably knew a great deal more about medicine than most doctors of the seventeenth century. The Empathizer might allow him to diagnose Mr. Lumley's condition. At the same time, however, he wondered what a simple blacksmith from 1668 might think of his battery-operated device. He decided the risk of raising suspicion was overshadowed by the possibility of curing Mr. Lumley's chronic discomfort. He pulled the Empathizer from his pocket.

"I'm not a doctor," began Mr. Cheeseman. "But I have this . . . tool . . . that might help us find out what's wrong with your head."

Mr. Lumley looked at the Empathizer and, as you might expect from a blacksmith, said, "Strange. What kind of metal is that?"

"It's plastic," said Teddy, this time unable to avoid a backhanded smack to the chest.

"Yes," said Mr. Cheeseman quickly. "It's a rare type of metal . . . called plastic. Comes from up north." He first placed the suction cup on his own head to assure Mr. Lumley that the device was perfectly safe; much safer than, let's say, having holes drilled in your skull. "Now," he said, "show me exactly where it hurts."

"Right here," said Mr. Lumley, indicating pretty much his entire forehead. Mr. Cheeseman affixed the second suction cup to his patient's forehead, then turned on the Empathizer. Immediately Mr. Cheeseman's face adopted the same scowl worn by Mr. Lumley.

"Wow," he said. "That is painful. But it's also familiar." Mr. Cheeseman turned off the Empathizer and disconnected the suction cups.

"Didn't work," said Mr. Lumley with resignation. "Head still hurts."

"It sure does," said Mr. Cheeseman. "It hurts the way my head hurts when I forget to wear my glasses for any amount of time. Have you ever been to an eye doctor?'

"They have a doctor just for eyes?"

"Well, some places they do. Here." Mr. Cheeseman removed his glasses and handed them to Mr. Lumley. "Try these." Mr. Lumley slid the glasses onto his face and almost immediately his eyes lost their squint and the scowl slowly faded until it had all but disappeared. He rubbed his head, perhaps to make sure it was still there.

"Well I'll be," he said. "You mean all this time I just needed to get me some spectacles?"

"Could be," said Mr. Cheeseman. "Like I said, I'm no doctor, but chronic eye strain is a common cause of headaches. And the light in here isn't the best."

Mr. Lumley nodded in agreement and right then decided that once he had completed work on the doorknobs and hinges for the governor's mansion, he would travel to Boston to be fitted with a pair of proper spectacles by a man who had once offered to drill holes in his skull. He removed the glasses and handed them back to Mr. Cheeseman. "I don't know how to thank you," he said. "You and that magical black box of yours."

"If anyone owes anyone a debt of gratitude, it's us," said Mr. Cheeseman. "We can't thank you enough for helping us out."

"No problem at all." He moved to the bin and slid out four rods of raw bronze, ideal for heating with a homemade blowtorch and reattaching ceilings to broken time machines.

"Does this mean we're going home now?" asked Teddy.

"Soon," said Mr. Cheeseman. "It's going to be dark in a couple of hours, so we should probably wait until tomorrow, get an early start." Mr. Cheeseman paid Mr. Lumley and thanked him once more. He turned to leave and then, just as quickly, turned back. "One more thing. Could you direct us to the nearest hotel?"

"Hotel?" said Mr. Lumley.

"Yes," said Mr. Cheeseman. "Or an inn or . . ."

"Ah, yes. An ordinary. There's one just down the road. But you can't stay there."

"We can't?" said Mr. Cheeseman. "Why not?"

"Because tonight you'll be staying with me."

"Oh," said Ethan. "Are you sure?"

"Don't I look sure?"

"Actually, you look mad," said Teddy.

Mr. Lumley squeezed the trace of a smile onto his grimacing face. "Come back in an hour. I'll take you out to my house. You see, unlike yourself," he said to Ethan, "my wife and I were never blessed with children of our own. She's a good woman and she loves to cook, so I hope you're hungry."

"Starving," said Teddy. "We haven't eaten in hundreds of years."

READ THIS ADVICE BEFORE IT IS STOLEN

When recently polled, thirty-two percent of Americans said that crime was a major concern. When polled at gunpoint that number rose considerably.

It would be fair to say that crime has been around for as long as there have been criminals, maybe even longer. You can bet that thousands of years before people were stealing cars, a few dishonest cavemen were involved in grand theft wheel. This led to the invention of the club and to the formation of the first caveman police force.

For these cave cops, fighting crime was not easy, as they had to do so without the help of DNA evidence, fingerprint technology, or pants. Just try chasing a suspect over a volcano while wearing only a loincloth.*

*Only joking. Please do not try.

In addition, police sketch artists were forced to create their drawings of suspects with only a chisel and a large flat rock.

"Does this look like the man who stole your water buffalo?"

"Yes, my water buffalo was stolen by a stick figure."

Of course, today's policemen have all kinds of modern equipment available to them, including pants. Still they struggle to get criminals off the streets and back onto the sidewalks where they belong.

So what is to be done to reduce crime? Some say we need to lock criminals up and throw away the key. Others insist the key should go into the recycling bin to help save the environment.

Still, there are those who believe we should do more to rehabilitate criminals. Of course, some criminals, like the evil Mr. 5, are so incredibly evil that there is no chance of them ever becoming good, law-abiding citizens. I would thereby advise those in the judicial system that people like him should be sent to prison for a very long time, should never be allowed to escape, and, by all means, should never be given access to a fully operational time machine.

CHAPTER 7

Since he had served twelve years in prison followed by three years as assistant to Professor Boxley, it had now been fifteen years since Mr. 5, now known as Gateman Nametag, had seen the Cheeseman family, though it had been only a few hours since they had last seen him, tied up in the back of an old school bus. Welcome to the strange and fascinating world of time travel.

Those fifteen years had not been terribly kind to Gateman, particularly to his aching joints. And you can be assured that trudging through an overgrown forest in fancy buckled shoes did them no favors. Adding to his growing discomfort, he recently learned that he had a nasty allergy to smog-free air, which caused his nose to run and his eyes to water.

"Do you have any idea where we are?" he sniped at Professor Boxley, whose nervous eyes were shifting back and forth between a map in one hand and a compass in the other. "My feet are killing me." Gateman sneezed so hard both his wig and toupee nearly fell off. This could be a problem. Though he complained about having to wear his 1668 getup, he was secretly very happy, as it would provide a means of hiding his true identity from the Cheesemans when he eventually ran into them, an event he looked forward to like no other.

"Quit your complaining. I'm trying to concentrate," Professor Boxley shot back. He turned his attention back to the map, which was—typical of maps of that era—not terribly accurate. "It looks like there's a small town called Shattuckton about two miles away. It appears to be the only town in the immediate area."

This bit of news was followed by much grumbling. "I thought I asked you to quit complaining," said Professor Boxley.

"I didn't say anything," insisted Gateman.

Another bit of grumbling and suddenly the two men realized they were not alone in that forest. They turned—just their heads—slowly in the direction of the noise. Standing a mere thirty feet away at the other side of a clearing was a rather large, rather irritated black bear. The two men spoke in whispers, scarcely daring to breathe. "Is that a bear?" said Gateman from the corner of his mouth.

"Either that or the world's largest chipmunk," said Professor Boxley. "What should we do?"

"Let's see. I think I remember reading that if attacked by a bear, you should punch him in the nose and swim away as fast as you can."

"That's a shark, not a bear."

Just then Gateman remembered something—a certain

bit of carry-on baggage he had brought along on this little trip through time. With trembling hands, he reached beneath his jacket and removed a handgun from its shoulder holster, careful not to move too suddenly. Professor Boxley seemed even more alarmed to see the gun than he had been to see the bear. "Why do you have a gun?" he hissed.

"I think, considering the circumstances, the better question might be, Why don't you?" Gateman turned to face the bear, whose grumblings had escalated into a growing crescendo of vicious snarling. Gateman raised the gun toward the bear, his hands shaking so badly he could barely hold on to it.

"You're not going to shoot him, are you?" asked the professor.

"Well I'm certainly not going to dance with him." Gateman's fiercely vibrating finger squeezed the trigger, sending a bullet screaming through the air, a good ten feet above the bear's head. Even though the bullet went nowhere near him, it is a well-known fact that some bears are frightened by loud noises. This bear, however, was not one of them. Rather than skulk away, the bear rose up on his hind legs and let out a roar that nearly blew the men's wigs off.

"Run!" shouted Professor Boxley.

In the following split second Gateman had the following thoughts:

1) Bears are able to run faster than humans.
2) With Gateman's achy joints and those terrible

buckled shoes, Professor Boxley would be able to run faster than he would.

3) The bear would most likely eat only one of them—the one he caught first.

4) Unless Gateman thought of something quickly, that person would be him.

In another split second, Gateman processed all of this information, then bent down, picked up a large stick, and hit Professor Boxley squarely on the knee.

"Aaaiiieeeee!" the professor wailed as Gateman took off running through the woods just as fast as his achy joints and his pointy buckled shoes would carry him. The professor took off after Gateman, limping as he went, and the bear took off after them both. "Bear!" yelled the professor. "Everyone out of the forest!" The ground trembled and tree branches snapped like chopsticks as the bear lumbered indelicately but with remarkable speed toward the professor.

The snarling grew louder and the ground vibrated more and more violently as the bear closed in. Professor Boxley tried to prepare himself mentally for what it might be like to slide a few notches down the food chain and become dinner for an animal with a brain the size of a pomegranate. Any hope that he had of escaping his oversized pursuer was dashed when his badly bruised knee gave out and he tumbled to the ground in a heap of buckled shoes, brass buttons, and artificial hair. He lay there, eyes clamped shut, preparing to be devoured. He covered his head and waited for the onslaught of teeth and claws. He waited, but it never came. Slowly he opened his eyes to see the bear a good twenty feet away. Between the professor and the bear stood a smallish girl dressed in buckskin and a dark blue baseball cap. Standing just behind her was a small brown fox, growling angrily.

The bear paced back and forth with a look on his furry face that seemed to say, "Not you again." The girl waved her hands above her head and yelled something in a language unfamiliar to the professor but, apparently, quite familiar to the bear, who decided he had had enough of this. Begrudgingly, he turned and ambled off in the direction he had come.

"O-nen," said the girl in the blue baseball cap to the slowly retreating bear. She then turned and walked toward a very traumatized Professor Boxley. "Are you hurt?" Digs trotted over and gave the professor's hand a good sniff.

"No, I'm okay," said the professor, failing to mention that he had just been kneecapped by his trusted assistant. "You saved my life."

Big responded with a quick one-shoulder shrug. "When it comes to bears you must be clear as to who is the boss. Nothing more, really." She extended her hand and helped pull the professor to his feet. "And, whatever you do, never run away."

If the professor knew nothing about bears, he knew even less about sports. For if he had any knowledge of the topic whatsoever, he would have known that, in 1668, baseball had not yet been invented, which would make the existence of baseball bats, baseball gloves, and baseball caps, like the one Big was wearing, completely unnecessary. But because he knew nothing about sports, he thought little of the blue hat with the white letter *P*.

"May I ask what it is that you're doing way out here in the woods?" said Big.

"We're lost," said the professor, looking about nervously. He brushed the dirt and leaves from his pants and jacket.

"We?"

"My assistant and I. He's run off, I'm afraid." The professor carefully examined the forest in the direction Gateman had run but saw no sign of him. "We were looking for a friend." Professor Boxley removed the magazine from his pocket and displayed it for Big. "This man."

Big crinkled her forehead and brought her fingers to the magazine cover. "This is a strange painting."

"Yes," said the professor. "It's a new style. All the rage in Europe."

"And this man is your friend?"

"Yes," said the professor. Though the gentleman featured in this new style of painting was twenty years younger, with a thin, wiry build and jet-black hair without the slightest sign of gray, he bore a remarkable resemblance to one Ethan Cheeseman.

"He looks very much like someone I met on the trail today," said Big.

This bit of information caused the professor's heart to palpitate. "Was his name Ethan? Ethan Cheeseman?"

"I did not learn his name," said Big. "Only the names of his children, Chip, Penny, and Teddy Roosevelt."

"Teddy Roosevelt?" said the professor excitedly. "Yes, that's got to be him. Do you know where I might find him?"

Before Big could answer, a sharp noise rang out in the distance. Professor Boxley recognized the sound right away as gunfire; one shot followed another.

In his hurry to avoid direct contact with the bear's claws, jaws, taste buds, and digestive tract, Gateman Nametag now found himself standing alone in the middle of the woods with no map, no compass, and absolutely no idea where he was.

"Help!" he shouted, firing another shot into the air. "Can anybody hear me? Heeelp!" Just as he was about to fire off a fourth shot he spotted something out of the corner of his eye. Turning, he found that something to be Professor Acorn Boxley, his arms folded across his chest. Standing next to the professor were Big and Digs.

"If it isn't my loyal assistant," said Professor Boxley, sounding none too pleased.

"Well, what do you know," said Gateman, chuckling nervously as he holstered the smoking gun. "You're . . . still alive. That's great news."

"Yes," said Professor Boxley. "Isn't it?"

"Hey, come on," said Gateman. "You would have done the same thing if you were in my shoes."

"I *was* in your shoes. About fifteen minutes ago. Remember?"

"Yes," said Gateman, all but giving up hope of being

able to justify his actions. He lowered his eyes in a practiced show of remorse. "I guess I panicked. I'm terribly sorry for anything that might be interpreted as me running away and leaving you to be eaten by a bear. But you see, I knew that someone as smart as yourself would find a way out of the predicament, and, as it turns out, I was right."

Professor Boxley sighed. "Okay. Just don't let it happen again." For a scientific genius, the professor could be quite gullible.

"So tell me," said Gateman. "By what brilliant means did you manage to escape?"

"There was nothing brilliant about it," said Professor Boxley. "This is Big. She and her little friend saved my life." Professor Boxley filled in the details of his narrow escape from death but Gateman failed to hear a single word he said. He was busy staring at that baseball cap. He hadn't seen it in fifteen years. It hadn't seen him in several hours.

"Where did you get that hat?" asked Gateman, interrupting Professor Boxley in mid-story.

"From a friend," said Big. Though she had just met him, she knew right away that she did not like this man with the hollow cheeks and clammy forehead.

"That hat belongs . . ." He stopped short. If he told Professor Boxley the hat belonged to Mr. Cheeseman's elder son, the professor would want to know how he came by this little bit of information. "That hat belongs . . . in a museum. It must be one of the first baseball caps ever made."

97

"Would you forget about the hat?" snipped Professor Boxley. "We've got more important things with which to concern ourselves. Big is a professional guide. I've hired her to take us to the nearest town. The same town to which she took our good friend Ethan Cheeseman earlier today."

"Well then," said Gateman with a smile. "I suggest we get moving."

The water shimmered in the soft, late-day sun as a weathered gray rowboat of guaranteed buoyancy, powered by a man with the strength of two and a half men, glided into Boston Harbor. In modern times, the harbor would be crowded with ships of all types and sizes, but in 1668, other than a few small fishing boats, there were only two of any size. Long wooden vessels they were, with towering masts and each armed with an impressive battery of cannons. One was a Dutch Fleut, the other an East Indiaman.

"Well, would you look at that?" said Jibby of the fleut. "If it isn't the *Sea Urchin*." The ship's prow featured a mermaid carved in wood. The mermaid's paint had chipped and faded and one side of her head was completely missing. Cannon fire would be a good guess as to the cause.

The ship's sides were stripped of pitch in many places, the bare wood graying and bloating badly. The black flag, which featured the image of a silver ring, hung from the main mast in tatters. "Looks like our old friend the Mailman is in town," said Jibby.

Sammy guided the boat to the dock and Aristotle tied it

to a pier next to several other boats, slightly larger in size, called tenders—rowboats used to ferry crewmen from the ships in the harbor to the shore and back again. On the dock sat two young boys fishing without much luck, their wooden bucket completely empty. They looked at Jibby and his boatload of misfits with annoyance for having disturbed the water and perhaps frightened away their dinner. Jibby climbed ashore and gave them a friendly nod, then extended a hand to his crew, beginning with his lovely wife, Juanita.

"So this is Boston," said Sammy, looking out at the bustling settlement before them. "Looks like a nice place."

"*Me gusta*," Juanita agreed.

"What do we do now?" asked Dizzy.

"Can't get to Denmark without a ship," said Jibby. "I think we should pay a little visit to the Mailman. And I have a pretty good idea where to find him."

Just a stone's throw away (perhaps two stones, depending on who was doing the throwing, but certainly no more than two), up the narrow cobblestone street that ran along the water, sat a white plaster-covered ordinary. Above the door, a large wooden sign suspended by chains marked it as THE ACKERMAN INN. It was a sturdy building and quite well insulated. From the street you might think that the establishment was closed or had gone out of business, but when an elderly gentleman with a curly mustache and a slight limp approached the inn and opened its heavy wooden door, the sounds of laughing, arguing, and yelling poured out like water from a hydroelectric dam. When the door swung closed behind the old man, the street quickly became a dry gulch of silence once more.

Inside the tavern, the air was thick with the stench and pother of seafaring men, all gathered around a table at the center of the room where an arm-wrestling competition was in progress. A crowd of fifty or more encircled the combatants, cheering for the one on whom they had bet their day's earnings, which for nearly all of them was hometown favorite Haystack Saunders, a man of such excess weight that the overworked wooden stool on which he sat could barely be seen.

When the battle first began, most of the onlookers assumed they would be cashing in on their bets in a matter of seconds. But now, nearly an hour later, the haystack-sized man had not been able to defeat his opponent, which was odd because his rival was but a third his size and not terribly muscled. In fact, as a matter of demonstration, you should know that the wiry man across from him had recently gotten a tattoo of a beautiful Polynesian girl in a grass skirt on the bicep of his right arm, the idea being that whenever he flexed his muscle she would appear to be dancing the hula. As it turned out, however, his arm was not sufficiently big to make the girl shimmy and shake her midsection. In fact, the best his undersized bicep could do was to make her wiggle the ankle of her left foot. The end result was a beautiful Polynesian girl who appeared to be dancing not the hula but the hokey-pokey.

"Wow. That lad is mighty impressive indeed," said the elderly man who had walked in earlier. He nudged the man standing next to him, who just happened to be Corben Ackerman, owner of the Ackerman Inn. "What's his name?"

"What's his name? Why, that's Haystack Saunders."

"No," said the elderly man. "The other fellow."

"Don't know his name," said Ackerman. "He's a privateer, I understand. And they call him the Mailman."

The Mailman, with his deficient biceps and hokey-pokey tattoo, was one of the fiercest and, dare I say, one of the ugliest pirates around. It should also be pointed out that, despite his name, he had nothing to do with the delivery of letters or parcels. He was known as the Mailman for a very different reason—or should I say about two hundred different reasons, because this is approximately the same number of piercings the man had on his face, each featuring a small gold or silver ring. He had enough rings on his left ear alone to hang a shower curtain. Rings lined each eyebrow and both lips and ran around each nostril. They covered a good portion of his neck and the areas of his shiny bald head where the skin was loose enough to be pierced.

Before the days of plate armor, the best way for medieval warriors to protect themselves against sharp swords was, well, to run away and hide. The second-best way was with another type of armor that consisted of thousands of metal rings all hooked together to form a barrier between flesh and blade. It was, essentially, a wearable chain-link fence and was known as chain mail or simply mail. And this is how the Mailman, with his multiringed face, neck, and head, came by his name.

His face jingled steadily as his scrawny arm pushed back against the meaty palm of his opponent, whose face grew a deeper shade of purple with each passing minute. The Mailman's face jingled ever more loudly. The hula girl wiggled her ankle as if to say, "That's what it's all about."

"You look terrible, mate," the Mailman taunted in his heavy cockney accent. "Like a four-'undred-pound sugar beet, ya do. Best maybe you lie down for a bit, eh? Take a wee rest. Come on, now. You've earned it, lad."

Haystack Saunders opened his mouth, ready with a witty retort, when suddenly he seemed to take the Mailman's unsolicited advice. In one instant, after a full hour of cheering, yelling, swearing, and purpling, Haystack's face lost all of its color, turning as white as the eyes that had rolled to the back of his head. He swayed—first left, then right, and finally all the way to the floor—but not before the Mailman had forced the back of his hand to the tabletop, winning the match. The victor leaped up and thrust his exhausted right hand triumphantly into the air, turning the hula girl tattoo upside down.

The crowd erupted in jeers at the loss by their

hometown boy and whispers of foul play on the part of the Mailman and his crew. The Mailman's first officer bent over the fallen Haystack and removed the golden ring from his left earlobe. He was a shifty-looking man by the name of Shifty. In fact, the other members of the Mailman's crew were similarly named, making them sound like the Seven Dwarfs gone bad. Besides Shifty, there was Flaky, Shady, Scurvy, Sketchy, Smarmy, and Doc, along with a half dozen other men, all of the same brutish ilk, with little to offer polite society and nothing to lose.

With a crooked smile, Shifty handed the coveted ring to the Mailman, who held it to the light and admired its sheen with no less appreciation had it been the very first he won.

Jibby and his crew walked in just as a half dozen of Haystack's supporters dragged him toward the door in hopes that some fresh air might revive him. They did this on orders from the old man with the mustache and the limp, the man known as Dr. Dignan.

"Hurry now," he commanded. "If he doesn't come around soon, we may have to bleed him. Or if that doesn't work, we may have to drill a few holes in his skull. Nothing serious. Six or seven at the most."

As the men lugged the unconscious loser—well, that's a rather harsh word; let's call him the second-place finisher—out into the fresh air, Jibby eyed the Mailman from across the room. "Well, Sammy?" he said. "You think you can take him?"

"With one hand tied behind my back," said Sammy, rolling up his sleeves.

"Good. Because we'll be betting our ship on you. Our ship against his."

"But we don't have a ship," said Aristotle. "Do we?"

"No, we don't," said Jibby. "But he doesn't know that."

ADVICE ON RESISTING PIERCE PRESSURE

There was a time, it seemed, when earrings were reserved strictly for ears. These days people's entire faces are being punctured with the frequency of a vice principal's tires.

I recently paid a visit to my local neighborhood coffee shop, where each of the persons employed there had no fewer than a half dozen metal objects attached to their faces. I asked one of the employees for a key to the restroom and noticed it was hanging from his left eyebrow. Handy.

Leaving the coffee shop and strolling through the downtown area, I spied a young couple walking hand in hand. Something (a severe vitamin deficiency, perhaps) had convinced these two that they should each have a ring inserted in their respective noses and that those rings should be connected with a long chain. I honestly have no idea what these people were thinking. I do, however, know what I was thinking: Red rover, red rover, send Cuthbert right over.

However, as strange as it might seem to me, I suppose this practice of self-mutilation is really nothing new and is no different than our forefathers growing sideburns the size of a badger or our foremothers plucking out their eyebrows only to paint them back on again with a colored pencil. So pierce away, but I advise you to be careful of this new craze. You may find yourself getting hooked on it, which might very well result in something getting hooked on you.

CHAPTER 8

Mr. Cheeseman and the children used the bronze rods as walking sticks and followed Mr. Lumley to a small wooden cottage next to a wide cornfield. There were flower boxes beneath the two front windows of the house, one of which was open with a pie cooling on its ledge, exhaling a sweet-smelling steam. Mr. Lumley led his new friends along a short walkway of flat stones and up the porch steps to the heavy wood-plank door.

"I like your house," said Penny.

"It could be a museum someday," said Teddy.

"Oh, I don't know about that," said Mr. Lumley with a scowly chuckle. "It's nothing fancy, but we like it. My father and I built it together. He's passed now. Ten years it's been."

When Mr. Lumley pushed the door open, Teddy was pleased by the wonderful mingling of smells that rushed to his eager nostrils. From the orchestra of aromas he could make out several individual instruments. There was black-berry pie, baked bread of some sort, and something kind of stewy. All in all, Teddy put the smell of the one-room house at a solid nine-point-six.

Pinky let out a low growl. The growl came not from her throat but from her stomach. If Teddy hadn't eaten in hundreds of years, then it could be fairly stated that Pinky hadn't eaten in thousands of dog years.

"We'd better leave these here," said Mr. Cheeseman, leaning his bronze rod against the porch railing. The children did the same, and Mr. Lumley escorted his new friends inside.

With the day's sun inching toward the horizon, the home was very dimly lit and Mrs. Lumley was left with just the glow of the fire and a few flickering candles by which to cook. She was a fair woman with naturally pink cheeks and dark, graying hair pulled back and pinned into a tight knob at the back of her head. The sight of her husband brought a smile to her face, which doubled in size when she saw that he had come home with guests, three of them children.

"Well, what have we here?" She put her work aside and cleaned her hands with her apron.

"I've got out-of-town visitors for the evening," said Mr. Lumley. He introduced Mr. Cheeseman and the children to his cheerful wife, who seemed to give absolutely no notice to their strange clothing or to the fact that their dog was completely hairless.

"It's an honor to have you in our home," she said. "What brings you to our fine little village?"

"Just in for some supplies," said Mr. Cheeseman. "Doing some repairs around the house."

"Speaking of repairs," said Mr. Lumley, "Ethan here has figured out the cause of my headache. Turns out it's my eyes. Just need a pair of proper spectacles is all."

"I suggested that months ago," said Mrs. Lumley, stirring the aromatic contents of a large cast-iron pot hanging above the fire.

"You did?" said Mr. Lumley.

Mrs. Lumley rolled her eyes and shook her head. "Men," she said. "Do they ever listen?"

"Not to me they don't," said Penny.

Mrs. Lumley smiled at Penny and hurried over to a long harvest table along the far wall. She pulled out a bench that ran the length of the table. At each end sat a small wooden chair. "Please, sit down," she said. "Dinner will be ready presently. Lamb stew with biscuits and blackberry pie for dessert."

Teddy removed the wad of flavorless gum from his mouth and, as a matter of convenience, stuck it to his forehead, as he often did while dining. "I love blackberry pie," he said.

"Me too," said Rat-Face Roy.

"Grrr," said Pinky's stomach.

While visiting the expansive home of Jacques Bon Mot, one might surmise that there is good money to be made in the business of witch hunting. In fact, the professional witch hunter just happened to be in the process of counting his money when there came a rather urgent-sounding knock upon the front door. Bon Mot looked up from his neatly arranged stacks of coins. There was a second knock on the door, prompting him to call out "Mortimer!" which he, in his thick French accent, pronounced "Mortimay." "Answer zee door, you wrinkled piece of sausage."

"Yes, your benevolence," said Mortimer in a weak, tired voice. The servant's ancient feet shuffled toward the front door as he muttered under his breath. "Stubby little snail eater."

"I heard zat," shouted Bon Mot, who was indeed a very short man and did enjoy eating snails on occasion.

When his eighty-year-old feet finally got him to the front door, Mortimer took the knob in his shaky, spotted hand and pulled it open to reveal the two horsemen, serious fellows by the names of Seth and Caleb, who just happened to have the misfortune of being the husbands of Appalling and Outrageous. They held their big buckled hats in their hands out of respect for and fear of the great witch hunter. Get on his bad side and you might suddenly find yourself accused of witchery.

"Yes?" said Mortimer. "May I help you?"

"We're here to see Monsieur Bon Mot," said Caleb nervously.

"I'm sorry," said Mortimer. "His supreme and wonderful lordship is busy counting his money at this moment. When he is finished, sometime later this week I would imagine, he has made plans to visit an orphanage so that he might have the opportunity to kick some children in the shins. But I will tell him you stopped by."

Suddenly Mortimer was brutally shoved aside and Bon Mot appeared in the space his servant had once occupied. "Pardon my valet," he said. "He's very old and feeble, I'm afraid. Just look at him, would you? His back is curved like a stale croissant. It was only out of zee kindness of my heart zat I agreed to take him in." Bon Mot looked at Mortimer, who was just standing there. "Well?" he said. "Don't you have some wood to chop or some cows to milk?"

"Yes, your squattiness," said Mortimer with a slight bend of his already severely bent spine. He shuffled off and Bon Mot invited Seth and Caleb inside.

"Zis way," he said, leading them to a well-appointed sitting room that featured fine French furniture and, hanging above the fireplace, a life-size portrait of Bon Mot, which was not as impressive as it might sound, considering Bon Mot's actual size. "May I offer you some cognac?"

"No thank you, sir," said Seth. "We're here on somewhat of an urgent matter. You see, your services are greatly needed in town."

Bon Mot's right eyebrow rose involuntarily as it always did at the thought of money to be made. "Please," he said. "Tell me more."

Bon Mot leaned against the fireplace, striking the very same regal yet stubby pose he held in the painting above. He listened intently as Seth and Caleb told him how four very strange-looking people had walked into town on the same day that two mysterious lights appeared in the sky, making it a foregone conclusion that those lights were the result of witches racing through the air on their magical brooms.

"But you said zat zare were four strangers," said Bon Mot. "Yet only two lights in zee sky."

"They must have been traveling two to a broom," offered Seth.

"Yes, I'm sure that's it," Caleb concurred.

"Two to a broom?" This was the first Bon Mot had ever heard of witches carpooling—or, should I say, broompooling.

"We hear tale that they carry with them long golden wands, which they use to cast horrible spells," said Caleb.

"And Lumley, the blacksmith, tells of a magic black box with strange, ghostly lights," added Seth.

"Yes," said Caleb. "And the witches travel with a hairless red wolf, so large it could swallow a man whole."

This was, without a doubt, the worst case of witchcraft Bon Mot had ever encountered. "Mortimay," he hollered. He waited and waited some more. He drummed his fingers impatiently on the mantel. He was just about to call out again when Mortimer appeared in the doorway, dragging behind him, with all his strength, a large splitting ax.

"What are you doing with zat thing?"

"If you recall," said Mortimer, "I was instructed by his supreme heightlessness to chop some wood. I thought I might start with the table in the dining room."

"Put zat down," snarled Bon Mot. "Zare is no time, for

today we go hunting for weetches! Now hurry off to zee stable and saddle my trusty steed."

"To do so would cause my spirit to soar like an eagle," said Mortimer as he dropped the ax handle to the floor and shuffled off toward the front door.

"I know sarcasm when I hear it," Bon Mot shouted after him. "I practically invented it, you know."

Bon Mot's horse was a snow-white stallion named Claude, which he valued nearly as much as he did his precious money. Mortimer led the prized animal to the front of the house where Bon Mot was waiting. Actually, it would be more accurate to say that Claude led Mortimer because, try as he may, there was no way the horse could walk that slowly.

He stopped near Seth's and Caleb's highly inferior horses, which were tied to the railing. Seth and Caleb each took a step away from the intimidating beast. It may be hard to imagine being intimidated by a horse, an animal whose two main sounds are known as whinny and neigh, but this was no ordinary horse. "Look at him," said Bon Mot, beaming with pride of ownership. "Seventeen hands high is he. I can assure you, zare is no better horse for zee hunting of weetches." He cleared his throat and waited.

"Yes, your dwarfishness," said Mortimer with a heavy sigh, as if he were on his way to the gallows. With the cracking of bones, joints, and cartilage, he lowered himself to his hands and knees next to the horse, offering his curved, brittle back as a footstool.

Seth and Caleb gave an empathetic wince as Bon Mot placed his boot squarely in the small of the old man's back, stepped into the stirrup, and swung his stubby leg over the horse. "I will be back by sunrise," said Bon Mot.

"I shall look forward to the event as if it were my very own birthday," grunted Mortimer from all fours.

"Good," said Bon Mot. "See zat my breakfast is ready upon my return."

Without assistance, Seth and Caleb mounted their horses. Bon Mot pulled on the reins and Claude reared up on his hind legs with a whinny that was mightier than most. Bon Mot prepared to ride off when he noticed that Mortimer had not moved.

"Mortimay. You can get up now."

"Can I?" said Mortimer. "I'm so glad you think so."

CHAPTER 9

Gateman readjusted his wig and Professor Boxley wiped the back of his neck. "For goodness' sake," spouted the professor. "Just once could you sneeze without sneezing on someone else?"

"Sorry," said Gateman, who had never been more unsorry.

Big was sorry. Sorry she had agreed to take these two squabbling buffoons anywhere. Friends of Ethan Cheeseman's or not, they were getting on her nerves. They neared the town, and she was relieved that the job would soon be over. As she lead Gateman and the professor over the bridge, the ground beneath their feet began to vibrate. They stopped and turned to see three horses galloping toward them. Atop two of the horses were men with hammock-shaped beards and big buckled hats, while the third, a white monster of a horse, carried a short, cruel, weetch-hunting Frenchman. Big quickly scooped up Digs in her arms, then jumped onto the bridge's railing.

Jumping was beyond the physical ability of both

Gateman and the professor, so they did their best to squeeze against the opposite rail as the horses bolted across the bridge, rattling it to the point that Gateman lost his balance and nearly toppled over the side and into the river. He managed to hang on, though his wig was not so lucky. It floated to the water below and began a leisurely cruise downstream.

"Watch where you're going!" Gateman said with a shake of his fist. His demeanor changed quickly when he inhaled the dust that the horse's hooves had kicked up. "Ah, now that's more like it."

Big watched the men ride off toward town. She didn't know where they were off to in such a hurry, but there was something about it that troubled her greatly.

Some thirty feet down the river, a beaver crawled out from his dam to see a white wig with a long ponytail float by. "Grandma?" he thought. "Is that you?"

Mrs. Lumley smiled and placed a small pot of honey and some freshly baked biscuits in the center of the table. "Please help yourselves while I dish up the stew. It's so nice to have a house full of children," she said. "You're a very lucky man, Ethan."

"I couldn't agree with you more," said Mr. Cheeseman, his voice rich with fatherly pride.

"Nelson and I were not so blessed, I'm afraid. Oh, well. There's a reason for everything, I suppose."

As a man of science, Mr. Cheeseman was not so sure

about this, but he was relatively certain that there was a very good reason why Pinky was standing near the door, growling steadily. And this growl had nothing to do with hunger. This was a growl of warning, the kind that had saved the lives of Mr. Cheeseman and his children many times over the years.

Chip looked at his father. "I know," said Mr. Cheeseman.

The sound of Pinky's growling was slowly taken over by the thunder of horses' hooves, galloping toward the house until it seemed as if they might come right through the front door.

"Sounds like we've got more company," said Mrs. Lumley. "I hope I've made enough stew."

"Nelson Lumley!" came a booming voice from just outside. "It is I, Jacques Bon Mot. I know zat you have weetches in your house."

"There are witches in here?" gasped Teddy. He looked under the table but saw only feet.

"I'm not sure," said Penny, "but I think he might be referring to us."

"But we're not witches," said Teddy.

"Of course we're not," said Chip.

"I'll take care of this," said Mr. Lumley. He slid his chair back and walked to the door. He slipped out onto the porch, closing the door behind him. Ethan and the others listened intently to the conversation outside.

"There are no witches here, Mr. Bon Mot," said Mr. Lumley. "So you can turn around and go home now."

"I will go nowhere until I have taken zee accused

weetches into custody," said Bon Mot. "If you do not send zem out, I will be forced to burn zee house down."

"Oh dear," muttered Mrs. Lumley.

"You have no right to do that," said Mr. Lumley defiantly.

"Haven't I? I am here by order of zee governor himself."

"What shall we do, Dad?" asked Chip. "We can't let them burn the house down."

"And we can't let them arrest us," said Penny. "We studied witch hunts in history class. If they catch us they'll probably hang us all."

"Hang us?" said Teddy. "I always thought they burned witches, but I guess I was wrong. I know you have to shoot werewolves with a silver bullet. For vampires you need to hammer a wooden stake into their hearts. And mummies? Hmm. I'm not sure how to kill a mummy. Poison darts, maybe."

Mr. Cheeseman thought for a very brief moment. "Teddy," he said. "That thing that Jibby gave you today? The one I told you not to use until tomorrow?"

"The cell phone?"

"Yes. I need you to use it now."

Mrs. Lumley watched with great curiosity as Teddy removed the cell phone from his pocket and flipped it open, lighting up the room with a cell-phoney glow.

At the same time, the standoff outside the cottage was growing more and more heated. Mr. Lumley steadfastly refused to hand over his guests to the witch hunters, and the likelihood of the stubborn Bon Mot giving up and going home seemed virtually nonexistent.

The argument attracted the attention of curious towns-people, who stepped out of their homes and wandered toward the commotion. Among them were Appalling and Outrageous. Bon Mot turned to Seth. "Burn it," he said with a nod toward the cottage.

Before Seth could hurl the torch onto the thatched roof of the lovely little house, the front door opened and out walked Mr. Cheeseman and his three smart, polite, attractive, and relatively odor-free witches. Children. Sorry, his three children. "No," said Ethan in a booming and powerful voice. "If you harm this house or anyone in it, you will pay the price."

"It is you who will pay zee price for your evil ways," said Bon Mot with a guttural laugh.

Mr. Cheeseman raised the cell phone above his head and hit the memo button. It was Teddy's voice that came forth. "Help! The witches have imprisoned me in this tiny box. Leave them alone or they will do the same to you. Heeeellllp!"

The growing crowd of onlookers quickly backed away. Seth turned white. Caleb turned green. Their horses turned around and galloped from the house as fast as they could. "Come back here, you cowards!" shouted Bon Mot.

Mr. Cheeseman hit the ring tone button and the tinny sounds of "The Girl from Ipanema" rang out. Luckily, Claude was not nearly as big a fan of the song as was Captain Jibby. The horse reared up on his hind legs and whinnied mightily, throwing Bon Mot to the ground, flat on his back, with spleen-rupturing force.

"Quick," said Mr. Cheeseman, pointing toward the cornfield. "Run!" Pinky and the children sprinted from the porch. "Sorry for the trouble," said Mr. Cheeseman to Mr. Lumley with a quick handshake. He poked his head inside the door. "And thank you for the biscuits." Mrs. Lumley joined her husband on the porch and watched in stunned silence as Mr. Cheeseman hurried off to catch up with the children.

"Well, that's a shame," said Mrs. Lumley. "Nice folks."

"Yes," Mr. Lumley agreed. "For witches."

With great effort and severe pain, Bon Mot pulled himself to his tiny feet. "You will not escape zee great Jacques Bon Mot," he shouted in time with his shaking fist. He tried to climb into the saddle, but without Mortimer's back to stand upon, his stubby leg would not reach the stirrup. He decided a running start might be the answer. He backed up ten feet, took a deep breath, and charged toward the horse. He sprang into the air, soaring gracefully like a flying squirrel, but without the bushy tail or the ability to fly. He slammed into the horse's flank with the sound of ribs cracking (not the horse's) and dropped quickly to the hard ground.

"Ouch," said Mr. Lumley, imagining how Bon Mot might feel right about now.

Bon Mot turned his head slowly. "Don't just stand zere, you weetch-loving peasants. Help me up at once."

The corn leaves tickled Teddy's ears as he ran down the narrow path between the rows, trying hard to keep up with Chip, Penny, and Pinky but losing ground. Suddenly something grabbed him and lifted him into the air. He tried to scream but a hand clamped down on his open mouth.

"Shh," said Mr. Cheeseman. He slung Teddy over his shoulder, fireman style, and quickly caught up with his other two children. Beyond the sounds of their pounding feet and pounding hearts, there was also the sound of a mob forming in the streets. Teddy gave this sound his lowest possible rating.

They ran and ran and, just as they were about to run out of breath, they ran out of corn. Chip was the first to reach the end of the line and the others soon joined him. He dropped to one knee and peered around that last stalk of corn. Back on the main drag, in the dim light, he could see two men walking by, one carrying a rifle, the other a pitchfork.

"What do we do we now?" he whispered.

"I don't know," said Mr. Cheeseman. He set Teddy down. "There's only one road out of town, and it's swarming with people who think we're witches."

Pinky growled and Chip grabbed her gently around the snout. "Yes, Pinky. We know. Good girl."

"Listen," said Mr. Cheeseman, looking back the way they had come. There was a definite rustling of the corn stalks that was growing louder by the second. Bon Mot was searching the cornfield. About fifty feet from its edge, on a patch of grassy land, stood a weathered gray barn. "Quick! To the barn."

Chip prepared to make a run for the barn across fifty

feet of naked ground. He inhaled deeply and took off with the others close behind, running bent at the waist to minimize their exposure.

As his feet pounded the ground, the blood pounded in Teddy's ears, a sound he rated at a surprising six-point-five because it meant that, for the time being, he was still alive. They dove behind the building, breathing as quietly as they could while the sounds of the angry mob seemed to grow angrier and mobbier by the second.

Mr. Cheeseman nodded toward a small door at the back of the barn. Chip crawled over and gave it a push. It opened with a painfully loud squeak. He ducked into the barn and the rest of his family followed.

Inside were many things you might expect to find in a barn. Two of those things caught Mr. Cheeseman's eye right away. The first was a wagon, its bed full of fresh, damp hay. The other was an old, sleepy brown horse. "The wagon," he said. "It may be our way out of here. Quick, let's get the horse hitched up."

"Dad," said Penny. "I don't think that horse is capable of outrunning anybody. I mean, look at him."

Mr. Cheeseman looked at the old horse, who seemed to say with his sleepy eyes, "She's right. I couldn't outrun a turtle with an artificial hip."

"Maybe we don't need to outrun anybody," said Mr. Cheeseman. "Maybe we just sneak by them."

"What do you mean?" asked Chip.

"If you kids were to hide under the hay, I could drive the cart all the way to the river. From there we could buy a boat and make our way to Boston, get some more rods for the LVR, and sneak back in a couple of days when the heat has died down."

"But they'll recognize you," said Penny.

"Maybe if we wait till dark," said Teddy.

"We can't afford to wait," said Chip. "They're bound to find us here. We've got to go now."

"You're right," said Mr. Cheeseman. "There must be a way. We just have to use our heads."

"Use our heads," said Penny. She repeated the phrase several times, then slowly moved her hand to her head and ran it down the length of her hair. "That's it."

She turned in a circle, her eyes scanning the barn, looking for something, anything sharp. They came to rest on an ax, its blade stuck into an old tree round. She ran to the ax and, with a couple of quick wiggles on the handle, pulled it from the stump. "Here," she said to her father. "Take this."

Perplexed, Mr. Cheeseman took the ax in hand and watched as Penny gathered her long auburn hair into a ponytail. She knelt down next to the stump and stretched her hair across its surface. "Now," she said, "chop it off."

"I don't understand," said Mr. Cheeseman. "You want me to chop off your hair?"

"We're going to make you a disguise," said Penny. "Now hurry up."

"Okay." With shaky hands, Mr. Cheeseman raised the ax above his head, paused for a moment, then brought it down slowly.

"What's wrong?" asked Penny.

"It's just that . . . Chip is quite a baseball player. It might be better to have him do it."

"Sure," said Chip. He took the ax from Mr. Cheeseman and positioned himself over the stump, digging his feet into the dirt for balance. Like a baseball hitter using his bat to measure the distance to the plate, he reached out with the ax and touched the area he meant to strike. Then, with a couple of quick breaths, he raised the ax above his head, brought it down, and severed Penny's head.

From her hair, that is. Sorry about that. He severed Penny's head from her hair. Or is it her hair from her head? Anyway . . .

Chip breathed a sigh of relief and Penny stood up, holding a twelve-inch length of freshly cut hair. "Nice job," she said. "Fastest haircut I've ever had." She looked around the barn once more. "We have your beard but we still need a way to stick it to your face."

"Maybe there's some glue in here," said Teddy, smacking his gum loudly.

"I doubt it," said Chip.

Penny strode over to Teddy, her palm outstretched. "Your gum. Hand it over."

"But it's my last piece," said Teddy.

"It might be the last piece you ever chew if you don't hand it over right now."

Without further hesitation, Teddy reached into his mouth and pulled out the giant wad of flavorless pink goo. He placed it in Penny's outstretched hand and watched with longing as she walked away. "Okay, Dad," she said, leading her father to the tree round. "Have a seat."

Mr. Cheeseman sat on the stump as he was told. "And hold this, please." Penny handed Ethan the beautiful hair of which she had been so proud because it looked so much like her mother's. She began working the gum with her hands like modeling clay, softening, flattening, and stretching it into roughly the shape of a miniature pink hammock. She pressed it to Ethan's face, laying the foundation for his future beard. Outside the barn, the sounds of the mob grew louder, closer. Pinky growled and Chip shushed her again. This was the first indication they'd had that having a psychic dog who growls at any sign of danger could be a drawback.

"We're aware of the danger, Pinky," said Chip. "We need you to stop warning us now." Pinky seemed to understand. She stifled her growling with a slight whimper and then lay down on the dirt floor. Chip gave her a reassuring pat on the head. After all, he didn't want to discourage her in any way. "Teddy, stay with Pinky. Make sure she doesn't growl. I'm going to get the horse hitched up."

"Do you know how to harness a horse?" Mr. Cheeseman asked.

"No idea," said Chip. "But I'll do my best." Chip approached the old horse slowly. "It's okay. We're gonna take you out for a little walk, that's all." Chip removed a set of reins from a hook on the wall and tried to make sense of what looked to him like a tangled mess of leather strips and metal hooks.

"There," said Penny when she had finished sticking the gum to Mr. Cheeseman's chin and cheeks. "Now, let's see that hair." She took the severed locks and measured them against her father's face. "Too long." She found the ax and handed it to Ethan, instructing him to hold it with the blade facing up. She grasped the hair tightly in both hands and ran it back and forth over the blade, slicing it half. Bit by bit, Penny fastened the hair to Mr. Cheeseman's face until he had his very own auburn-colored, hammock-shaped beard. Penny stepped back to size up the job she had done.

"Well?" said Mr. Cheeseman, trying hard not to move his face when he talked. "How do I look?"

"Hmm. Like the son of Abraham Lincoln and Wilma Flintstone."

"That bad?" said Mr. Cheeseman.

"Your hair doesn't match your beard." She looked around the barn and spied a straw hat hanging from a nail. She grabbed it and tossed it to Mr. Cheeseman. "Try that." Mr. Cheeseman donned the hat and Penny gave a nod of approval. "Perfect. Except for your clothes. Here." Penny grabbed an old tattered coat from a hook on the wall and handed it to her father.

"Okay," said Chip. "I think I got it." He gave the reins a good tug to make sure they were fastened correctly, then led the horse over to the cart. That was the easy part. The hard part was getting the animal to back up to the cart so he might be properly harnessed. Though his father had taught him to drive a car, both standard and automatic,

Chip had no idea how to put a horse in reverse. "He won't go backward."

"That's okay," said Mr. Cheeseman. "We'll just wheel the cart around behind him."

The cart was heavier than it looked, and it took all four of them to move it into position behind the horse. They found they had to zigzag it several times to line it up properly. Mr. Cheeseman had never hitched a horse to a wagon before. In fact, he had never hitched anything to a wagon before. But as a brilliant scientist, he was relatively sure he could figure out the mechanics of such a thing. At least he hoped that he could. For if he failed, it could be the end of them all.

ADVICE TO THE PUBLIC ON PRIVATEERS

It's sometimes easy to forget that pirates are criminals—people who take what is not rightfully theirs—like bank robbers, shoplifters, or your older brother. And while there are but a few famous shoplifters, there is no shortage of well-known pirates, including: Henry Morgan, Captain Kidd, Blackbeard, Bluebeard, Yellow Beard, and Yellow Beard with Black Roots, who surmised that, if blondes have more fun, then blond pirates must have a heck of a lot more fun.

But what is our fascination with pirates, and why do we treat them differently than we do other lawbreakers? For instance, pirates are the only type of criminal after which it is acceptable to name a sports franchise. While we have teams known as the Pirates and the Buccaneers, it is unlikely that you will ever find yourself watching a game between the Kansas City Thieves and the Arizona Arsonists. (If you do, I would strongly advise against putting your money on the Thieves.)

Just as sports enthusiasts are tolerant of this type of behavior, the pirate is the only parent-approved, robbery-themed Halloween costume. While each year children by the thousands adorn their faces with eye patches and coffee-ground beards and venture out into the neighborhood in search of sugary loot, you will see very few kids dressed as pickpockets or Mafia kingpins.

I believe the fascination with pirates has less to do with all the stealing and plundering and more to do with adventure on the open sea (now open twenty-four hours for your convenience). After all, is there anything more exciting than a hunt for buried treasure? To find out, I recently purchased a metal detector and brought it to a nearby beach in search of excitement and underground riches.

I learned rather quickly that hunting for buried treasure can be quite dangerous because you can actually die of boredom. After four hours in the blazing sun, everything I had dug up included six nails, eleven bottle caps, and a skeleton holding a metal detector. I would thereby advise you that a pirate's life is not all it's cracked up to be and, though dressing as one for trick-or-treat may be fun, entering into an agreement with one could be deadly.

CHAPTER 10

As his crewmen counted their winnings while swilling celebratory tankards of ale, the slow-witted Mailman sat at the table probing his hideous head and face, searching for any remaining spot with skin loose enough to pierce so he might properly display his latest trophy. He found no vacancy and turned his attention elsewhere, finally settling on his right elbow, which was currently ring free. "Right 'ere," he said, stretching out the skin as far as it would go.

To his left sat his loyal first mate, Shifty, holding a needle over the dancing flame of a candle. Though the Mailman had been pierced on hundreds of occasions, it still hurt like the dickens every time that needle poked through his skin. He winced in advance, preparing for the sting as Shifty placed the needle against his elbow and, with a pop, drove it through. The Mailman let out a hiss, then quickly inserted his newly acquired earring into the freshly made hole.

"Well, mates?" he said, standing and exhibiting his latest disfigurement for all to see. " 'Ow do I look?"

"Like a big ugly tambourine with legs," came a voice from behind him. The Mailman's soulless eyes narrowed. He turned, curious to see who had the guts to throw such an insult his way. He was surprised to find a familiar face looming above him. It was Captain Jibby, his big white smile framed by his red shrubby beard.

"Well, what 'ave we 'ere?" said the Mailman with a smile of his own as he turned to face Jibby and his crew. It was not necessarily a friendly smile, though not an unfriendly one either. "If it ain't Gentleman Jibby Lodbrok," he said, his face jingling not at all unlike a tambourine. The Mailman's crew—Shifty, Flaky, Shady, Scurvy, Sketchy, Smarmy, and Doc—did likewise, taking up a position behind their captain in a shifty, flaky, shady show of unity.

"It's been a long time, jingle face," said Jibby.

"Indeed it 'as, you old rust bucket," the Mailman agreed. "No 'ard feelings, I trust. That bit of nastiness back in Denmark was all business, you know. Nothing personal."

"Most men who steal from me don't live to tell about it," said Jibby.

"I ain't most men," said the Mailman with a short burst of laughter. While most people's laughs tend to fade away gradually, the Mailman could go instantly from snicker to sneer, which could make things very awkward in a hurry, especially if you were caught still laughing after he had stopped. He sized up Jibby's crew and was shocked at how haggard they looked. He had no way of knowing that Jibby and his crew had spent the last eight years in the future working as a traveling circus sideshow, and thus were all eight years older than the last time he saw them—only three months before off the coast of Denmark.

"Blimey, lad," he said when his eyes landed upon Jake. "What the devil 'appened to you, Four-Eyed Jake?"

"Uh . . . it's Three-Eyed Jake now, I'm afraid," said Jake. "Little sword-swallowing accident. Missed my mouth and, well, you get the picture."

The Mailman did get the picture and shuddered, causing his face to jingle like wind chimes. "You look 'orrible. In fact, you all look awful. Like death warmed over, ya do. All but the beautiful Juanita, that is," he said with a leer.

Juanita stared at the Mailman and uttered something unsavory in Spanish. Jibby draped his arm protectively across her shoulders and the Mailman gasped at the sight of Jibby's severed right hand.

"Ahh," said the Mailman, making no effort to hide his repulsion. "Your 'and. Where the devil is your 'and?"

"Not sure where it is, to be honest," said Jibby. "Perhaps the tiger knows."

"Your 'and was eaten by a tiger?"

"Actually, I believe he spat it out. Too tough for him, I imagine."

"Or too sour," countered the Mailman with another quick laugh that he shut off like a kinked garden hose. "So tell me, Jibby old boy, what brings a man of such fine breedin' into a place like this?"

"Heard you were here," said Jibby. "Thought you might be interested in a little wager."

132

The Mailman laughed and his greasy-looking crew laughed with him at the absurdity of such a statement. To suggest that the Mailman might be interested in gambling would be similar to asking a mouse if it might be interested in a bite of your cheese sandwich. Again the Mailman's laugh stopped abruptly, like a test car hitting a wall at forty miles per hour. "You know me too well, Jibby," he said. "I'd welcome the chance to take your money. That and those lovely earrings on your lovely wife's lovely little ears. I've got just the place for them."

"No," said Jibby. "I'm thinking of a much bigger wager, actually."

"Oh?" said the Mailman.

"You against Sammy here. My ship against yours."

The Mailman looked a bit thrown. "You mean to say you would risk losing the *Bella Juanita*? She's your pride and joy."

"I don't plan on losing," said Jibby.

"They never do," said the Mailman, laughing for a full three seconds. "And if you win, what will you do with two ships?"

"By the looks of yours, I'd have little choice but to sell it for firewood."

The Mailman's eyes narrowed once more, becoming mere slits on his jingly face. "Be careful there, matey," he sneered. "It's one thing to insult the Mailman and quite another to speak poorly of 'is ship."

"Fine," said Jibby. "I shall reserve my comments for after she becomes mine."

"We'll see about that," said the Mailman. "Very well, then. Your ship against mine. When do we start?"

"We're ready whenever you are," said Jibby. "Right, Sammy?"

Sammy nodded confidently. He loosened up by shrugging his shoulders and rolling his head from side to side. As the two men were about to take a seat at the table, Shifty cleared his throat and said, "Permission to speak freely, sir."

"Go ahead," said the Mailman impatiently. Shifty leaned in and whispered something in the Mailman's ear.

"I don't follow you," said the Mailman. Shifty leaned in and delivered a longer message this time.

"Oh, riiiiight," said the Mailman. "Excellent point. Smart one, 'e is." Shifty's round, bearded face lit up with pride. "All right then, lads. Let the contest begin. Me against your boy Sammy. The *Bella Juanita* against the *Sea Urchin*. A balancin' contest. 'E who can stand on one foot the longest wins." The Mailman did a couple of deep knee bends to get the blood flowing.

"Balancing contest?" said Jibby.

"That tiger didn't bite off your ears too, did 'e?"

"No, it's just that . . . I assumed it would be arm wrestling."

"Not sure if you had occasion to notice," said the Mailman, "but I just finished arm wrestlin' a man ten times me size. Needless to say, me arm's a bit spent, as you might imagine. Besides, I'm not stupid enough to go up against someone with the strength of, uh . . ." He turned to Shifty. "What was it again?"

"Two and a half men."

"Right. Two and a half men. No, I'm afraid it'll 'ave to be balancin'."

Jibby turned to Sammy. "How are you with balancing on one foot?"

Sammy shrugged. "Not bad, I suppose."

"Not bad? What do you mean by not bad?"

"Well, I mean not very good."

Jibby felt a tug at his sleeve. It was Dizzy, volunteering for duty. Of course, thought Jibby. Dizzy, with his specially made earmuffs, was the perfect candidate for the job.

"Dizzy is our man in this fight. The most stable fellow on one leg." He gave Dizzy an encouraging pat on the shoulder and then, with a smile and a wink, leaned in and whispered, "If you lose, I'll break both your legs."

Word of the contest spread quickly among the crowd and bets were laid as the Mailman's crew moved tables and chairs to make room for the upcoming battle of the well balanced. Dizzy removed his shoes. He always had better equilibrium without them.

Shifty laid down the ground rules and the two balancers faced each other. "Ready, Dizzy boy?" asked the Mailman. Dizzy took a deep breath and nodded confidently. "Really? 'Cuz you don't look so good. A little shaky. Last chance to back out."

"I'm fine," said Dizzy.

"All right then. On the count of three."

Shifty counted to three and Dizzy lifted his right foot off the ground while the Mailman went with the left.

Always looking for an edge, the Mailman made sure he was farthest from the door to avoid even the slightest draft. To further increase his advantage, his men stood behind him, slowly swaying from side to side in hopes of confusing Dizzy's perspective. Still, the Mailman had no idea that Dizzy had his own edge. Those silly-looking earmuffs, designed by the greatest scientist of all time, would keep Dizzy in perfect balance for as long as he needed. Or at least he hoped they would, for if not, there would be trouble. Big trouble.

CHAPTER 11

This is as far as I go," said Big, standing at the outskirts of town with her two squabbling clients. "You will find the ordinary on this very road on the right-hand side."

"Ordinary?" said Gateman.

"It's like a hotel," said Professor Boxley, who had done some research before departing for the seventeenth century.

"Excellent," said Gateman, rubbing his hands together excitedly. "I can't wait to order some room service. A massage would be nice, too."

"I said it's *like* a hotel," said the professor. "It's not a hotel. It's an ordinary. Remember, this is 1668."

What an odd thing to say, thought Big. To remind someone what year it was.

"I'm sure they must have an extraordinary," said Gateman. "Something with a nice bar and a pool? After all, this seems like a lively little town."

Gateman was right. From where they stood, it did seem like a lively town, with all the people running back and forth and all the shouting. But Big knew this was not a lively town. Something was going on. Something unusual.

"Well, thank you for your help, young lady," said the professor. "Best of luck to you. We'll be sure to say hi to Ethan Cheeseman for you."

Big forced the slightest of smiles but kept her eyes down the road on the quiet town that was, for some reason, no longer quiet. As her customers continued on, Big stood and listened to what sounded to her like an angry mob.

If there is one good thing about an angry mob, it's that they are often so focused on being angry and mobbish that they sometimes miss little things. Things like a horse-drawn cart being driven by the very person who has made them so angry and mobbish in the first place.

With his three children secreted beneath a pile of moist hay, Mr. Cheeseman, disguised with a straw hat and a reddish beard, guided the cart from the barn toward the main drag, which by now was teeming with people carrying torches, pitchforks, and rakes, and one very confused man who apparently had mistaken the mob for a parade and was marching around with a Swedish flag.

As the cart made its way toward the center of town, never before had the Cheeseman children had such fond recollections of their family station wagon. It may have been old and beat-up, but at least it had padded seats, shock absorbers, and did not smell of wet hay.

In addition to being very hard on one's backside, the bumpy ride also had the undesirable effect of loosening the bubble gum's grip on Mr. Cheeseman's face. The left side began to peel away and he quickly pressed it back on just as two men holding long wooden clubs ran by.

Beneath the hay, the children could see nothing but they could hear a great deal, even over the din of the iron-rimmed wheels grinding along the cobblestone street. They could hear footsteps rushing in all directions and Jacques Bon Mot barking out orders in the distance from atop his mighty steed. They could hear shouting and a man loudly singing patriotic songs in Swedish. They could hear female voices just clear enough to make out the words *appalling* and *outrageous* as the two plump women walked straight toward the cart, each carrying a long-handled sharp object equally suited to tilling the earth or bludgeoning witches. Mr. Cheeseman tensed at the sight of them.

As world-class busybodies, the women knew everyone in town, and this red-bearded farmer with his hand pressed to the left side of his face was not at all familiar to them. They sized up Mr. Cheeseman carefully as he passed. He held his breath and hoped the women scrutinized every-one in such a way. Once the cart had gone by, Mr. Cheese-man let out a huge sigh of relief. That sense of relief lasted all of about two seconds because just then he was reminded that he knew nothing about hooking up a horse to a seventeenth-century wooden cart. With a heart-sinking *thud*, the cart's sidebars fell to the ground. The horse kept moving. The cart did not.

"Why are we stopping?" whispered Teddy.

"Shh," said Chip.

The sudden quiet caught the ears of Appalling and Outrageous. They turned and looked at each other, then walked back to the motionless cart. "Pardon me, good sir," said Appalling, "but it doth appear that your horse is leaving you behind."

"Yes, it . . . doth appear that way, dothn't it?" said Mr. Cheeseman with a chuckle. He could feel the right side of the beard start to loosen and he quickly slapped his other hand to his face.

"Is there something the matter with your face?" asked Outrageous.

"Huh? Oh, yes. Toothache. Two. Two toothaches. One on each side. On my way to Boston to see the dentist. I'm . . . paying him in hay."

"I see. Perhaps you should fetch your beast," said Appalling, "lest he find himself taken captive by the witches for use in their unholy rituals."

"Witches?" said Mr. Cheeseman as if he had never heard the word before.

"Surely you've been told," said Outrageous, adjusting her glasses to get a clearer look at Mr. Cheeseman. "Our town has been besieged by them. You shouldn't be traveling without something with which to defend yourself." Then, without warning, she tossed her gardening implement to Ethan. Instinctively, he reached out with both hands and caught it. Without support, the beard slowly peeled away from his face on both sides.

The women gasped. "It's him!" cried Outrageous. "The leader of the witches!"

"Outrageous!" said Appalling.

"Appalling!" said Outrageous.

"Run, kids!" said Mr. Cheeseman.

The children jumped to their feet, throwing the damp hay aside, large chunks of it smacking Appalling and Outrageous in their faces, leaving them even more appalled and outraged than before. While Penny and Pinky hopped out of the cart, Chip lowered Teddy to the ground and then jumped out himself. Mr. Cheeseman peeled the sagging beard from his chin and tossed it aside. It soared through the air and landed, quite unintentionally, right on Appalling's well-groomed hair, gum side down. Perhaps, then, everything does happen for a reason.

Appalling screamed and fussed and generally ran around in panicky circles, trying to pull the sticky bubble gum from her hair. The accused witches took off on foot, quickly passing the old horse, still loping along and completely unaware that the wagon had come unhitched. As they ran by he gave them a look that seemed to say, "Hey, I know those guys."

"Ahhh, my hair!" cried Appalling. "The witches have cursed me! Oh, what a world!"

Jacques Bon Mot heard the cry as he emerged from the cornfield. Looking toward the main drag he saw the four dangerous witches; their hairless, man-eating pet wolf; and their pink-eyed, bilingual sock puppet running in the direction of the bridge out of town . . . and directly toward

Gateman Nametag and Professor Acorn Boxley as the two men strolled into town, looking for the ordinary. Mr. Cheeseman and his children did not recognize Gateman as the evil Mr. 5, thanks to his toupee, goatee, and fifteen years of aging. In fact, they didn't even bother to look at him as they practically flew by.

Professor Boxley stopped and whirled around. "I don't believe it."

"Agreed," said Gateman. "That man should learn to control his children."

"No," said the professor. He pulled the magazine from his pocket and checked the photo on the cover. "That was him. That was Ethan Cheeseman. Come on, let's go." The professor took off down the road after the Cheeseman clan and Gateman followed, the thought of imminent revenge bringing a sudden ear-to-ear grin to his hollow cheeks.

Fueled by fear and adrenaline, the Cheesemans ran until the cobblestone turned to dirt and angled toward the bridge. If they could just get to the river they might have a chance, thought Mr. Cheeseman. A natural athlete, Chip was the fastest and had gained a considerable lead when he saw, standing on the path just up ahead, a familiar silhouette. He would have been overjoyed to see Big if he had not been preoccupied at the moment with not being killed.

"Chip," she said. "What's wrong? What's happening?"

"They think we're witches," said Chip breathlessly.

"Who thinks you're witches?"

"Everybody. The whole town."

"So that accounts for the commotion," she said. "We've

got to get you out of here. It will not go well for you if they catch you." Mr. Cheeseman, Penny, and Teddy caught up. Pinky greeted Digs with a friendly nudge, then turned and growled. Running toward them were Professor Boxley and Gateman Nametag and, farther down the road, Jacques Bon Mot and his massive horse, galloping at full speed.

"We'll never make it," said Mr. Cheeseman.

"You go ahead," said Big. "Continue over the bridge and down along the river to Crazy Nellie's shack. I'll catch up to you."

"What are you going to do?" said Chip.

"I'll be okay. Just go. Now!"

Reluctantly, Chip turned and sprinted down the road. The others followed, Pinky being the last to pull herself away. Big clapped her hands and pointed to a spot on the ground near her feet. "Digs. Right here."

Digs began digging furiously, carving out a six-inch-deep hole in no time. "And here." Digs dug another hole. Twice more Big pointed to spots on the ground, and each time Digs tore at the earth like a backhoe.

Bon Mot was not about to let these witches escape and ruin his perfect witch-hunting record. He kicked Claude in the ribs to hurry him along. Claude thought briefly about how nice it would be to kick Bon Mot similarly but instead did what he was told and increased his speed. All that stood between Bon Mot and his prey were several hundred feet of dirt road, a young girl in a blue baseball cap and her small brown fox, and two men in knee-length pants, hobbling along in their big-buckled shoes.

"Out of zee way, you wig-wearing simpletons!" he shouted. "Zay are getting away!"

When Gateman and the professor saw the tiny Frenchman atop the mighty, arrogant horse charging directly toward them, their faces nearly exploded with fear. Quickly they dove out of the way, one to each side, and rolled across the dusty ground just as Claude thundered by, right where they had stood a fraction of a second before. This marked the second time that day that they had been run off the road by horses and, despite the refreshing cloud of dust kicked up by Claude's hooves, Gateman was not happy.

"You'll pay for this!" he shouted as he and the professor stood up and dusted off their knee-length pants and fancy buttoned jackets. "Well, I must say, I can't wait to get back home, where there are five-star hotels and crosswalks."

"He seems to be after Ethan Cheeseman," said Professor Boxley. "But why? Who would want to hurt the greatest scientist of our time?"

"Yes," said Gateman. "What kind of . . . sicko would want to do something like that?"

"Hurry, Digs!" shouted Big as Bon Mot closed to within a mere fifty feet. Digs completed one last hole and then he and Big turned, ran, and hoped for the best.

Bon Mot leaned forward in the saddle to decrease wind resistance and improve his aerodynamics. The horse lengthened his gait. His oversized hooves punished the ground beneath them. Then, quite suddenly, the ground had its revenge as one of those obnoxiously large hooves—the right front one to be exact—landed in a freshly dug hole just deep enough to cause the horse to stumble forward.

Bon Mot took to the air like a circus clown shot from a cannon. A second later, the hard, angry ground offered his tiny body a most unpleasant welcome.

He landed chest first, his ruffled shirt providing little padding as he slid across the path, down a slight embankment, and into a good-sized blackberry bush. If it had been his habit to do so, he would have rated the sharpness of the stickers at an impressively high eight-point-nine. And if the fall hadn't knocked the wind out of him, he certainly would have been screaming in pain by now. Instead he just lay there, surrounded by thorns, afraid to move.

And so Claude did the moving for him. The horse walked down to where Bon Mot lay and took the heel of his master's protruding left shoe between his enormous white teeth. Claude put himself in reverse and dragged the battered witch hunter from the bush. Bon Mot made a wobbly transition to standing and gasped at the sight of himself. His white ruffled shirt was covered in blood. He gasped again, until he realized the blood was actually blackberry juice. Claude gave him a lick. Yes, definitely blackberry juice.

But there was no time for a Bon Mot smoothie right now. The witches were heading to the river. While Bon Mot searched the area for a way to get back onto his horse, the two men he had nearly run over just moments before came sprinting toward him. He moved to the middle of road and waved his arms, determined to flag them down.

"Stop! It is I, Jacques Bon Mot, and I command your assistance!"

Professor Boxley gave Bon Mot no assistance. Nor did Gateman, who instead gave him a hard hip check as he ran by, causing Bon Mot to topple over and slide down the embankment into the blackberry bush again. With his face somewhere in the middle of the undergrowth, Bon Mot missed out on seeing a most rare occurrence in nature: the sight of a horse smiling.

As a thin sliver of moon appeared in the sky, Crazy Nellie didn't expect any more business this late in the day. With the money Captain Jibby had paid her earlier, she walked out the rickety door of her equally rickety shack and prepared to set out for town when who should come running down the path along the river but another customer, a boy with a wiry, athletic build and a mustache that resembled poorly watered alfalfa sprouts in all but color.

"Excuse me," said Chip, trying to temper the urgency in his voice and sound as casual as the circumstances would allow so as not to raise suspicion. "Are you Crazy Nellie?"

The old woman flashed her shiny, tip-jar grin. "What can I do for you today?"

Nellie was pleased and surprised to see three more customers come running up, along with the strangest-looking dog she had ever seen. This was turning out to be a very good day indeed. "We need a boat," said Chip. "Our friend Big told us you have boats for sale."

"I do indeed," said Nellie. "Right this way."

"Any sign of her?" Chip asked his father as Crazy Nellie led her new customers down to the waterline.

"I don't see her," said Mr. Cheeseman, looking back over his shoulder.

"She'll be okay, Chip," said Penny. "Don't worry."

"I have two left," said Nellie. Chip paid little attention to the boats, gently nudging each other in the shallow water of the river's edge. Instead he kept his eye on the road, waiting and hoping that any second Big and Digs would appear.

Mr. Cheeseman looked doubtfully at the two boats. "I don't know," he said. "Are they seaworthy? We need to get to Boston Harbor."

"They're one hundred percent guaranteed," said Crazy Nellie. "Except the blue one, which comes with a free bailer." She looked around in the tall grass for the cast-iron pot but couldn't find it. "Hmm. It was here a minute ago."

"We'll take the red one then." Mr. Cheeseman dug into his pocket and pulled out a handful of coins.

"Excellent choice," said Crazy Nellie. "Will you be needing any oars with that?"

"It doesn't come with oars?"

"No, but if you buy three I'll throw in a free vest."

"Two oars will be fine. Listen, we're in a bit of a hurry here."

"It's a very nice vest. Even comes with a free bonus sleeve."

147

While Mr. Cheeseman negotiated with Crazy Nellie, Chip wandered back up the path, looking, waiting, and hoping. Pinky followed, also looking, waiting, and hoping. Despite all the looking, waiting, and hoping, they saw nothing but trees running along each side of an empty path.

"Chip! Let's go!" Penny, Teddy, and Rat-Face Roy sat in the creaky red rowboat and Mr. Cheeseman prepared to push off. Chip took one last look and Pinky took one last sniff before they started down toward the boat. Chip lifted Pinky into the boat, then climbed in himself and sat next to Teddy, who looked a bit shaken.

"You okay, Teddy?" asked Chip.

"Hmm?" Teddy certainly did not look okay. In fact, he couldn't remember a time in his young life when he had felt worse. He gave this horrible nauseated feeling an equally horrible rating of zero-point-zero.

With everyone aboard, Mr. Cheeseman waded into the ice-cold water, pushing the boat toward the swift center of the river. He was about to step into the boat when he heard, "Dad, wait!"

In the fading light, Chip was sure he saw a swatch of blue moving through the trees. Mr. Cheeseman waited for a moment but saw nothing. "Chip, I'm sorry." Chip offered a slow nod of resignation. Mr. Cheeseman climbed into the boat that he hoped was sufficiently seaworthy to take them, by oar and by current, to Boston Harbor.

Crazy Nellie barely had the chance to admire the shiny new coins Mr. Cheeseman had given her when two tired men came chugging down the path just in time to see the red rowboat disappear around the corner.

"There they go," said Professor Boxley. "We have to catch them. We need a boat."

"You've come to the right place, sir," said Crazy Nellie. "I've got one left and she's a real beauty."

Gateman and the professor looked at the faded blue boat, full of patches and utterly lacking in beauty. A good two inches of water had collected in its hull.

"Is it seaworthy?" asked the professor.

"One hundred percent guaranteed," said Nellie, "or your money back."

"Good. We'll take it."

The river grew wider, noisier, and splashier with every stroke of the oars that took Mr. Cheeseman and his family away from the angry mob, away from the LVR, and nearer to safety but farther from hope.

There was no conversation now. Just a sense of relief and a sense of dread mingling in the air above them. Ethan rowed steadily and mechanically while the children sat and stared at whatever happened to occupy the space directly in front of them.

What occupied the space in front of Chip was the forest—trees of green and brown and, for a brief moment, what looked possibly like a tiny patch of blue. But he'd been wrong before and so he chalked it up to a fluttering blue jay perhaps, or, more likely, wishful thinking.

As the red rowboat continued downstream, it took its silent, sullen crew around a long, sweeping bend. The first star appeared in the sky and Chip made a wish. Penny made a wish too. Teddy just stared straight ahead. Then Chip saw it. Not a tiny, possible splash of blue but a real, definite splash of blue.

It sat atop Big's head in the form of a Police Pals baseball cap. She and Digs stood on a fallen tree that stretched out over the river, perhaps five feet above the surface. "Look!" Chip shouted over the rush of the water. "It's Big." Chip waved and Big smiled ever so slightly. She crouched down as the boat neared and Digs inched forward to the very edge of the log. Chip and Teddy moved aside to make room. Though it had been years since he'd been at the oars, Ethan was still an expert rower, having been captain of the sculling team at Southwestern North Dakota State University. Deftly he guided the boat directly toward Big and Digs. He hoped the fragile boat could withstand the impact.

Big and Digs jumped, taking into account the speed of the boat and the distance to the water. What they did not and could not take into account was the boat meeting with a strong undercurrent, causing it to yaw sharply to the left at that very moment. Digs landed in Penny's lap, knocking her backward and nearly forcing the wind out of her. Big missed the boat altogether. Actually, she didn't quite miss it entirely. Her right arm collided with the side of the boat as she plunged into the cold, white water, disappearing in an instant.

"Big!" yelled Chip, searching for a sign of her in the churning river. A second later he saw the blue cap spring to the surface. But just the cap and nothing else. Quickly he removed his shoes.

"Chip, wait!" said Mr. Cheeseman, fighting to keep the boat from spinning around in the absolute wrong direction. But Chip did not wait. He dove into the river and vanished beneath the swirling rapids. Mr. Cheeseman knew that his son was a good swimmer but not a great swimmer, especially in conditions like these.

Under the water, Chip could see nothing but the water itself, full of bubbles, sand, and debris. He searched and searched with his hands, groping into the murky river for any sign of Big. By now his lungs were full of air but very little of it was oxygen. He needed to surface but was unable to determine which direction was up. Then he saw something float by, only inches from his face. It was bright red and light blue—the beads on Big's ponytail.

"Chiiiiiip!" yelled Penny. It had been nearly a full minute since her brother disappeared beneath the water's surface. Teddy just sat mumbling, tears streaming down his face.

Finally, after the longest sixty seconds in the history of mankind, Chip surfaced with a desperate gasp for air that might have been heard miles away. He'd been dragged downstream, ahead of the boat. "There he is!" Penny alerted her father. Mr. Cheeseman dug in and paddled toward his son. Chip swam for the boat as best he could with only one arm, the other wrapped around Big, towing her behind him. Big helped paddle with her left arm, the right one having been rendered completely useless by its collision with the boat.

Chip took hold of an oar and his father reeled him in, bit by bit, until Chip was able to grasp the side of the boat. Mr. Cheeseman and Penny grabbed Big's buckskin shirt and dragged her aboard, then pulled Chip from the freezing water.

For the first few moments, no one said a word. Chip and Big coughed up the water they had swallowed while Penny fought to catch her breath and Teddy rocked back and forth, his top teeth grinding against the lower ones. Digs sat in Penny's lap, whining softly.

"Are you okay?" asked Mr. Cheeseman when he had regained control of the boat. Chip nodded and noticed Big was clutching her right arm, her face locked in a grimace. Chip knelt over her.

"Your arm? Is it broken?"

"I'm not certain," said Big.

"Dad," said Chip. "The Empathizer."

Mr. Cheeseman tucked one oar under his arm, then reached into his pocket and fetched the magical black box. As the river tossed the boat violently, Chip attached one suction cup to his temple. "Where does it hurt?"

Big put her hand to her shoulder. Chip reached beneath her buckskin sleeve and attached the second suction cup. He powered up the Empathizer and Big watched as it came alive with lime-green light. Chip cried out and quickly turned off the machine.

"Broken?" said Penny.

"I don't think so," said Chip. "Feels like the time I dislocated my shoulder diving for a ground ball."

"Okay," said Mr. Cheeseman. "There's not much we can do about it now. Just make her as comfortable as possible and we'll get it looked at the minute we get to Boston."

"Looked at?" said Chip. "By the guy who drills holes in people's heads? I'm not letting him near her." Chip placed his hand beneath Big's head, giving it some manner of cushioning against the hard wooden hull of the boat. Though he was wet, cold, and near exhaustion, he honestly couldn't remember the last time he had been so happy to see someone.

"You saved my life, Chip," said Big, clutching Chip's hand in hers.

"Just paying you back for saving ours," said Chip.

"My friend Digs did all the work. All I did was nearly get you killed by taking you to that awful little town. And I'm sorry you never got to see your friends."

"Friends?" said Chip. "What friends?"

Big described the two wigged men she met in the woods and how one of them carried a strange painting of a very young Ethan Cheeseman. In addition to Mr. Cheeseman's likeness, the painting featured words as well and, though Big could not remember all of them, she did recall the phrase "Scientist of Tomorrow."

Mr. Cheeseman considered it necessary, under the

circumstances, to deny any knowledge of such a painting. But to Ethan and his children, Big's story could only mean one thing: someone from the future was looking for them. The very thought of it consumed their imaginations and momentarily drew attention away from the forest that ran along the river. For if they had been watching, they might have noticed a splash of white moving swiftly through the trees.

CHAPTER 12

Their feet were numb, their ankles swollen, their grasp on reality waning. Three and a half hours after the competition began, there was no end in sight to the battle of Dizzy and the Mailman. (Incidentally, a very good title for a sitcom. *Dizzy and the Mailman.* Thursdays at 8:00.)

Each man was soaked with perspiration and drowning in fatigue. The Mailman's crewmen were leaning ever farther to one side, by now listing at a near forty-five-degree angle. Dizzy tried not to look at them, instead focusing his gaze on a painting hanging on the wall, which, unbeknownst to him, Shifty had tilted to one side. Still, he kept his balance.

Tension in the crowded room grew by the second. The onlookers either cheered or groaned each time one of the balancers teetered or tottered.

Captain Jibby was not cheering. He just sat, biting his knuckles. The stakes were too high. If Dizzy won, they'd have the ship they needed to sail to Denmark and return the White Gold Chalice, thus ending the terrible curse. If Dizzy lost, they'd have no ship and a lot of explaining to do.

Then, just when it seemed the battle would go on forever, the Mailman appeared to be wavering. Dizzy's victory seemed a foregone conclusion when suddenly there could be heard, over the clamor of the crowd, a very high beeping noise. It came in three short, consecutive beeps. No one knew quite what to make of it, since they lived in a time long before beeping had been invented. No more than a half-minute had passed when the strange sound occurred again—and it seemed to be coming from Dizzy's head.

It may have seemed that way, but it was actually coming from Dizzy's earmuffs, which were, at the most inopportune time imaginable, emitting a low-battery signal. Because Mr. Cheeseman had given Dizzy the earmuffs just a few weeks ago (or several hundred years from now), he had never found it necessary to change the batteries and, in fact, had never given it much thought at all.

The beeping sounded once more, and then it was Dizzy's turn to panic. The earmuffs went dead and Dizzy's artificial sense of balance died with them. Dizzy nearly fell over that very instant but managed to avoid it by taking two giant hops to the left and then three hops backward. Then he began hopping forward, unable to stop.

Jibby removed his knuckles from his mouth and shouted, "No!"

The crowd parted down the middle and Dizzy hopped across the room, right for the opposite wall, stopping just inches short of slamming into it face-first. He hopped backward, then did a quick pirouette and hopped straight for the exit, where Dr. Dignan was now standing.

"Quick!" shouted Jibby. "Open the door."

While there were definite rules about using people or things to help contestants maintain balance, there was no rule stating that they had to remain in the room or in the city of Boston or even in the Northern Hemisphere, for that matter. The doctor opened the door and Dizzy hopped out into the street. The crowd followed while Jibby and Shifty stayed back to keep an eye on the Mailman, whose confidence seemed to have returned as quickly as Dizzy's had left him.

And if Jibby had any hope at all that his man Dizzy could somehow snatch victory from the jaws of defeat, it faded quickly when he heard a loud splash followed by cheers of triumph and moans of disappointment. The Mailman's multiringed lips curled into a smile most smug. He lowered his foot to the floor and was immediately greeted by a sharp pat on the back from Shifty. Moments later, Sammy and Aristotle dragged Dizzy, soaking wet from his recent plunge into Boston Harbor, back into the ordinary. The crowd came in on their soggy heels, losers begrudgingly paying winners.

"What the devil happened?" Jibby demanded.

"What do you think happened?" said Aristotle. "It's the curse."

The Mailman swaggered over. "Well, you can't win 'em all," he said. "I can, but you can't." The Mailman punctuated his remark with a quick two-second laugh. "Now, about me new ship."

"Yes," said Jibby. "About your new ship. You see, here's the situation."

The Mailman's countenance grew dark. His crewmen moved their hands to the grips of their cutlasses.

"The situation is . . ." Jibby appeared to be leaning toward the door when he said, "It's all yours. Without a doubt, the best man won today. Congratulations."

"Why, thank you," said the Mailman, a little thrown by Jibby's sunny disposition while standing in the shadow of defeat. His men relaxed and removed their hands from their weapons. "Now, I trust you'll need some time to remove your personal effects from the ship before I officially take 'er into me possession. Of course, me men and I will want to accompany you, just to make sure you don't run off with me *Bella Juanita*." He winked at Juanita when he said this, and Jibby fought off the urge to punch him in the nose.

Meanwhile, Jibby's crew looked to their captain, wondering how he would get them out of this mess. He had certainly gotten them out of jams before, but this one seemed particularly dicey. Jibby slapped his hand on the table. "No," he said. "We won't be needing our personal effects. They're all yours."

"I'm confused," said the Mailman.

"We don't need possessions to be happy," said Jibby. "All we need is each other. Right, men?" With a hearty laugh, Jibby threw his arms around Sammy and Aristotle. His crewmen tried their best to hide their confusion and forced out laughs of their own.

"Riiiight," said Three-Eyed Jake. "All we need is each other."

"You bet," said Jibby. "We've given up pirating and have decided to become shepherds, living the simple life."

The Mailman snorted out a quick one-second laugh. "Sorry, mate, but I have trouble imagining you as a shepherd. Just the sight of you all is guaranteed to frighten the sheep away."

"We'll see," said Jibby. "Now, let's go have a look at your new ship, shall we?"

Jibby led the way down along the water and the Mailman and his crew followed. Dizzy leaned against Sammy and Three-Eyed Jake for support. When they arrived at the pier, the two boys were still fishing and still had caught nothing other than a soggy white wig.

"There she is," said Jibby, looking out with pride at the ship to the right of the *Sea Urchin*. Beneath the light of a tiny slice of moon, it very well could have been the *Bella Juanita*. "Your new ship."

"She's a beauty, all right," said the Mailman, rubbing his palms together with excitement. "Just like her namesake. Okay, men, let's have a look at our new 'ome upon the sea." The Mailman and his crew climbed into their tender and prepared to row out to what they assumed to be the *Bella Juanita*.

Jibby's crew still had no idea what their captain was up

to. Once the Mailman got to the ship, he would find out rather quickly from whoever was onboard that it was not the *Bella Juanita*. When the Mailman and his crew had rowed a fair distance out into the harbor and were out of earshot, Three-Eyed Jake turned to Jibby. "What do we do now, run?"

"Run?" said Jibby. "Can't run all the way to Denmark." He walked down to where the young boys sat, one of them wearing the waterlogged wig. "Excuse me, lads. Don't seem to be having much luck there."

The boys looked up at Jibby, not sure whether he was being empathetic or rubbing it in. "What's it to ya, mister?" said the boy in the wig.

"Well, it's gotta be one of two things," he said. "Either you're lousy fishermen or your equipment's no good. By the looks of you fine fellas, I'm willing to bet it's the latter and not the former."

The boys had no idea what Jibby had just said. He dug into his satchel and pulled out some coins. "Tell you what. I'll buy those poles off you. For a good enough price that you can go out and get yourselves some proper equipment." The boys quickly agreed and handed over the poles in exchange for a small sampling of gold coins, then ran off, leaving their empty wooden bucket behind.

"Okay, then," Jibby said to his crew. "Let's move out."

They followed Jibby to the gray rowboat. He stepped in, then offered his hand to the others. "Where are we going?" asked Sammy.

"Where are we going?" Jibby repeated. "Why, to Denmark, of course."

"In a rowboat?"

"No," he said. "Not in a rowboat. Don't be ridiculous."

"Wait a minute," said Dizzy. "We're going to steal the *Sea Urchin*? I thought you said our stealing days were over."

"We're not stealing it," said Jibby. "We're borrowing it. Nothing wrong with borrowing things as long as you give them back when you're done."

"But we can't sail her with the numbers we've got," said Aristotle.

"We can and we will," said Jibby.

When the Mailman's tender glided up next to his new ship, he reached for and grabbed a rope ladder hanging over the side. "Follow me to our new 'ome, boys," he said before beginning his ascent. Halfway up the ladder, he was greeted by the barrels of six long rifles staring down at him, along with one angry face belonging to the ship's captain.

"Who are you?" the captain demanded. "And what manner of business have you aboard my ship?"

"Your ship? But I won the *Bella Juanita* fair and square."

"*Bella Juanita*? This, sir, is the *Saratoga*. Now I suggest you be on your way lest you find even more metal in your face."

The Mailman's eyes turned red at the thought of being had. "Why that no good son of a walrus," he said, dropping back into the tender. "He has designs on me ship. Scull the rudder! Top speed to the *Sea Urchin!*" The tender was equipped with four sets of oars and could move through the water much faster than Jibby's dilapidated old rowboat. The Mailman stood at the bow of the tender and drew his sword.

"Ramming speed!" he cried.

"Here they come," said Captain Jibby. "Right on time." Even from such a distance, he could see the fury on the Mailman's well-decorated face.

Three-Eyed Jake made a quick visual assessment of the distance between the rowboat and the *Sea Urchin* as well as the distance between the rowboat and the Mailman's fast-approaching tender. Taking into account the speed of each boat, he came to a conclusion. "We'll never make it."

"What are you going to do?" asked Aristotle.

"I'm going to do what I always do when things get a little too stressful," said Jibby. "I'm going to go fishing." He picked up one of the fishing rods he had just acquired and stood in the center of the rowboat, trying to steady himself.

The rowboat lurched closer to the *Sea Urchin* with every thrust of the oars while the tender sped along its collision course. Soon, the Mailman and his crew trailed the rowboat by a mere thirty feet, also known as shouting distance.

"You oughtn't 'ave done that, mate," shouted the

Mailman, the blade of his cutlass shimmering in the moonlight. "Now you'll 'ave to pay with your life."

Jibby brought the rod back and snapped his wrist in the direction of the Mailman. The hook floated silently through the air, eventually finding its way to one of the many rings on the Mailman's lower lip. Before the Mailman could say what was on his mind (which was "Oh no!"), Jibby pulled on the rod and sent him tumbling into the bay. The extra fifteen pounds of metal on the Mailman's face made it very difficult to keep his head above water.

Jibby tossed the rod overboard. "Ah, the one that got away," he said with a shake of his head.

While the Mailman's crew stopped to rescue their captain, the rowboat pulled up alongside the *Sea Urchin*. Jibby picked up the second fishing rod and cast the line high into the air. It disappeared into the darkness and over the side of the ship. He gave it a quick tug, and a rope ladder tumbled down from the ship's deck all the way to the waterline.

"Ladies first," he said. Juanita took the ladder and climbed up. While the others followed, Jibby held the ladder, watching as Shifty grabbed the fishing line floating on the water and pulled hand over hand until the Mailman's head appeared, his lower lip stretched to its limit. The men hauled him aboard like a common mackerel, but by the time they were able to remove the fishhook from his lower lip, Jibby had nearly finished his climb up the ladder—which was no easy task with only one hand and a can opener to work with.

"You won't get away with this, Lodbrok!" the Mailman shouted, along with a few other words that I will not repeat. He seethed with anger, which caused his face to jingle and his hula girl tattoo to put her left foot in and shake it all about. "I'll have my revenge if it's the last thing I do!"

Jibby scoffed at the threat and stood on deck, pausing for a moment to soak in the feeling of being aboard a sailing ship for the first time in eight years. Boy, did it feel good to be back. "Weigh anchor and heave in the mainsail!" he shouted. "Hard about on the helm. Let's get this ship turned around."

Jibby's crew went to work, expertly working the rigging as if they hadn't missed a day in the last eight years.

The Mailman and his crew could do nothing but watch as Jibby "borrowed" their ship.

While they sat in stunned silence, a small red rowboat glided quietly into Boston Harbor. "We made it," cried Penny. "We're in Boston."

"Hey, look at that," said Mr. Cheeseman. With an oar he reached out and lifted a blue baseball cap from the bay.

"My hat," said Chip.

"I think you mean my hat," said Big.

"Right," said Chip, shaking the water from the cap. "Your hat."

Rowing farther into the bay, they could see quaint shops

and beautiful houses and a very short man sitting atop a very large white horse, cackling loudly. The man, that is. The horse was far too proud to cackle.

"He followed us," said Mr. Cheeseman.

"What do we do now?" asked Chip. "We can't go ashore."

Mr. Cheeseman looked over his shoulder and thought of rowing back up the river and escaping into the woods. But he quickly set that idea aside when he saw a blue rowboat with two strange men coming toward them.

"Dad, look out!" cried Chip.

Mr. Cheeseman whirled around just in time to see a large, barnacle-covered ship heading directly for them at full sail. "I see it," said Mr. Cheeseman, taking evasive action.

The ship was making a 180-degree turn and its stern swung past the rowboat, missing it by mere feet and tossing it about in its wake. From the ship's deck, Jibby barked out commands loud enough for all to hear, including those being bounced around in tiny rowboats far below.

"Ready to tack! Now steady up and set course for Jutland!"

"It's Jibby," said Penny.

"Are you sure?" asked Ethan.

"I recognize his voice. And Jutland is exactly where he said they were headed. We've got to get on that ship." Penny stood and shouted to Jibby through cupped hands but to no avail.

Mr. Cheeseman rowed toward the ship but his two

oars were no match for the mighty sails of the *Sea Urchin.*
"I know," said Chip. He quickly found the end of the rowboat's tether rope. "Big, I need an arrow."

Big nodded. Chip slid one of the handmade arrows
from Big's quiver and began tying it to the tether. Big
managed to sit up. She lifted her bow over her head with
her good arm and handed it to Penny. "You can do it," she
said.

"I hope so," said Penny.

Chip handed Penny the arrow. "Don't miss."

Penny didn't answer. She placed the arrow against the
bowstring, steadied herself as best she could, and drew it
back. She inhaled and held her breath for a moment, then
released the arrow and sent it, strong and true, into the
side of the *Sea Urchin* with a decisive thump.

"Nice shot!" yelled Chip, offering a rare compliment to
his younger sister.

"Hang on," said Mr. Cheeseman as the *Sea Urchin*
quickly took the slack out of the rope and yanked the little
rowboat along. They were safe. Well, as safe as you can be
while sitting in a rickety old rowboat that is being dragged
along by a rickety old pirate ship toward the open ocean.
If they were not able to signal Jibby to drop down a ladder and take them aboard, they would eventually be cap-
sized by the growing waves or dragged beneath the ship
and drowned.

But Jibby was occupied with the business of trying to sail
a ship with a crew half the size of what is normally needed,

which is especially difficult when that crew includes one man who is incredibly dizzy, another with a bad back, and yet another who can't seem to remember things from one moment to the next. So no matter how loudly Mr. Cheeseman and his children yelled, their voices were lost among all the shouting on deck.

"Okay, quiet everyone," said Mr. Cheeseman. "I have an idea." He reached into his pocket and removed the cell phone. He flipped it open, held it as high in the air as he could, pressed the ring tone button, and waited. After several bars of "The Girl from Ipanema," there was still nothing but shouting on board. Ethan pushed the button again and, just a few seconds in, all the yelling from above stopped. Jibby leaned out over the starboard side, searching for the source of his favorite song. Mr. Cheeseman and his children yelled and waved their arms wildly. In the dark, Jibby could see only the glow of the cell phone, moving back and forth, but that was enough. "Drop ladder!" he wailed. "Crew members coming aboard!"

Within seconds a ladder came tumbling over the side. Mr. Cheeseman took hold of the tether and began pulling the rowboat closer and closer to the *Sea Urchin*, all the while hoping that the one tiny arrow would not come loose and set them adrift straight into the hands of a persistent witch hunter. When the rowboat pulled parallel to the *Sea Urchin*, Chip took hold of the ladder and guided Teddy to it. "Hang on tight, now. We'll be right behind you. And whatever you do, don't look down."

With shaky hands and quivering lower lip, Teddy and Rat-Face Roy started up the ladder. Penny placed Digs on her shoulder and followed. Ethan helped Big to stand. "Come on," he said. "I'll carry you."

"No," said Big. "I'm okay." Big, her right arm hanging useless at her side, started up the rope ladder, alternately using her one good arm and her teeth to propel herself upward. Chip was the next to go. Mr. Cheeseman slung Pinky over his shoulder, but as he reached for the ladder the arrow snapped in half, instantly separating the rowboat from the ship. The gap widened quickly. Mr. Cheeseman dove from the rowboat and managed to catch the very bottom rung of the ladder with one outstretched hand. Pinky clung to him tightly, digging her nails into his back and shoulders, as the ship dragged them along danger-ously close to its hull, which was coated with razor-sharp barnacles.

"Dad! Hang on!" yelled Penny from the deck.

Mr. Cheeseman managed to get both hands on the ladder and pull himself and Pinky from the water. His palms were blistered, his arms were spent from three hours at the oars, and the climb was slow and painful. Finally, two rungs from the top, Sammy and Jibby reached over the edge and dragged Pinky and Mr. Cheeseman aboard.

"Don't you people ever get tired of being rescued?" said Jibby with a twinkle in his eye. "What in the name of Rag-nold's bunions brings you here?"

"Hunters," said Penny.

"Hunters? Which hunters?"

"Exactly," said Penny.

"Is this your ship?" asked Chip. "Is this the *Bella Juanita*?"

"This bundle of kindling?" said Jibby. "Not even close. No, this is a different ship."

"Where'd you get it?" asked Penny.

"Borrowed it," said Jibby. "Now, let's get you folks belowdeck and into some dry clothes."

The others followed as Aristotle scooped Big up and carried her down to the captain's quarters, only to find the door locked. "Stand back," said Sammy. "I'll break it down."

"Easy there, Sammy boy," said Jibby. He retracted the hole punch from his Swiss Army hand. "There's not a lock I can't pick with this thing." Jibby knelt in front of the door and worked the lock only for a matter of seconds before it responded with a decisive click. He smiled with satisfaction, turned the knob, and pushed the door in.

Aristotle lowered Big onto the captain's bed. Chip took her hand and held it tightly. Her face was awash in pain and cold sweat.

"There's no easy way to do this," said Jibby. He offered Big a piece of rawhide on which to bite down, but she refused with a quick shake of her head. "Okay, then. Take a deep breath." Under Chip's watchful and protective eyes, Jibby pressed on Big's shoulder with one hand and rotated her arm upward with the other, stopping only when there was an audible *pop*. Big exhaled. A single tear ran down her cheek but she did not cry out.

"Now," said Jibby, "fetch me some cloth for a sling. This arm is to stay put for at least a week."

169

Once Big's arm was taken care of, Mr. Cheeseman focused his attention on young Teddy, who had not spoken for hours and now sat on a chair near the bed, rocking back and forth and grinding his teeth.

Mr. Cheeseman knelt in front of his son. "Are you okay, Teddy?"

Teddy gave an unconvincing nod.

"Looks like he's got the fever," said Sammy. "If he does, we're all doomed."

Mr. Cheeseman put his hand to Teddy's forehead. It was not hot but rather quite cool and damp. "Chip," he said, "the Empathizer." Chip tossed the device to his father and Mr. Cheeseman suctioned it to his temple, then asked Teddy where it hurt.

"Doesn't hurt," mumbled Teddy. "Just feels . . . bad. Very bad."

Mr. Cheeseman chose Teddy's forehead as a good starting place. He attached the suction cup, then flipped on the Empathizer. In a moment, his hands began to tremble ever so slightly. "Strange."

"What is it?" asked Penny.

"I remember feeling like this a few years ago when I quit drinking coffee. But this is much worse. I could be wrong but it seems like Teddy might going through some type of withdrawal."

"Withdrawal?" said Chip. "But Teddy doesn't drink coffee."

"I know," said Mr. Cheeseman. "It doesn't make a whole

lot of sense. I think the best thing is to get him off to bed. It's been a long day. For all of us."

As the *Sea Urchin* left the protected waters of Boston Harbor and glided into the open ocean, Mr. Cheeseman looked concerned, Teddy looked pale and drawn, and Rat-Face Roy looked nervous—very, very nervous.

Chapter 13

When Professor Boxley walked downstairs to the main room of the Ackerman Inn, he found Gateman in a heated discussion with the owner, Mr. Ackerman, who was busy sweeping up the mess from the previous night's debauchery—mud, broken glass, a few scattered teeth.

"You've got no indoor plumbing, the food was questionable at best, and the bed was horribly lumpy. I've slept on prison beds that were more comfortable. The mattress felt like it was filled with corn husks."

"It is filled with corn husks," said Mr. Ackerman. "What did you expect it to be filled with, sir? Goose down?"

"That would be a good start. And how about some proper towels? Oh yes, and would it kill you to offer room service and a complimentary continental breakfast?"

"A continental what?"

"You know. Muffins, coffee, diced fruits."

"Diced fruits?" Mr. Ackerman ceased his sweeping and turned to face Gateman. "Pardon me for saying so, sir, but you are being quite ridiculous."

On his way to the door, the professor did not break stride as he grabbed Gateman and dragged him along. "Please excuse my friend," he said. "He's not himself today. And thank you for your fine hospitality."

"I'm being ridiculous?" said Gateman, refusing to let the matter rest. "This whole town is ridiculous, with its lumpy beds and its ridiculously clean air."

"Come on now," said the professor. "Let's go."

"I hope your fleabag hotel is shut down by the Boston health authorities! And I hope the Red Sox lose!"

"What was that all about?" asked the professor, once he had successfully hauled Gateman out of the inn and into the ridiculously clean air and the bright sunshine glistening on the bay.

"Perhaps you find such shoddy accommodations acceptable, but I do not."

"That's it," the professor said. "I refuse to listen to your incessant complaining. Any more bellyaching out of you and you're fired."

"Fired? You can't fire me."

"I can and I will. Then you'll have to find your own way home."

If only I knew how to work the LVR-ZX, Gateman thought. Then it would be the professor worrying about finding a ride home. "Fine then." Gateman pouted. "I will try and resist the temptation to complain. I just hope the ship has properly appointed cabins and a nice buffet."

"Ship? What ship?"

"Last night you said we were going to Denmark."

"Yes," said the professor, leading Gateman across the street to an awaiting horse-drawn coach. "But why go by ship when you can go by time machine? It will take Ethan Cheeseman nearly a month to get there by sea. We'll set the LVR-ZX for three weeks from now, destination Jutland, Denmark. Then all we have to do is watch and wait."

"I hate waiting," said Gateman. "Uh . . . I mean, except in Denmark, that is. In fact, there's no place I'd rather wait than in Denmark. Yessiree. Sometimes I go to Denmark just to wait around. I'll stand there on the corner all day just waiting for . . ."

"Okay. I get it," said the professor.

The two men climbed into the coach and started out for the woods near Shattuckton, where the LVR-ZX sat waiting. On the way, they passed a small Frenchman on a large white horse. Bon Mot knew that his once-shining reputation as the world's greatest witch hunter was sure to fade when he returned to Shattuckton empty-handed. His shoulders slumped forward, his eyes cast downward, he made the long, lonely ride toward the reassuring comforts of his beautiful home, where he would find a fire blazing in the fireplace and his dining room table missing.

Her sails puffed and rounded like a baritone's chest, the *Sea Urchin* moved east by northeast through the spiky waters of the Atlantic. Any illusion Mr. Cheeseman and his children may have had that they were guests aboard Jibby's borrowed ship was quickly dispelled with a sharp call: "All hands on deck! No layabouts allowed!"

Chip opened his eyes and tried to shake the sleep from his head. His first few moments of consciousness were spent attempting to figure out just exactly where he was, trying to piece together the strange sequence of events that, in the last twenty-four hours, had led him from a small town in the twenty-first century to an even smaller town in the late 1600s . . . and finally to a hammock hanging between two cannons on the darkened gun deck of a damp, creaky pirate ship bound for the Danish province of Jutland.

When Jibby once more sounded the call for all hands, Chip swung his legs over the edge of the hammock and dropped to the floor. In the hammock below him, Mr. Cheeseman sat up with a groan. Daylight leaked in through the shuttered gun port doors. "Come on, gang," he said. "Sounds like we're needed above."

Penny and Big crawled out of their hammocks, Big struggling to do so with her right arm immobilized by Jibby's homemade sling. Chip extended a hand and helped her to her feet.

"Thanks," said Big quietly. She took much pride in her self-reliance and did not like the idea of having to depend on others for the most simple of tasks.

Penny's first thought was to find a brush and untangle

her long auburn hair, as she did each and every morning. She was both surprised and amused when she remembered it had been hacked off and was last seen firmly stuck to Appalling's pompous and ignorant head.

Her new lack of hair reminded her of something else as well. "I saw Mom," said Penny. "She spoke to me."

"I dreamed about her as well," said Mr. Cheeseman.

"No," said Penny. "It wasn't a dream. It was more like a . . . like a vision."

"Vision?" said Chip, trying not to roll his eyes. Penny was always seeing ghosts or visions. Chip often thought she made these things up in order to get attention.

"Yes," said Penny, aware of Chip's skepticism. "She was floating out over the water like an angel. And she spoke to me."

"Okay," said Chip. "What did she say?"

"It was weird. She said, 'Round and round, it never ends, north is south, then north again.' "

"What the heck does that mean?" said Chip. "Sounds like she's saying we're going the wrong way."

"It does sound like that, doesn't it?" said Penny. This is the point at which Mr. Cheeseman would have expected Teddy or his pink-eyed sock puppet to pipe in with a wisecrack. But there was absolute silence from Teddy's bunk.

"Teddy?" said Mr. Cheeseman. "Are you awake? Let's go now. Rise and shine." Mr. Cheeseman waited but there was no movement from Teddy's hammock. "Teddy?" He waited again but still there was no response. Mr. Cheeseman rushed to Teddy's hammock and threw back the covers. Teddy was gone. Mr. Cheeseman called out for him once more, thinking he might be hiding somewhere among the cannons. When he received no answer he practically flew up the stairs to the ship's deck, where he saw Sammy, Dizzy, Aristotle, and Juanita working the rigging and adjusting the sails as Jibby shouted out commands from the front of the ship. There he also found his youngest child at the wheel, helping Three-Eyed Jake steer.

"Hey Dad, look," Teddy said when he saw his father approaching. "Captain Fabulous is driving the ship."

Mr. Cheeseman was relieved not only to find Teddy but to find him in such a fine state of repair. His color had returned and no longer was he rocking, mumbling incoherently, or grinding his teeth. He was smiling and happily whistling a sea shanty that Three-Eyed Jake had taught him while Mr. Cheeseman had been sleeping below.

"I found Teddy," said Mr. Cheeseman as the others climbed on deck, shielding their eyes against the low-lying sun. "You had me worried there for a moment."

"Why? I'm fine," Teddy insisted.

"He's fine," Three-Eyed Jake agreed, scruffing up his helper's hair as people seemed to enjoy doing to those with spiky hair like Teddy's. "It's the rest of you I'd be worried about. Sleeping till the morn's half gone. You'd best report to the captain." Three-Eyed Jake thrust his one good eye in the direction of the ship's bow, where Jibby stood taking in as much sea air as his lungs could hold.

"Right," said Mr. Cheeseman, acutely aware that he was no longer in charge. He reported to Captain Jibby and the others joined Teddy and Jake near the helm. "Good morning, Jake," said Penny.

" 'Tis indeed," said Jake. "Finer conditions for sailin' I've rarely seen."

"You're looking a lot better today, Teddy," said Chip.

"I feel a lot better," said Teddy, his jaw moving rhythmically up and down.

Penny exchanged a look with Chip. "Teddy?" she said.

"Yes?"

"Where'd you get the gum?"

Teddy's face froze and turned suddenly red. His forehead became instantly shiny with perspiration. "Hmm?" He turned away as if studying the billowy clouds resting on the horizon.

"You're chewing gum. Where'd you get the gum?"

Teddy's eyes danced about, contemplating an answer. "Uh . . . found it?"

"Found it?" said Chip. "Is that true, Rat-Face Roy?"

"*Sí*," said Rat-Face Roy, keeping his back to his inquisitors.

"You really should look at people when you're talking to them, Roy," said Penny.

"*Sí*," said Rat-Face Roy once again. Penny bit her cheeks. It was all she and Chip could do to keep from laughing. Even Big smiled as they hadn't seen her do since Penny shot the arrow into the outhouse roof.

Suddenly, Penny turned and pointed wildly off to the starboard side. "Hey, look. A mermaid!" When Teddy turned to get his first ever glimpse of a half woman, half fish, Penny stepped forward and took hold of her brother's left arm, holding it up for all to see. Chip and Big feigned shock, gasping at the sight of a sock puppet with no face. "Teddy," said Penny with mock astonishment. Teddy hung his head in shame. "You ate Rat-Face Roy's face?"

Tears streamed down Teddy's cheeks. "I couldn't help it," he blubbered. "I need my gum. I just can't think without it." Teddy's crying intensified until it interfered with his breathing and soon he was speaking in staccato bursts. "Besides, I . . . didn't eat his . . . face. I'm just . . . chewing on it for a while until we . . . get back home and I can get some more . . . gum."

Chip and Penny suddenly felt ashamed of themselves. It had been their intention to have a little fun at their brother's expense, not to make him cry. Chip placed his hand on the back of Teddy's neck and gave him an affectionate squeeze. "It's okay," said Chip. "You did what you had to do. In the meantime, Rat-Face Roy will just have to go by a different name."

"May I suggest No-Face Roy?" said Big.

"Sounds good to me," said Chip. "What do you think, Roy?"

"Who said that?" said No-Face Roy.

Just then, a long shadow fell over them all. The source of the sudden shade was Captain Jibby, eclipsing the sun with his six-foot-six frame. Standing next to him was Mr. Cheeseman.

"Fall in!" barked the captain.

Chip and the others weren't sure what to do. They looked at one another and shuffled their feet. "Fall in means stand at attention," whispered Three-Eyed Jake. "Single file."

Chip, Penny, Teddy, Pinky, and No-Face Roy lined up next to Mr. Cheeseman and stood at something that would be called attention in only the least disciplined of navies. "All of you," said Jibby, with a stern eye toward Big.

"I don't take orders," said Big. "From anyone." Digs took up position at her feet and gave a look that seemed to make the same declaration.

"When you're aboard my ship, you do," said Jibby. "I know we're all friends here and I'd like to keep it that way. But out on the open sea, allegiance to your captain is essential for survival, and I require nothing less than complete obedience. We have just enough hands to get this ship safely to Denmark. And if you landlubbers are to learn the ways of the sea, you'll have to pipe down and listen. And, I'm afraid, you'll have to take orders."

"I'm sorry. I don't take orders," said Big once more.

"Then you'll have a long swim back to Boston," said Jibby. His eyes locked with Big's in a battle of wills. "Won't be easy with one arm, I imagine."

Chip cleared his throat. "Permission to speak with Big," he said. "Uh . . . privately."

"Permission granted," said Jibby with a sideways nod.

Chip pulled Big aside, taking her by her uninjured arm. "What are you doing?" he said gently.

"I don't know what you mean."

"You do know what I mean. Listen, it's like Jibby said. He needs every one of us to cooperate if we're to get to Denmark safely. We all need to pull together here for the good of the team." Chip realized he was quoting his old Police Pals baseball coach, but it seemed to fit the situation, so he saw no reason to stop. "We've all got to give a hundred and ten percent."

"That's mathematically impossible," said Big, whose birth had preceded the advent of sports clichés by several hundred years.

"I know," said Chip. "But making it across the Atlantic might be impossible too if we all don't pitch in. Just try not to think of it as taking orders. Think of them more as suggestions." Big's expression was unreadable and Chip wondered if he was getting through to her. "Do it for me."

Big smiled. "Is that an order or a suggestion?"

"It's a request," said Chip. The faint smile that accompanied Big's sigh let Chip know that his little pep talk had been effective. He and Big joined the others at attention and Jibby gave Chip a wink in appreciation of his diplomatic skills.

"All right then," he began as he paced back and forth, his arms tucked behind him. "It takes years to learn all there is to know about sailing a ship like this. But you scalawags are going to learn it all in just a few hours, so pay attention because our very lives may depend upon it. Out here on the open seas, you never know when you're gonna run into bad weather." Jibby narrowed his eyes and gazed out at the distant skyline. "Or, worse yet, bad people."

CHAPTER 14

Unlike Ethan Cheeseman's LVR, the newer version was equipped with a homing device, so the professor and his assistant knew exactly where to find it.

One full day since it had first arced across the sky and set down in the forest of New England, the LVR-ZX lay in the same spot in which Gateman and the professor had left it, and in the same condition other than the fact that it had attracted a few leaves and branches blown by the wind and several thousand very busy red ants. Professor Boxley's precise scientific calculations had enabled him to make certain the LVR-ZX would land on flat, solid ground in a remote location while avoiding things like the ocean, steep hillsides, or the interior of a volcano. No amount of calculating, however, could ensure that it would not land on a rather large anthill.

"It's covered with ants," said Gateman, bitterly watching the industrious bugs crawling about with no obvious purpose in mind other than to carry him to a new level of irritation.

"I can see that," said Professor Boxley. "Well, don't just stand there, get rid of them."

"Me? Why should I have to get rid of them?"

"Because you're my assistant. If you can't be counted upon to perform simple tasks, like bringing me my coffee or getting rid of swarms of ants, then what good are you?"

Seething, Gateman reached beneath his jacket and removed his gun.

"Now, now," said Professor Boxley. "There's no need to threaten me with that."

"You? It's not for you. It's for them." Gateman waggled the gun in the direction of the ants.

"You're going to shoot the ants? How many bullets do you have in that gun?"

Gateman thought about this for a moment. He looked at the gun, then at the thousands of scrambling insects and did some quick math in his head. "Yes, I see. Well maybe if I just shoot one of them. You know, as an example to the others."

"You couldn't hit a bear, remember? What makes you think you could shoot an ant?"

"I can get much closer to an ant," said Gateman, moving the gun in close to one of the ants climbing up the side of the LVR-ZX.

"Are you crazy?" shrieked Acorn Boxley. "Get that gun away from my machine. You'll put a hole in it and we'll be stuck here forever."

Too busy arguing about whether a gun was a suitable device for getting rid of bothersome ants, the two men failed to notice that a few hundred of the tiny creatures were now crawling up their stocking-covered legs. Of course, as stealthy as ants may be, eventually someone is going to notice a small army of insects climbing up his leg. The sensation of being bitten on the legs, right through his white stockings, was sent to Professor Boxley's brain, which sent the following message to his mouth: "Ahhhhhhhh!"

From a distance it might have looked to the average person like folk dancing, the two men hopping about and slapping rhythmically at their legs. But to the large black bear watching them, it only looked like dinner; dinner he was determined not to be deprived of again. One hungry roar later and the two men stopped dancing and turned to see the ill-tempered beast, his slobbery tongue hanging from his mouth like a flag on a windless day.

"Quick. Let's get out of here!" cried Professor Boxley, forgetting all that Big had taught him about the ways of bears. He hurriedly keyed in the code to unlock the pod door and pushed it open. The bear, sensing that the opening of the pod door meant that the buffet was about to close, took off running in their direction. Gateman quickly shoved Professor Boxley to the ground and dove into the time machine. As the bear closed in, Professor Boxley scrambled to his hands and knees, crawled into the LVR-ZX, and kicked the door closed.

"You did it again," said the professor, rising to his feet. "You left me to be eaten by a bear. That's twice."

"All's well that ends well. That's what I like to say," said

Gateman. In the commotion, the two men had forgotten that they were awash in fierce biting ants. And that commotion continued when the bear, having just been denied a rather sizable pre-hibernation brunch, angrily attacked the LVR-ZX, slamming his rotund body against its vulnerable outer shell and rocking it to the point that it nearly rolled onto its side.

"Come on, let's go here!" screamed Gateman.

"I'm trying!" countered Professor Boxley.

"Well try harder!"

Professor Boxley quickly entered the necessary data into the navigation system while muttering to himself. "Longitude: 56.42 degrees north. Latitude: 9.5 degrees east. Factoring curvature of the Earth. There, that should do it. Jutland, Denmark, three weeks from today. Hold on!" Professor Boxley hit the ignition switch just as the bear hit the LVR-ZX again, rocking it violently. The engines whirred and hummed but the date on the chronometer did not move forward. Not by three weeks. Not by three seconds. Not at all. "Uh-oh."

"What? What is it?"

The bear collided with the machine once more.

"It won't let me go forward."

"What do mean it won't let you? You've got to let it know who's in charge here." As if he weren't irritated enough as it was, Gateman's legs chose that very moment to remind his brain that they were being ravaged by nibbling insects. He screeched loudly and resumed his highly entertaining folk dance while Professor Boxley reentered the data and tried again, stopping when necessary to slap a few biting ants. He flipped the switch, but still nothing. "I don't understand it. For some strange reason we can't go forward in time."

"Then go backward! Just get us out of here!"

With a hungry bear attacking from the outside and pesky ants attacking from within, the professor had no choice. He quickly adjusted the date for yesterday and, once again, punched the ignition button. This time the machine did just as it was told, taking them, in a matter of a few seconds, to Jutland, Denmark, one day before.

"It worked. I think," said the professor when the engines wound down to the point that he could be heard. "We should be in Jutland and it should be yesterday."

"Good. Now let me out of here! These bugs are eating me alive!"

"Wait," said the professor. "Let me run a quick atmospheric test to make sure it's safe out there."

"I don't care," said Gateman. "I just want these bugs off me." He pushed Professor Boxley aside, opened the door, and ran out—right into a massive spiderweb strung between two trees. "Ahhhhhhh!" From a distance it may have looked as though he were possessed by evil spirits as he made a desperate attempt to get the webbing off his face while simultaneously slapping at the ants, which had continued their journey northward to his arms and neck. But to the pack of wolves watching him, it looked like dinner.

Professor Boxley stepped out into the Danish forest and immediately saw the wolves beginning to circle, though

Gateman was so busy trying to de-web himself that he failed to notice. "Maybe next time you could set this thing down on a hornet's nest," he snipped. "Or hey, how about a pit of poisonous—"

"Wolves," said the professor.

"Wolves do not live in pits," said Gateman. "They live in forests and . . . oh." Gateman finally noticed the wolves that had been noticing him for quite some time. His webby face went white. Quickly, he shoved Professor Boxley aside and ran back into the LVR-ZX. Professor Boxley followed, angrily slamming the door behind him.

"For goodness' sake. Just once could you manage to think of someone besides yourself?"

Gateman shrugged. "Like who? There are only the two of us here."

Professor Boxley sighed and groaned at the same time. "Why couldn't I have hired that nice fellow from Nebraska? Okay, here we go. I'm going to try and send us to this exact location but three weeks ahead. Hopefully, the wolves will have moved on and Ethan Cheeseman will be nearing shore. Now hold on." The professor entered the pertinent data and hit the ignition switch. The engines wound up, drowning out the sounds of the growling wolves outside. Still, as loudly as the engines groaned, the chronometer simply refused to budge.

"I don't understand it. It won't move forward."

"Then go backward again," yelled Gateman. "Just get us out of here."

"I'll set it for yesterday, same location." This time the

machine acted predictably and instantly took them back one full day, landing in the exact same location.

"It worked," said Professor Boxley. "I wonder why it won't . . ."

Gateman pushed the professor aside, opened the door and ran out, right into the same spiderweb, hanging between the same two trees. "Ahhhhhh!" He frantically wiped the web from his face. Professor Boxley, stepping out into the forest, could not help but laugh.

"What's so funny?" sneered Gateman, hunting down the last few remaining ants and flattening them with his palm.

"You ran into the same spiderweb twice," chuckled Professor Boxley. "You have to admit, that is pretty funny."

"And you have to admit that you are an idiot!"

Professor Boxley had had just about enough and he cautioned Gateman to mind his tongue.

"I will not mind my tongue," Gateman bellowed. "I am tired of minding my tongue. You, sir, are an idiot, because you have invented a time machine that doesn't work."

"It does work," said Professor Boxley. "It's just that it goes back in time but won't go forward."

"Then fix it so it does," barked Gateman.

"That's the problem," said Professor Boxley. "There's nothing wrong with the machine. It's the science. Something's wrong with the science behind it."

"Well, then fix the science."

"Don't be ridiculous," said Professor Boxley. "You can't fix science. It is what it is."

Gateman grabbed the professor by his puffy shirt and pulled him close to his clammy, shallow face. "Are you telling me we're stuck in this miserable place in this miserable time with its miserably clean air for the rest of our miserable lives?"

"I can't answer that," said the professor. "The only person who might be able to is Ethan Cheeseman. I'm afraid the man we came here to rescue may now be our only hope of getting home again."

SOME TIMELY ADVICE FOR TIME TRAVELERS

No one has done more to help us understand the concept of time than celebrated physicist and part-time hand model Albert Einstein, whose theory of relativity tells us that time is relative to the circumstances of the individual. For example, we all know that when an elephant sits on the fence it's time to get a new fence, unless it's an electric fence; then it's time to get a new elephant.

Time, you see, moves at different rates for all of us. Even a time period as short as a second can mean different things to different people. Consider how when your big brother says, "Hey, let me see your bike for a second," what he really means is, "I am going to take your bike and ride it until the chain falls off."

Or something like that. Actually, I must admit I have absolutely no idea what Einstein is talking about—and it has nothing to do with that German accent. It has to do with the fact that I failed high

school physics because I mistakenly thought I was taking a class called psychics.

This is why, when it comes to explanations of time
and space, I rely on the theories of celebrated rock
star and part-time physicist Steve Miller, who points
out that time keeps on slipping, slipping, slipping into
the future.

And though time may be slipping into the future,
the closest most of us will ever get to traveling forward
in time is when, each spring, we fearlessly set our clocks
one hour into the future for daylight savings. We take
this annual trip into the future despite the risk that we
may awaken the following morning to find that our
planet has been taken over by renegade robots, talking
apes, or—worst-case scenario—talking renegade robot
apes. (Another very good title for a sitcom.)

I thereby advise anyone who wishes to go slipping,
slipping, slipping into the future that you may not like
what you find once you get there. And for those who
choose to slip into the past, I hope very much that you
do like what you find, because there is the very real
possibility that you may be stuck there forever.

CHAPTER 15

Sailing a ship the size of the *Sea Urchin* requires a great deal of work, and by the end of the first day both Jibby's crew and the newcomers were fairly exhausted. But with a steady wind at their backs and calm seas ahead, there was time for all to grab a little rest after a delicious supper that Juanita had managed to whip up with the limited provisions stored in the galley.

Mr. Cheeseman was leaning against the ship's rail, taking in the sunset and trying to imagine how someone from the future with an old magazine was able to track them down. He was nowhere near coming up with a logical explanation when Juanita approached with a plateful of food. "You eat, *sí*?" she said. "*Para fuerza.*" She flexed her right bicep. "For the strength."

"Thank you." Mr. Cheeseman smiled. He took the plate and looked at its contents.

"Try. *Es muy bueno.* Very good."

"I'm sure it is. It's just that I don't seem to have much of an appetite these days."

"You miss her, *sí?*" said Juanita.

Mr. Cheeseman nodded. *"Sí. Mucho."* The dull pain that followed caught him quite by surprise. It started somewhere deep in his chest and moved swiftly upward, as if trying to escape his body, finally finding a way out through his eyes. He wiped the tears with his shirtsleeve and turned away.

"Lo siento," said Juanita. "I am sorry."

"It's okay," said Mr. Cheeseman, feeling more than a little embarrassed. *"No problema."*

"You see her again. Pronto. Soon."

Mr. Cheeseman's smile did not match his mood in any way but smiling seemed like the polite thing to do. He did not want Juanita to feel bad for trying to cheer him up. But he had to wonder if she was right. At this point, it seemed the likelihood of seeing Olivia was fading away as quickly as the day itself.

Chip was wondering the same thing as he leaned against the railing next to Big, the two staring at the same setting sun from the rear of the ship. "What's it like?" asked Big after a long silence.

"What's what like?"

"The future."

Chip laughed, turning from the sea and leaning back against the railing. "I was only kidding about that."

"I don't believe that you were," said Big, her face completely void of expression. "When I saw you in the forest, when you stepped out of that strange device, I knew you were not of this time. I believe it to be true, as the painting said, that your father really is a scientist of tomorrow."

The first thought Chip had was that, before saying anything, he should discuss the matter with his father. But he had just traveled several centuries into the past, had been chased by witch hunters and pirates, had nearly drowned in an ice-cold river, and had just put in a full day's work aboard a borrowed ship bound for Denmark. All this, he decided, earned him the right to speak without consulting his father or any other adult.

"Yes," Chip relented. "We did come here from the future."

"It is most wondrous? The future?"

"It is pretty great," said Chip. "We have airplanes, giant metal birds that carry people through the sky. And we have cell phones and pizza. And baseball."

Big noticed a fresh sparkle in Chip's eyes when he mentioned baseball. She wanted to know more about this thing that had so obviously captured his imagination. Chip tried his best to explain the game, but Big found it confusing.

"And a home run is when the batter hits the ball out of the park," he explained.

"And this is a good thing?"

"It's a very good thing if you're the hitter. Not so good if you're the pitcher."

"I don't quite understand it," said Big. "But I get the feeling you're quite good at this baseball."

"I'm not bad, I guess," said Chip with a shrug. "I'd like to pitch in the World Series someday. That is, if we ever make it back home."

"Perhaps I could go with you. And I could watch you pitch in the World Serious."

Chip smiled, thinking there was nothing he would like better than for Big to one day watch him pitch in the World Serious. "I don't know," he said. "It'd be great if you could come with us, but I don't think you'd like it very much."

"Really? And why do you say that?"

"Well, for one thing, you said you don't care too much for towns. In the future, there are towns everywhere. And cities. Huge noisy cities with buildings so tall they vanish into the clouds. And trucks, trains, and cars. Millions of cars."

"Cars?"

"Automobiles. Think of a horse-drawn carriage but with a kickin' sound system, cup holders, four hundred horsepower, and no horses. I can drive one, you know. I mean, technically, I'm not old enough, but my dad taught me just in case."

"In case of what?"

"Ah, it's a long story," said Chip, turning back to the sunset.

Big looked out at the endless expanse of water. "I think we've got time."

As Chip started in, the sun soon retired for the evening and, over the next couple of weeks, the days passed one much like the other. Ethan and the children worked hard to master the art of sailing. They learned how to trim and reef the sails and how to tie a host of essential knots: the French bowline, a Tom Fool knot, the lighterman's hitch, and the highly intricate double carrick bend.

They learned the proper names for all the parts of the ship. Port was the left side and starboard the right. The rear of the ship was known as the aft or the stern, while the front was called the fore or bow. They learned that a staircase was a companionway and the kitchen was known as the galley.

But most important, they had learned to duck when Three-Eyed Jake turned the ship's wheel hard to port or starboard, sending the massive wooden boom of the mainsail sweeping across the aft deck with enough force to send anyone in its way careening over the rails and into the drink.

All in all, the newcomers adapted quite well to life at sea and even found themselves enjoying the adventure of it all. Teddy never missed a chance to help Jake steer the ship. Big's arm improved and so did her willingness to take orders, though Jibby still had strong reservations about her. Pinky and Digs slept a lot, usually curled up together inside a large coil of rope. Ethan replaced the batteries in Dizzy's earmuffs with those from the Empathizer and once again the former tightrope walker was a climbing machine, scaling the shroud to the crow's nest each day, searching for any sign of bad weather or bad people.

One day, he spotted both.

Dead ahead, purplish black clouds hung low over the water. A shard of lightning shot down from the darkened sky all the way to the growing swell. Dizzy pulled the earmuff away from his head, then cupped his hand around his ear and counted. He got to eight when the thunder caught up to the lightning with the sound of a low, slow timpani roll. A few moments passed before the next lightning strike. This time Dizzy counted to seven before the thunder arrived, sharper and more crackly than the last burst. It was a pretty nasty-looking storm, and they were headed right for it.

As he turned to begin his downward climb on his way to make a full report to Captain Jibby, he saw something in the other direction that gave more cause for concern than the electrical storm ahead. It was a ship far off in the distance, approaching from the stern and becoming less distant with every second. Dizzy slipped his spyglass from his pocket and brought it to his eye.

The first thing he noticed was that the ship, a quick and agile sloop, sailed without a flag, a practice common among pirates. The next was a strange shimmer coming from the ship's deck. As the vessel moved closer, the sparkle seemed to be emanating from a man standing on deck or, more precisely, from the man's head. One more look and Dizzy realized the true source of the light. It was the sun, dancing on the two hundred shiny gold and silver rings that covered the hideously ugly face of the Mailman.

Long before Dizzy had spotted the approaching ship, Captain Jibby knew that something was not right. For the past ten minutes or so Pinky had been standing at the ship's stern, her front paws upon the railing, growling steadily. Jibby lowered his spyglass and handed it to Mr. Cheeseman.

"The dog's right, I'm afraid. Looks like we've got company." Ethan took a look for himself. No question, the sloop was gaining rapidly.

"Who is it?" asked Chip.

"It looks to be me old friend the Mailman," said Jibby. "Must've stolen himself a ship."

This news seemed to invigorate young Teddy. "I hope we get a letter," he said.

"*Sí,*" said No-Face Roy. "Or a huge package. Filled with bubble gum."

"This is not the kind of Mailman with little blue shorts and a big bag full of letters," said Jibby. "This Mailman would just as soon gouge your eyes out as look at you."

"Then I hope we don't get a package," said Teddy.

"Can we outrun them?" asked Mr. Cheeseman.

"In this glorified piece of driftwood?" said Jibby. "Not likely."

"Then what's our plan?"

"Don't really have one right now," said Jibby.

"You mean we just wait until they pull alongside us and this Mailman character blasts us out of the water?"

"Oh, he won't blast us out of the water," said Jibby a little too casually, considering the situation.

"Why not?" asked Penny.

"Because this is his ship."

"His ship?" said Chip. "I thought you said your thieving days were behind you."

"Didn't say I stole his ship. Just borrowed it for a while."

Dizzy rushed up, out of breath. "Sir," he began. "I regret I have some dire news to report."

"Yes, I'm aware of the problem," said Jibby. He walked toward the wheel where Three-Eyed Jake stood, happily whistling a sea shanty, completely unaware of the troubles that lay ahead and astern.

"Yes, sir," said Dizzy, struggling to keep up. "But are you aware of the other?"

"What other?" asked Jibby. A distant rumbling answered the question for him. By now the storm was close enough that Jibby could smell it. He took in a chest full of air. "Amazing, isn't it? That something so deadly could smell so darned good."

"Like bacon," offered Teddy.

"Bearing off," said Jake. He began to turn the ship away from the storm but Jibby stopped him.

"No," he said. "Steady up. Continue on."

Jake looked at Jibby as if he must be mad. "But Captain," he said. "What about the curse? Surely you haven't forgotten the last time we sailed into such a storm."

"Of course I haven't forgotten. But we've got no choice as I see it. In fact, the storm might be our only chance of survival. If we can get to it before they overtake us, we might be able to lose them."

"We might lose them by sinking to the bottom of the ocean," said Jake.

"We might indeed," said Jibby. "Break out the foresail! Full and by!"

Penny ran up and handed Jibby the spyglass. "They're gaining on us." Jibby didn't need the spyglass to confirm this little bit of information as fact. There it was, the nimble sloop, with sails full of wind, dead astern and approaching quickly.

"Battle stations!" shouted Jibby, preparing the crew for

the inevitable. "We'll fight to the last man. Arm yourselves with anything you can find and prepare to be boarded."

Jibby spat out a list of orders with rapid-fire delivery, giving each crew member a specific task. When he got to Big and the Cheeseman children, the order was the same for all of them: go belowdecks and wait there until the danger passed.

"Belowdecks?" said Chip.

"That's an order," snapped Jibby. "All children will go below until I say otherwise. Anyone who disobeys my order will be dealt with harshly. You have my word on that. And I never go back on my word." Jibby turned to walk away, but Chip grabbed hold of his buttoned sleeve.

"You said you would welcome a man of my caliber aboard your ship anytime," said Chip, his voice deeper than it had ever been. "You said man, not child. Now, you're not going to go back on your word, are you?"

Jibby opened his mouth but words did not follow. He looked to Mr. Cheeseman, who offered only a shrug. He puffed up his cheeks and let the air out with a slow shake of his head. "I am the captain of this vessel and all orders come from me. But as far as this matter is concerned, I will allow you to answer directly to your company commander." He said this with a nod toward Mr. Cheeseman.

Chip smiled. "Well, Dad?"

"Okay," said Mr. Cheeseman. "You can stay."

"If Chip stays, I stay," said Penny, hands on her hips.

"And I as well," said Big, striking an identical pose.

"Me too!" shouted Teddy.

"I can't see a thing," said No-Face Roy.

Mr. Cheeseman secretly wished he hadn't raised such brave children. In this situation, a band of cowards would have been much easier to deal with. He answered by not answering, then turned to Jibby and asked, "What are our chances? If they catch us."

"You mean when they catch us. This is sailing, not rocket science. The facts are plain and simple. They've got the faster ship and the Mailman knows his business."

"Hold on," said Penny. "You said this isn't rocket science. But we've got cannons, right?"

"Yes," said Jibby.

"Can they be moved?"

"With great effort they can." A wicked snap sent lightning sprinting across the sky ahead. "So tell me, young lady, what exactly do you have in mind?"

FIGHTIN' WORDS

The simplest advice I can give you on the subject of fighting is *don't*. However, sometimes we may find ourselves in a situation that requires us to practice the art of self-defense. Long before I became a remarkably successful purveyor of unsolicited advice, I was bullied on a regular basis all through junior high because I was the smallest kid in my class.

You've heard of the ninety-pound weakling? Well, he used to beat me up on Thursdays. This is what happens when you are a fifty-three-pound weakling. And believe me, it's not easy to put on weight when you are constantly on the run from bullies.

Adults rarely have good advice on this subject. My mother offered up this timeless bit of wisdom on the matter: "He who fights and runs away lives to fight another day."

I believe this was Mother's way of saying, "Always fight to the death."

My father suggested that I simply tell the bully to pick on someone his own size, which resulted in the bully going to my house and beating up my dad.

If suggesting to the bully that he pick on someone his own size doesn't work for you, it may be necessary to get professional help. I'm talking about enrolling in a martial arts class. Personally, I have been practicing martial arts for years. I recently earned a pink belt in karate and am proficient in the tiger position, the cobra position, and the fetal position, which is the best way to protect your internal organs and is a method of self-defense I will always recommend over fighting to the death.

Chapter 16

The Mailman's face jingled in the breeze, the sound growing stronger each moment as the sloop inched closer to the dangerous storm and dangerously close to the *Sea Urchin*, pulling up fast just off her port side. He could barely contain his excitement. It had taken two weeks to catch her and now she was finally within his grasp. It wasn't so much the thought of getting his ship back but the opportunity for revenge that was causing him so much happiness.

While he compiled a mental list of all the horrible ways he could inflict pain upon Jibby and his crew, Scurvy approached in a state of alarm. "Pardon me, sir. Not sure if you've noticed, but we're heading right into a pretty nasty mess."

"Worry not, Scurvy old boy. We'll catch 'er before we get there. Did you 'ear that, Lodbrok? You can't outrun us! Ha ha!"

Then the Mailman saw something he couldn't remember having ever seen before. It was a trunnion—a wheeled wooden base for a cannon—being hoisted through the hold door of the *Sea Urchin* and pulled onto the main deck by Sammy and Aristotle. A moment passed before the barrel of a cannon followed and was remounted on the trunnion. From there, Ethan, Chip, Penny, and Big rolled the cannon to the far aft of the ship while Teddy and No-Face Roy hitched a ride.

"What the devil are they doing?" said Shifty.

Another trunnion appeared on deck, followed by yet another cannon barrel. When the two parts were reassembled, Juanita and Dizzy rolled it back, parking it next to the first.

"Fools!" shouted the Mailman as yet another trunnion was hoisted from the gundeck below. "They're making 'er top 'eavy. She'll founder for sure. If they sink me ship I'll kill 'em, I will."

"Weren't you going to kill them anyway?" asked Shifty.

"Then I'll double kill 'em!"

Soon, a full dozen cannons were in place, side by side, spanning the full width of the *Sea Urchin*'s aft deck.

"I hope you know what you're doing!" shouted Jibby.

"Sir Isaac Newton's third law of motion," said Penny. "To every action there is always an equal and opposite reaction. So I'm pretty sure this will work."

"It should," said Mr. Cheeseman, his chest swelling with pride. "But for us to get the kick we need, the cannons need to become part of the ship itself."

Under Mr. Cheeseman's instructions, Dizzy and

Aristotle used a large mallet to knock the wooden wheels off the trunnions while Chip followed with a hammer, pounding nails right through the trunnions and into the ship's deck until they were firmly attached.

"Let's move it here," shouted Jibby. "Time's a wastin'." By now the bow of the sloop was even with the *Sea Urchin*'s stern and a mere thirty feet off her port side. In another five minutes the Mailman and his bloodthirsty crew would be boarding the *Sea Urchin*, and, just like the Mailman himself, it would not be pretty.

As each cannon was firmly adhered to the deck, Big and Teddy loaded them with powder. Chip and Penny followed with ammunition, dropping the heavy lead cannon shot into the awaiting gun barrels.

"Prepare to die!" shouted the Mailman with a malicious laugh as the sloop came alongside the *Sea Urchin*. Scurvy stood on deck with a sharp butcher knife clenched between his teeth. His hands clutched a thick rope that hung from the mainmast. The Mailman nodded and Scurvy left his feet, the rope carrying him through the air like a human tetherball. Were it not considered unmanly (or un-pirately) to do so, he might very well have shouted "Wheeeee!" as he flew toward the *Sea Urchin*.

"Fire!" hollered Jibby. With that one word, the power of a dozen cannons was unleashed all at once, causing a deafening blast that sent the *Sea Urchin* lurching forward, exactly as Penny and Sir Isaac Newton had promised it would. When Scurvy reached his apex—the point at which he would normally have dropped down onto the deck of the

Sea Urchin—he encountered a slight problem. The ship was no longer there. The propulsion of the cannons had taken it twenty feet ahead of where it had been just seconds before. This forced Scurvy to revert to plan B, which was to continue holding on to the rope until it swung back to the sloop, where he would plow, full force, into the hard wooden mast.

Captain Jibby ordered the cannons reloaded, this time with double powder, as the sloop regained the ground it had lost, again pulling up alongside the *Sea Urchin*. So close was the sloop that Chip felt he could reach out and touch it. He loaded the last cannon, then covered his ears and waited.

"Fire!" The roar of the guns coincided with a fierce blast of thunder as once more the cannons helped propel the creaky old ship through the stormy waters. The sun disappeared behind the purple clouds and a cold rain began to coat the deck. Teddy and Big primed the cannons again, while Chip and Penny reloaded.

"Permission to speak freely, sir," shouted Shifty over the increasingly gusty winds.

"What is it?" snarled the Mailman.

"Well, sir. Do you think it wise to follow them into the storm?"

"May not be wise, but if you've got another idea on 'ow to get me ship back, I'd love to 'ear it."

"Well, I was just thinking. I mean, we have this ship now." Shifty chose his words carefully. "And no offense to the *Sea Urchin*, but this ship is a somewhat nicer vessel."

"This isn't about the ship. This is about winning. And I always win."

A third blast from the cannons and, just like that, the *Sea Urchin* was in the thick of the storm. "Batten down the hatches," shouted Jibby. "Reduce the sails. Reef the main and trim the fore!" Jibby's crew sprang into action while Chip, Penny, and the rest of the newcomers put what they had learned over the past two weeks to the test.

Young Teddy Roosevelt took his position at the helm next to Jake and held tightly to the wheel as huge waves swept across the deck, one nearly washing Penny over the side. If Teddy hadn't reached out and grabbed her as she slid by, she would surely have been sent to a watery grave. "You saved my life," she said, wiping the cold water from her eyes and struggling to regain her breath. "Thank you."

"Thank you . . . ?" Teddy hinted. By the smug look on his face, Penny knew what he was after.

"Thank you, Captain Fabulous," she said with a roll of her eyes, even though she thought Teddy had rightfully earned his title.

"You're welcome," said Captain Fabulous.

In good conditions, having twelve iron cannons lined up at the stern of a ship's top deck could prove dangerous. In this weather, it was suicide. The top-heavy *Sea Urchin* heeled port, then starboard.

"Lighten the load!" shouted Jibby. Chip, Ethan, Sammy, and Aristotle began detaching the cannons from the trunnions and hurling them overboard. Other than Jibby's Swiss

Army-knifed hand, Big's knife and bow, and a few forks from the galley, they were now completely weaponless. Their only hope was to lose the Mailman in the storm. But as good a sailor as Jibby was, the Mailman was better. And despite pleas from his terrified crew, he sailed forward into the squall. Electricity shot across the sky while rain crashed down upon the dueling ships. Jibby continued to shout out orders but little could be heard over the crashing, mashing, and gnashing of the waves and the thunder from above, which rang out every few seconds accompanied by jagged bolts of lightning.

So far the storm had done nothing to throw the Mailman off their port side. He pulled alongside the *Sea Urchin*, perilously close for two ships so utterly out of control. He took hold of the rope that hung from the mainmast and stepped back, pulling it taut. He would succeed where Scurvy had failed. He would board the ship, and when the others followed, Captain Jibby and his crew would be sorry they had double-crossed one of the meanest pirates on the seven seas.

"Here they come," said Jibby. "Dig in and never say die!"

Big drew an arrow from her quiver and loaded her bow. She drew the bow back but the rain-washed deck was too slippery and far too unsteady to line up a shot.

Chip stumbled to the helm where Three-Eyed Jake was working doggedly to maintain course for the center of the storm. "Excuse me," he said, nudging Jake and Teddy aside and taking the wheel. Jake was confused but there was no time for explanation as the Mailman lifted his feet and took to the air, swinging toward the *Sea Urchin*, his eyes ablaze with anger, his mind full of malicious intent, his face full of metal.

Chip knew he had one shot and one shot only. This would be the most important at-bat of his baseball career. He cranked the wheel hard to the right and the boom swung around like a giant baseball bat. The Mailman saw it coming but it was too late. He barely had time to wince before the solid oak beam met him in midair, sending him flying back the way he came, over the deck of the sloop, as his men watched helplessly from below.

Just before he started his descent to the churning waters, the Mailman learned a very valuable lesson, which is this: never go willingly into an electrical storm if you have a face covered in metal rings. A shard of lightning sent a powerful current skittering from earring to nose ring to elbow ring and back again until his entire body both looked and smelled like barbecued chicken. He plopped into the ocean with the sizzle of a burger hitting a red-hot grill.

"Nice job, Chip!" shouted Penny.

Chip smiled, then turned and shouted to Big. "That," he said, "is a home run."

"Now I understand," said Big, returning the smile.

Jake took the wheel from Chip, but not before giving him two hearty thumbs up.

Jibby gave him one thumb and a can opener up. "Good work, everybody," he said.

As the Mailman's crew focused their attention on fishing their half-baked captain from the sea, Jibby and his crew seized the opportunity to escape, sailing deeper into the seething maelstrom. In minutes, the Mailman's sloop disappeared among the watery mountains and valleys of the violent Atlantic. "We lost him!" said Sammy.

"Three cheers!" said Dizzy.

"Hip, hip, hooray!" shouted the group. But the celebration would be cut short, for they were only one *hip* into the second cheer when a bolt of lightning crackled overhead. It was so close it made their hair stand on end, and it reminded them that while they had successfully rid themselves of one danger, they still had to contend with a savage storm.

A sudden wave, some thirty feet high, slammed into the *Sea Urchin*'s hull, nearly capsizing the old girl. Jibby lost his balance and hit the deck hard. When he did, the leather pouch on his belt, the one that carried the White Gold Chalice, broke away. "Nooo!" he shouted as he watched the pouch skate along the deck toward the ship's railing. Big saw it too. She released her grip on the mainmast and sprinted after it. Just as another colossal wave attacked the ship she took to the air, landing on her belly and sliding across the deck, reaching out for the precious pouch. Chip watched in horror as Big and the satchel tumbled over the railing, out of sight.

"Man overboard!" shouted Jibby.

"Big!" cried Chip, struggling to make his way to the other end of the violently pitching ship. Halfway there, a third giant wave knocked him off his feet, forcing him to crawl the rest of the way. He grabbed the railing and pulled himself up. He looked over the edge, desperately scanning the turbulent water for any sign of Big, but he could see nothing.

He heard a grunt and looked to his left. There she was, dangling above the water, clinging tenuously to the spindles of the railing. Clamped between her teeth was the leather pouch. "Hold on," Chip commanded. He shinnied along the railing, then leaned over as far as he could, reaching for Big. He grabbed one wrist and then the other and had just begun to pull when another vicious wave washed across the deck. Chip felt himself going over the railing, helpless to stop his inevitable plunge. It seemed that he and Big would drown together. Then, just like that, his forward motion stopped and his jeans tightened around his waist.

"Pull her in, lad!" yelled Captain Jibby, the bottle opener of his Swiss Army hand hooked on Chip's back pocket, his hand gripping the line to the foresail. With all his strength Chip pulled Big up and over the railing and they tumbled to the deck in a heap.

"What were you thinking?" Chip yelled, the stress of the situation coming out in the form of anger. "You could have been killed. We both could have been killed."

Big removed the satchel from her mouth. "And you could have been cursed forever," she shot back. She turned and handed the pouch to Jibby. "I believe you dropped this."

Jibby smiled and took the pouch. "I did indeed."

"We're takin' on water!" shouted Dizzy from below.

"Man the bilge pump!" yelled Jibby. He turned to Chip and placed his hand on his shoulder. "I need a volunteer. Someone who can get the job done. And I've chosen you."

Big watched as Chip trudged off toward the companionway without a word.

It was not long before Chip began to regret his demand to be treated as an adult. The bilge pump was located, as the name might imply, in the ship's bilge, the very bottom of the hull. Here fresh air was in short supply and, as Dizzy and Chip worked fervently to rid the ship of unwanted water, Chip's stomach began to churn like the sea outside and his face turned a similar color of green. It seemed like forever, though it was probably just over an hour before Dizzy finally noticed.

"You all right there, lad?" he asked. Chip tried to nod yes but instead answered by leaning over and losing his lunch. Actually, he didn't lose it, technically. He knew exactly where it was: right at his feet.

Now, when someone throws up, there is something peculiar in human nature that causes people to think they can make that person feel better by telling them about times they threw up.

"Don't worry, son," said Dizzy. "First time I worked the pump I got sick myself. I'd just eaten a whole plate of greasy fried oysters and a half-dozen boiled eggs and I wasn't feeling too good to begin with. So, anyway . . ."

Dizzy's vividly detailed account did not make Chip feel better at all. In fact, it seemed to have quite the opposite effect and soon everything went black.

When Chip regained consciousness, the first thing he noticed was how strangely quiet it was. There was no thunder and there were no waves splashing over the side of the ship. Nor was there any yelling or running about. All he could hear was the sound of the water lapping gently at the hull and the soft susurrus of the sails. All he could see was a pretty girl in a blue baseball cap leaning over him.

"You're alive," said Big with a smile that carried with it much information. It suggested to Chip that the storm was over and that all was well once again.

"I'm sorry, Big," he said. "I'm sorry I got angry with you. I was just scared, that's all."

"I know," said Big.

"We sure showed the Mailman and his crew a thing or two, didn't we?"

"We sure did."

Chip pushed himself up to his elbows and surveyed the deck to find it littered with the tired bodies of his family members and Jibby's crew, sprawled out in various degrees of exhaustion.

Two of those bodies, Sammy and Mr. Cheeseman, came to life and dragged themselves over to check on Chip's condition. "Are you okay, Chip?" his father asked.

"Just a little queasy. What happened?"

"You got sick working the bilge pump."

"Nothing to be ashamed of," said Sammy. "The first time I worked it I got sick myself. Now picture this. I'd just eaten an entire rack of lamb . . ."

CHAPTER 17

In the hands of Jibby's expert crew, the sails were in constant harmony with the ever-changing winds of the high seas. The *Sea Urchin* cut through the water at top speed, which, I should point out, was not nearly fast enough for those on board.

As each day passed, the ship's inhabitants grew increasingly restless, weary, and hungry for dry land, a change of clothes, and a good meal. After three and a half weeks at sea even a gourmet cook like Juanita had a hard time putting together something edible from the ship's dwindling supplies. As Penny sat in the galley poking at the porridge with her spoon, she was sure she knew why sailors kissed the ground when they finally went ashore. The ground was probably much tastier than anything they had eaten in a very long time.

"I can't wait to eat real food again," she said.

"When we get to Denmark, can we get pizza?" asked Teddy, nudging his porridge around the edge of his bowl.

He plucked the bubble gum from his forehead and popped it back into his mouth, having all but given up on the meal.

"I wouldn't count on finding any in Denmark," said Mr. Cheeseman. "The Danish are not exactly known for their pizza."

"What are they known for?"

"Danishes," said Chip, causing Big and Penny to snicker.

"Really?" said Teddy.

"I hope so," said Mr. Cheeseman, who was known to have a terrible sweet tooth. "I love Danishes."

"Hmm," said No-Face Roy. "I wish we were going to Turkey."

There is much debate over which are the two sweetest words in the English language. While some will say *french fries*, others would opt for *free cash, frosted doughnuts*, or *no homework*. But to those who had spent nearly a month aboard the *Sea Urchin*, the two words they most longed to hear were, "Land ho!"

Dizzy shouted it out again from the crow's nest and all hands rushed to the bow. There it was: the coast of Denmark, a mere sliver of land on the distant horizon but the most beautiful sliver of land any of them had ever seen.

A spontaneous celebration erupted with much hugging, cheering, and dancing as Jibby broke out his fiddle for the first time since he played at Steve the sock puppet's funeral. But this was not a funeral dirge. This was a reel, a lively

Scottish folk song, perfectly suited to kicking off a bona fide wingding, which, as Jibby would be happy to tell you, is just like a shindig but without all the hullabaloo.

Chip was surprised to find that Big was a very good dancer and equally surprised to discover that he was not. But Big was patient and a very good teacher as well, and soon Chip found himself nearly able to keep up with her.

When the wingding finally came to an end, the ship was only a mile from shore. They could see the outline of a gray stone castle resting high atop a rocky cliff.

"Wow," said Teddy. "Is that where we're going?"

"That's where we're going," said Three-Eyed Jake.

"Grrrr," said Pinky.

Jibby ordered the sails at full and, as the shore grew nearer, the ship moved faster.

"Pardon me, Captain," said Penny with an urgent tug on Jibby's buttoned sleeve, "but shouldn't we be slowing down a bit?"

"Nope," said Jibby. "We've got no tender to shore, so the only way to get there is by swimming or running her aground and I have no intention of doing any swimming today. So the farther up the beach I can take her, the better." Jibby gave the order to hold tight and prepare for a bumpy landing. Penny wrapped her arms around the mainmast and waited for impact.

The keel met with the sandy ocean floor, grinding its way up the beach. The sudden jolt caused Teddy to lose his grip on the wheel and he was sent hurtling along the deck until Penny reached out and grabbed him by the ankle as he tumbled by.

"Thanks," said Teddy, rubbing a brand-new bump on the crown of his head.

"Thanks . . . ?" Penny arched her eyebrows and waited.

"Thanks, Queen of the Universe," said Teddy with a smile.

"Happy to help," said Penny Nickelton, Queen of the Universe.

As the ship continued to slice its way through the sand, it began to heel sharply to the left. Just when it seemed the ship would roll right over onto its side it ground to a stop, resting at a near forty-five-degree angle.

The crew members were lowered by rope—women and children first—to the shallow water where they could easily wade ashore. Penny was neither the first nor the only one to kiss the ground as everyone, it seemed, considered this to be a good idea.

"Yes, that's definitely them," said Professor Boxley from his position on the bluff about a half mile to the south, where every day for the past three weeks he and Gateman Nametag had scrutinized every ship that passed by. The Danish province of Jutland offered a long coastline and featured many small villages. The fact that Professor Boxley had been off by only a mile or so was impressive. He lowered the spyglass and Gateman grabbed it eagerly. Though waiting in Denmark may have been one of his most favorite things to do, he was happy the wait was almost over.

"They're kissing the ground," he said. "Disgusting."

"I guess they're glad they're here," said the professor.

"Not nearly as glad as I am." Gateman chuckled and the professor shot him a quizzical look. "I mean . . . I'm very happy for them. As you might imagine."

"Yes," said the professor. "Now let's hurry along before we lose them."

The route from beach to castle was a series of steep switchback trails that would take Captain Jibby and his crew to the top of the bluff. The climb was difficult enough without the sensation of the ground constantly moving back and forth, a feeling brought on by weeks at sea.

"Don't worry, lad," said Sammy, scooping Teddy off his wobbly legs and placing him on his shoulders. "You'll get your land legs back in a day or two."

Pinky growled louder and more steadily with every unsteady step they took toward the imposing gray castle, home to the Duke of Jutland. A small village spread out around the massive structure and people scurried about on its stone streets. There was certainly no shortage of strange looks from the villagers, but this time, with Jibby and his crew at their side, Mr. Cheeseman and his family did not find the quizzical stares intimidating.

"I don't know," said Ethan. "Something about that castle is causing Pinky concern."

"Well, it is a pretty creepy-looking castle," said Chip.

"*Es bastante escalofriante,*" said Juanita.

"*Sí,*" said No-Face Roy, who could only imagine what Juanita had just said.

The dark stone walls of the fortress reached forty feet into the air, and its four circular towers rose another fifteen feet beyond that. Armed sentries patrolled the catwalk above. Creepy or not, they continued walking into the expansive shadow of the castle. When they neared the gatehouse, two stern-looking guards with lances at the ready stepped forward and shouted something in a language that was, if not Danish, certainly very Danishy sounding.

Jibby had grown up in Scotland but his grandfather was Danish and he seemed to understand at least a little bit of what the guards were saying. He uttered a few Danishy-sounding phrases of his own, then removed the White Gold Chalice from its pouch. The guards immediately looked less stern and one of them cupped his hand around his mouth and shouted to the catwalk above. In a matter of minutes there was more shouting from above and the two guards stepped to the sides as the drawbridge lowered.

When the drawbridge touched down upon the ground, a thin man with a rather large nose and a bushy blond mustache was waiting in the archway. "Velkomstord," he said with a deep bow. "Welcome. My name is Yannick."

"Is that the duke?" whispered Teddy with a tug on his father's hand.

"I don't think so," said Mr. Cheeseman. "I think it's just one of his helpers."

"You mean like the Santa Claus at the mall?"

"Uh . . . sort of," said Mr. Cheeseman.

"I understand you have something for the duke," said the duke's helper.

"Do indeed," said Jibby, displaying the famous chalice.

"I will be more than happy to take it to him," said Yannick, reaching for the cup.

Jibby pulled it away quickly. "Sorry," he said. "This item is to be hand delivered."

"Very well. If you insist." Yannick offered a tight-lipped smile, which faded when his eyes set upon Pinky and Digs. "I'm afraid that animals are most definitely not allowed in the castle. They will have to wait outside."

"No," Penny blurted out. "I'm not leaving Pinky out here all by herself." She knelt next to the hairless dog and gave her a tight squeeze.

"It's okay, Jibby," said Mr. Cheeseman. "We'll wait here for you."

"Are you kiddin' me?" said Jibby. "Remember what happened the last time I left you people alone?" Jibby shook his head in mock disgust, then turned to Yannick and threw back his shoulders, towering over the much smaller man. "Nope," he said. "The animals come with us or we don't come at all."

Yannick tightened his lips once more, then spat out a sigh. "Very well, then. Follow me." Despite Pinky's growling, they did just that.

With an officious stride, Yannick led them down a long,

dim corridor and into the great hall, a cavernous room with large stained-glass windows, its cold stone walls festooned with brightly colored tapestries. The group continued on through the echoey room toward a set of large double doors at the far end. Two heavily armed guards opened the doors and the menagerie of misfits entered another hallway.

"Now, when you meet the duke," said Yannick, "there are a few things to remember. First, you must never look the duke directly in the eye. Never touch the duke. Never speak to the duke until he first speaks to you. Never turn your back to the duke. When the duke makes a joke or delivers a witty rejoinder, always laugh heartily—but not too heartily. Never make mention of other dukes while in the presence of the duke."

"This duke sure has a lot of rules," whispered Penny as Yannick prattled on with his long list of nevers and alwayses.

"Yeah," Chip agreed. "Who does he think he is, a rock star?"

"Or a sock star?" said No-Face Roy.

"I just hope he's happy to see us," said Ethan. "Because if he's not, he sure has a lot of weapons at his disposal."

"After all we've been through," said Penny, "he'd better be happy."

They took a sharp left down another long hallway and nearly ran over their guide when he stopped abruptly in front of another large wooden door flanked by two more heavily armed guards. He shushed the group and directed his gaze at Big, motioning for her to remove her hat, which she did without protest. He knocked and waited until he heard, "Kommer!"

He pushed the heavy door inward and led the visitors into a room of spectacular opulence. Enormous floor-to-ceiling mirrors and priceless works of art adorned the walls, which featured but one small window overlooking the surf below. It had obviously been designed for security and not for the view. Marble stairs led to a raised platform, which featured an oversized canopy bed, draped in the finest linens. Next to it stood a gong, eight feet in diameter and cast in bronze, suspended from a fabulously ornate frame. Adjacent to the gong was a chair, beautifully carved in mahogany and heavily decorated with jewels of various colors, shapes, and sizes. Sitting in that chair was a plump man with thick lips and a small collection of chins.

"I give you Duke Ulrik of Jutland," said Yannick.

The duke raised an eyebrow and said something in Danish.

"Greetings, your lordship," said Jibby, trying very hard to avoid direct eye contact. This was not easy to do because the duke, as it turns out, had one eyebrow that was much wider and bushier than the other, giving his face a certain lopsided quality. "My Danish is a tad rusty, I'm afraid. I don't suppose you speak any English."

The duke chuckled at the absurdity of such a remark. "Ja," he said. "I shpekken prefekt Engelsk."

Jake leaned in and whispered to Jibby, "What did he say?"

"I think he said 'I speak perfect English.' "

"Ja," said the duke with a jowly grin, his out-of-control eyebrow arcing upward. "Merry goot Engelsk." With a grunt he forced himself out of the chair, his chins wobbling on the way. "Jai oondershtand dar haven der vide guld jallus?"

"The . . . what?" said Jibby. "Oh, the White Gold Chalice. Yes." Jibby held up the highly coveted goblet. At the very sight of it the duke's eyes sparkled like the chalice itself.

"Ahhh, ur esh beautyshmuckle. Jai dink dette kulls for ein vingdingle. Ha ha!" He grabbed a mallet hanging on the wall next to the gong and took a swing, putting his full weight behind it. The gong barely moved but its vibrations filled the room, shaking the mirrors and the paintings on the wall.

In a matter of seconds, the door to the room opened and two servants appeared. "Ja, Hertugen?"

The duke spoke to them in Danish. The only word the non-Danish speakers in the room could make out was *vingdingle*. Duke Ulrik, it appeared, was planning to throw a wingding in honor of the occasion. This seemed like a good idea to everyone but Pinky, whose constant growling indicated that she was somewhat less than fond of the chubby, jowly Duke of Jutland with his one rogue eyebrow.

Chip knelt next to Pinky and gently grabbed her snout. "Shh." Though he didn't want to discourage the use of her psychic abilities, he feared the growling might insult the duke and result in an even more dangerous situation than the one Pinky foresaw. Pinky stopped growling but did not look happy about having to do so.

225

The servants hurried off to prepare for the vingdingle and the duke waddled down the stairs toward Jibby, who took a knee out of respect for royalty. Tension filled the air as the duke's plump fingers reached for the chalice. Once he officially took possession, as the cup's rightful owner, the curse would finally be broken. The duke lifted the cup from Jibby's outstretched hands and a collective sigh of relief rippled through the room. The relief soon turned to jubilation. The curse was over.

Penny hugged Teddy and scruffed up his hair. Jibby hugged his wife and planted a furry kiss on her lips. Chip looked at Big and thought of doing the same but the very idea of such a thing was frightening. Kissing someone for the first time is always fraught with danger. Will they kiss you back or turn away, leaving you standing in a pool of awkward embarrassment? Though he had risked his life to save Big on more than one occasion, this was a risk that Chip found himself unwilling to take. He gave her a hug and that was all. He had successfully maintained his dignity, though inside he cursed himself for his failure to seize what seemed like a perfect opportunity.

"Well," said Dizzy with the biggest grin his face had ever known. "Now that the curse is over, I guess I won't be needing these." He removed the completely unnecessary earmuffs and prepared to toss them aside when he promptly lost his balance and fell to the ground.

Jibby threw him a dirty look and apologized for the

disruption as Sammy helped Dizzy to his feet, throwing his back out in the process.

Sammy wailed in pain but the duke paid little attention to the commotion. He was busy admiring the chalice as well as his reflection in its polished surface. When he finally tore his eyes away from the cup, he made an announcement in prefekt Engelsk. He declared that this was too great an occasion to be celebrated with a mere vingdingle. This magnificent event could only be properly observed with a bona fide shindiggle.

He waddled back up the stairs and took the mallet once more. With the chalice in one hand, he struck the gong with the mallet. Instantly the giant bronze disc fell from its fancy frame and landed directly on the duke's right foot. The pain was so intense that the duke found himself unable to scream. His eyes bugged out of his head in opposite directions as the gong rolled off his foot and bounced down the stairs with a sound that was torture to the eardrums. *Gong! Gong! Gong!* Each step louder than the last. Juanita grabbed Teddy and pulled him out of the way as the massive gong rolled across the room until it met with a very large mirror, smashing the glass into thousands of pieces and sending everyone running for cover. The empty frame dropped from the wall and began to fall like a giant redwood, its enormous height covering the entire length of the room. It crashed to the ground, narrowly missing the duke but successfully demolishing his bed and chair, turning them to splintered wood and scattered jewels.

The gong spun and spun, faster and faster, with an unbearable racket until finally it lay flat on the floor amid the broken glass.

The door opened and the two servants reappeared. "Ja, Hertugen?"

SOME PREDICTABLE ADVICE ON PSYCHIC POWERS

Admittedly I am a fierce skeptic when it comes to the topic of psychic abilities, most likely because I am a Libra and we tend to be that way.

You can't help but be doubtful about things like astrology when you see the constellations on which the signs of the zodiac are based. These figures in the sky were named by the ancient Greeks, who were able to gaze upon a grouping of eight stars and determine that it looked like a crab, which is a ten-legged animal. To me the constellation of Cancer looks more like a sombrero. The ancient Greeks, however, did not wear sombreros and so they opted instead for the crab, which, I imagine, is a lot tougher to match with a pair of slacks.

But who could have predicted that thousands of years later, astrology (unlike the sombrero) would be more popular than ever? Today, there are psychics everywhere, and they are not cheap. A psychic reading can cost as much as a couple hundred dollars. For twenty dollars you can go to a Chinese restaurant, get some moo goo gai pan, an order of pork fried rice, and your fortune wrapped in a crispy cookie. How many psychics do you know who will give you, in addition to predictions about your future, a crispy cookie? Exactly.

Now, I know what you're thinking. You're thinking, "If there's no such thing as psychic ability, then how do you know what we're thinking? And, furthermore, how do you explain Nostradamus?"

Actually, I have no explanation for why someone would name his child Nostradamus. For those of you unfamiliar with the man, Nostradamus was a sixteenth-century astrologer who accurately predicted the occurrence of various wars, earthquakes, floods, and the seventeenth century, which nobody saw coming.

His predictions, though amazingly accurate, did nothing to change the events he forecast. The point is, despite our desire to know the future, there is very little we can do about it and the only time a star will ever play a part in our destiny is when our own sun explodes millions of years from now and bakes us all like a crispy Chinese cookie.

I would thereby advise you that even if your psychic hairless dog warns you of impending danger, sometimes there's nothing you can do but ride it out and hope for the best.

CHAPTER 18

When Gateman and the professor arrived in the tiny village, the professor removed the magazine from his pocket and the two men began the arduous task of going door to door, showing Ethan's photo to everyone they met, asking if they had seen the brilliant scientist. They asked at the inn, the bakery, the fish shop, the vegetable market, and every little house within walking distance, but no one could remember having seen Mr. Cheeseman. This may have been due to the fact that he was the most normal-looking member of his traveling group.

"I knew it," said the professor, angrily stuffing the magazine back into his pocket. "As long as it took us to get here they're probably long gone by now."

"I told you I can't walk fast in these shoes," Gateman retorted. "Besides, there's still one place we haven't checked."

There had been a changing of the guard by the time Gateman and the professor approached the castle. Two fresh sentries with fresh lances (or the exact same lances, hard to tell) watched the two bickering men waddle up to the gatehouse. The guards shouted a warning in Danish and the professor responded with one of the few Danish words he had learned over the last three weeks of waiting around in Denmark. "Hej," he said.

"Hej," said the guards.

"We're looking for a friend of ours."

The guards seemed confused and muttered something in Danish. The professor repeated his words, this time louder and more slowly. If the guards didn't understand English, he reasoned, perhaps they would if it was presented to them at a slower pace and a greater volume.

The guards responded by repeating what they had said, louder and more slowly. The professor looked confused and said, even more loudly and slowly than the previous two times, "WE'RE . . . LOOKING . . . FOR . . . A . . . FRIEND . . . OF . . . OURS!" Gateman rolled his eyes and shook his head. At this rate, he thought, they would all grow very old and very deaf before anything was accomplished. "Show them the picture," he urged with an elbow to the ribs.

"Oh, yes," said the professor, removing the magazine from his pocket. "This man. We're looking for this man."

The guards leaned in for a closer look. "Ja," said one guard, nodding and pointing over his shoulder with his thumb. "Der vide guld jallus."

"What the heck is a vide guld jallus?" said Gateman.

"I don't know," said the professor. "But it seems as though Ethan Cheeseman is somewhere inside this castle. Did you hear that? We've found him! We've found him at

last!" The professor was so happy he almost hugged Gateman before quickly remembering that he had a rather strong
dislike for the man. Instead, he turned to the guards and
explained, very loudly and very slowly, that he and his
assistant needed to see the man in the picture immediately.

The guards shook their heads and ran off a long explanation in Danish, pointing to the castle and miming the
acts of eating and drinking.

"What did they say?" asked Gateman.

"I'm not sure," said the professor. "But I think I heard
something about a shindig. I guess we'll just have to come
back later." The professor walked away and Gateman
hurried after him.

"Later?" The professor's lack of assertiveness was making Gateman crazy. "Don't you know anything about
getting past security? Give me some coins."

"What?"

"Some money. Give me some money." Gateman thrust
his open palm a little too close to the professor's face.

After nearly a month of waiting around in Denmark,
staying at inns and eating at restaurants, the professor's
cash reserves were running dangerously low. He pulled
a couple of the few remaining coins from his pocket and
handed them to Gateman. "Are you sure you know what
you're doing?"

"Watch and learn," said Gateman. He approached the
guards with a casual swagger and a smarmy grin. "Hey
fellas, looking good today. I simply must get the name of
your tailor. And who does your hair? You have to tell me

his name and what size bowl he uses. Now listen. I realize we don't have an invitation to this little shindig of yours, but perhaps my good friend, misterrrrr"—Gateman paused to check whose likeness appeared on the coins—"fat guy with a beard might convince you to let us in."

With a wink he handed the coins to the guards, who thanked Gateman with wide smiles and eagerly pocketed the money. Gateman waited, but the guards did not give the signal to lower the drawbridge.

"Okay," he said, "this is the part where you turn the other way while we sneak inside." The guards smiled and nodded but did nothing else. "All right listen, you simpletons. Haven't you ever taken a bribe before? This is ridiculous. I'm dealing with a bunch of amateurs here."

Professor Boxley grabbed Gateman by the elbow and pulled him away from the scene. "Nice job," he said. "I learned a lot. Now let's go back to the inn. They've got to come out of the castle sooner or later. And when they do, we'll be waiting."

"More waiting?" huffed Gateman. "I mean, more waiting. Hooray!"

The long, narrow banquet table of the great hall was set with fine china and polished silver of the quality that one might expect to find at a shindig in honor of the White Gold Chalice being returned to its rightful owner.

Various smells wafted in from the kitchen, all of which received no lower than an eight-point-four rating from

Teddy, who had already planted his bubble gum firmly on his forehead in anticipation of the coming feast. "I'm starving," he said. "When do we eat?"

"We can't eat until our host arrives," said Mr. Cheeseman. "It takes a long time to tend to a broken foot."

"I like it here," said Teddy, taking in the splendor of the room. "Do we have to go back on the boat right away?"

"I think we could all use some time ashore," said Mr. Cheeseman. "But we shouldn't leave the LVR sitting where it is for too long. It'll be winter by the time we get back. Besides, the way Pinky's been growling, I don't think we should stay here any longer than we have to."

Trumpets sounded, temporarily drowning out Pinky's growling. All rose as the duke hobbled into the room on his heavily bandaged foot with the help of two servants, who escorted him to the head of the table, where the precious chalice awaited him.

Big leaned across the table and whispered to Chip and Penny, "Pinky's not the only one who thinks little of this duke character. I can say without reservation that I am not so fond of him myself."

"I know what you mean," said Chip. "There's something a little off about him."

"I'm hungry," said Teddy.

"*Sí*," said No-Face Roy.

The duke's servants pulled out his chair and he lowered his wide posterior to the seat. Instantly, and without warning, the chair collapsed as if it were made of Popsicle sticks, sending the duke's plump backside and his broken foot crashing to the hard stone floor. The duke said something in Danish that sounded to Teddy like swear words. In fact, to Teddy, most words in Danish sounded like swear words. The duke's servants hurried to help him up and called for a replacement chair.

"The duke seems to be having a run of bad luck," said Jibby.

"Yes," said Penny. "It's almost as if he's . . . cursed."

"Are you sure the Duke of Jutland is the rightful owner of the chalice?" Mr. Cheeseman asked.

"Sure as can be," said Jibby. "I've done my research well, I can promise you that."

When the duke's backup chair arrived, he ordered three of his servants to sit in it at once, one on top of the other, in order to check its sturdiness. It passed the test and he took a seat, then cleared his throat.

"Velkomstord til alla jer. Jai vil leeken du maak en toashte!"

"What did he say?" whispered Jake.

"I think he said, 'I would like to make a toast,'" said Jibby.

"Well," said Sammy. "It's a good thing he speaks perfect English."

The duke raised the White Gold Chalice and the dinner guests hoisted their glasses as well. "Til mein jonored gesten!" He drank to his honored guests, then clapped his hands twice sharply, and out came the food. Platters of fine delicacies arrived one after the other. Among the happiest to see the food were Pinky and Digs, whose ribs were beginning to show after nearly a month at sea, and they quickly devoured their platefuls of Danish sausage and waited for more.

Teddy gave all of the food a very high grade but rated none higher than the gravy, which he found to be absolutely perfect. Not for eating but for something else. When he was certain no one was looking, he dipped his finger into the bowl and then dabbed at his sock puppet. He dipped and dabbed twice more and that's how, in a matter of seconds, No-Face Roy, formerly Rat-Face Roy, became Gravy-Face Roy.

"This is the best meal ever," said Teddy. "No offense, Juanita."

Juanita smiled her warm Spanish smile and scruffed up Teddy's spiky hair. *"Sin ánimo de offender adoptadas."*

"I couldn't agree more," said Gravy-Face Roy.

And that was about the extent of the conversation at the table. Everyone was so hungry they could not stop eating long enough to engage in idle chitchat. Finally, Yannick spoke loudly over the sounds of enthusiastic chewing. "Well," he said, breaking the awkward silence. "Perhaps his lordship would be kind enough to regale us with one of his many humorous anecdotes."

"Ja," said the duke, his mouth full of partially chewed sausage. If the duke's English was less than perfect, it was even less than less than perfect with a mouthful of sausage. He started into a story that included the phrases, "look out!" "millions of noodles," and "buried alive," which turned out to be the punch line. Yannick laughed heartily but not too heartily and the duke's honored guests followed suit. The duke laughed too. Then he suddenly stopped laughing. He also suddenly stopped breathing. He reached for his throat. His face turned purple.

"Something's happened to the duke!" yelled Yannick.

"He's choking," said Penny.

Mr. Cheeseman sprang to his feet, knocking his chair over in the process. He sprinted the length of the table and positioned himself behind the purple duke. He wrapped his arms around their choking host, placing his fist just below his sternum.

"What are you doing to his lordship?" shouted Yannick. "Assassin! Assassin!"

Guards rushed toward Ethan. He drove his fist into the duke's chest but nothing happened. He tried again, and just as the guards were about to descend upon him, a large piece of sausage shot forth from the duke's throat like a rocket to the moon.

With quickness never before seen from a man his size, the duke reached out and caught the meaty projectile in midair, like a shortstop stretching out for a sharp line drive. He inspected the sausage briefly, then popped it back into his mouth and swallowed it with a satisfied grunt.

"You saved the duke's life!" exclaimed Yannick.

"Ja," said the duke, helping himself to another plateful of sausage. "Du har zaven mit live." As he continued eating, he spoke to Yannick at great length. Yannick did not seem at all pleased with what the duke was telling him. The two argued back and forth until Yannick finally gave in. He pressed his lips firmly together and addressed Mr. Cheeseman.

"The duke is most grateful. He wishes me to tell you that you and your friends are welcome to stay for as long as you like."

This was excellent news for the weary travelers. After dinner they were given the opportunity to bathe and each was presented with a change of clothes and a fine silk sleeping gown.

Despite all the growling from their hairless psychic dog, the duke was turning out to be a fabulous host. Perhaps Pinky was losing her touch, thought Penny. After being fed two platefuls of delicious sausage, Pinky also thought she might be losing her touch. Maybe she'd been wrong about the duke after all.

The castle was large enough that they could each have their own room but creepy enough that none of them chose to do so. Jibby's crew all paired off while Penny and Big agreed to share a room and Mr. Cheeseman opted to bunk with Chip, Teddy, and Gravy-Face Roy.

After sleeping in hammocks on a moving ship for the past three and half weeks, the down-filled beds were like heaven and soon everyone fell into coma-like sleep. Everyone, that is, but Teddy, who could not stop thinking about all the delicious food he had eaten earlier. His stomach was calling for more and would not take no for an answer.

Quietly, he slipped from beneath the covers and stepped

over Pinky and Digs, curled up together and snoring softly at the foot of his bed. He successfully tiptoed from the room without waking his bunkmates and set out to find the kitchen.

Candles along the walls provided poor lighting for the long hallway and Teddy quickly became confused. He took a turn down another hallway and followed it until it ended, forcing him to go either right or left. He took a right and soon found himself at the end of this hallway as well. But this time there was no left or right, just a closed door that Teddy had no reason to believe did not lead to the kitchen.

He turned the knob and opened the door to find not the kitchen, but a small empty room. A rug had been rolled away to reveal an open hatch with stairs leading down, perhaps, he thought, to the kitchen. His stomach urging him on, Teddy descended the stairs slowly, as the light below was quite dim.

At the bottom of the steps, Teddy found himself in another hallway, the ceiling low and the air damp and musty. The floor beneath his bare feet had turned from stone to cool earth. As he inched forward down the dank corridor, confidence in his ability to find the kitchen dwindled with each and every step. He was about to turn back when suddenly he smelled food. Yes, definitely food. He quickened his pace and walked to the end of the hall, turned left, and screamed at the sight of a man coming toward him. The man screamed, too, and ran headlong into Teddy, dropping the tray he was carrying, dishes smashing and cutlery clanging off the hard dirt floor.

The man looked at Teddy with rage in his eyes. "What are you doing here?" Yannick demanded.

Teddy stepped back slowly. "I was hungry," he said apologetically. "I was looking for the kitchen."

"The kitchen?" said Yannick, softening his tone. "Now why on earth would you think the kitchen is down here?"

"I smelled food."

"Uh, yes," said Yannick with a chuckle. "Easy explanation for that. I was just . . . feeding the cats, you see."

Teddy looked at the broken dishes and the cutlery on the ground. "You feed them with a fork?"

"They're very particular, I'm afraid," said Yannick. "You know cats."

"But I thought you said there were no animals allowed in the castle."

"Did I?" said Yannick with a forced chuckle. "Well, when you think about it, this isn't really part of the castle."

"It isn't?"

Yannick bent to gather up the mess on the floor. "No, it's the basement."

"Looks like a dungeon," said Teddy.

"Sure does," said Gravy-Face Roy.

"A dungeon?" said Yannick, incredulous at the very thought. "That's absurd. We have no use for such things around here. Now, what do you say we go to the kitchen and get you something to eat?"

Penny recognized the feeling. It was the same one she had when her family once stayed at a bed-and-breakfast and she had woken in the middle of the night to find a ghost roller-skating back and forth at the end of her bed. The feeling, the sense of a strange presence in the room, was the same, but this time she opened her eyes to find that the ghost was not on roller skates. The spirit appeared to be that of an older man with a gray beard and garments befitting nobility. Penny thought of crying out for her father as she had done at the bed-and-breakfast, but she realized she was strangely unafraid of this ghost with his pathetically sad face.

He said nothing but seemed to beckon her to follow before vanishing through the chamber door. Careful not to awaken Big, Penny crept across the room and out into the hallway, where she saw the ghost disappear behind a rounded door on a curved wall. She hurried across the hall to the door and opened it to find a spiral staircase leading upward.

As she climbed, around and around, up and up, she soon became aware that she was inside one of the castle's four massive towers. The higher she climbed the colder the air became until finally she ran out of stairs. She stepped through an archway to the rooftop of the castle, where a billion blinking stars coated the sky, providing a spectacular backdrop to an autumn moon that was sharp, brilliant, and nearly full.

Far below, waves could be heard belly flopping onto the beach, one after the other; heard but not seen, as the land and sea below were shrouded in a blanket of thick, low-lying fog. It was nearly November and Penny's silk nightgown offered scant protection from the frigid breeze. With no sign of the ghost, she had just made the decision to return to her chamber when she heard a voice.

"Mark me," it rang out, deep and hollow. She turned to find the spirit hovering but a few feet away.

"Who are you?" she demanded. "What do you want?"

"I am Penfold," the old man droned in a highly dramatic tone. "Doomed for a certain term to walk the night, and the day confined to fast in fires, till the foul crimes done in my days of nature are burnt and purged away."

Penny wrinkled her nose. Something wasn't quite right here. "Wait a minute," she said. "I'm sorry, but isn't that from *Hamlet*?"

"What?"

"That whole thing you just said. Those are lines spoken by the ghost in Shakespeare's *Hamlet*."

Penfold hemmed and hawed. "I'm sure you must be mistaken," he said with minimal conviction.

"I don't think so," said Penny, who had somewhat of a Shakespearior attitude when it came to the greatest playwright of all time. "I should know, I've read it twice and I received one hundred percent on my report in advanced English." Penfold seemed to lose some of his ghostly pallor and Penny wondered if he wasn't blushing. "What do you want from me, anyway? Why are you here?"

The ghost raised his eyes to the stars. "But that I am forbid to tell the secrets of my prison-house," he emoted.

"Uh, that's also from *Hamlet*," said Penny flatly, her patience waning. "It's cold out here. Now, if you'll excuse me, I'm going back to bed." Penny turned to leave and the ghost reappeared in front of her, blocking her escape.

"Okay," said Penfold, quickly dropping his dramatic flair. "Here's the deal. I'm the guy who first stole the White Gold Chalice all those years ago, all right?"

"You're the one?" said Penny, her disdain for the ghost reaching new heights. "You stole the White Gold Chalice? From a dead guy? And left all those poor souls stranded at the gates of Valhalla?"

Penfold hung his head. "Uh, yes. I'm afraid so. But now that you're here, that's all about to end."

"What do you mean about to end? It already has ended. We returned the chalice to the duke this afternoon."

"Or did you?" said Penfold.

"What do you mean?" asked Penny.

"What I mean is, you must be wary of those in lofty towers who are not themselves. Instead, place thy faith in dwellers of dungeons dark, betrothed to fortune but wed to fate, and foul deed of kin but not of blood. Wrote that one myself. Not bad, huh?"

"Not bad," said Penny. "But what does it mean?"

The ghost began drifting away, slowly fading from view. He threw the back of his hand across his forehead. "My hour is almost come when I to sulphurous and tormenting flames must render up myself."

"Also from *Hamlet*," said Penny.

244

"What*ever*!" And in a snap, Penfold the plagiarist ghost melted into thin air, leaving Penny alone to try and decipher his words.

She crept down the tower steps and into the pale light of the hallway. She nearly jumped out of her skin when she bumped into a small creature with three eyes. By the time she inhaled enough oxygen for a good-sized scream, she realized that the three-eyed creature was Teddy, his bubble gum stuck to the center of his forehead. Luckily, his mouth was too full of food to cry out with surprise. Penny grabbed him roughly by the arm and he nearly dropped his bowl of rice pudding. "What are you doing out here?"

"I was hungry, so I got something to eat."

"You just went to the kitchen and helped yourself to some food?"

"No," said Teddy. "I ran into Yannick when he was feeding the cats and he took me to the kitchen."

"Cats?" said Penny. "But it was Yannick himself who said that animals were not allowed in the castle."

"I know," said Teddy, taking another spoonful of the pudding, which came in at an impressive nine-point-three rating. "But they're not really in the castle. They're in the basement. It just looks like a dungeon but it's really a basement."

"Dungeon?" gasped Penny. "The ghost said something about dungeons dark."

"Ghost?" said Teddy. "You saw another ghost? How come I never get to see ghosts?"

"I can't speak for them personally but it might have something to do with that gravy-stained sock on your arm. Now, can you show me where this dungeon is?"

"It's a basement," said Gravy-Face Roy indignantly. "Not a dungeon."

Teddy and Roy retraced their steps and Penny followed closely. The rug in the empty room had been rolled back over to cover the hatch. "It's under there," said Teddy.

Penny peeled the rug back and, with a grunt, pulled open the heavy door. "You're right," she said, peering down the stairway. "It does look like a dungeon." Cautiously, and against her better judgment, she made her way down the stairs and Teddy followed close behind.

"Can we pet the cats?" he whispered.

"Shh," said Penny. "Hear that?"

Teddy cocked his head to one side and raised his eyes for better listening. He did hear something coming from the end of the hall. It sounded like growling. "I've changed my mind," he said. "I don't want to pet the cats."

"Come on," whispered Penny. Teddy followed his sister as she walked, ever so slowly, to the end of the dark corridor. The flickering candles cast long, unsteady shadows along the cold stone walls. The broken dishes had been completely cleaned up and fresh broom strokes marked the dirt. The growling grew in volume as they turned left, down the very passageway from which Yannick had come earlier before bumping into Teddy. As they continued on, the corridor became smaller and darker and the growling became louder but now sounded less like growling and more like . . . snoring.

"I think the cats are asleep," whispered Teddy. "We should probably go back now so we don't wake them up."

But Penny kept moving and Teddy had no choice but to follow. They reached the very end of the damp tunnel and there he was, the source of the noise, lying on a small bunk in a tiny windowless cell in the far corner of the dungeon. Sorry, basement. The chubby man lay on his side, his face to the wall. "Pssst," said Penny but the man did not wake. "Hey," she said louder. Still nothing. She grabbed Teddy's spoon from his hand and dragged it across the metal bars, back and forth, but the racket failed to stir the man. "Oh for crying out loud." Penny heaved the spoon at the sleeping prisoner.

"Hey," Teddy protested.

The spoon bounced off the back of the man's head and hit the stone wall with a *clang*. He uttered a few words in Danish that sounded like swear words to both Penny and Teddy. He spun around and stood up. Penny and Teddy gasped in unison at what they saw.

"It's the duke," said Penny.

The man's chubby face registered utter confusion at the sight of his two visitors. "Who are you?" he asked, rushing frantically to the bars, his chins jiggling like Teddy's rice pudding. Penny and Teddy backed away. Though he spoke with a strong Danish accent, his English was otherwise perfect. "You must help me. Please."

"Wait a minute," said Teddy. "He's not the duke. The duke talks funny and has a crazy eyebrow."

"But I *am* the duke," insisted the man, who seemed to share every facial feature with their gracious host; every one, that is, but the overgrown eyebrow. "I am Ulrik, the Duke of Jutland. The man of whom you speak is an impostor. His name is Wenzel and he is my evil step-twin. His cousin Yannick imprisoned me here and positioned Wenzel in my place, where he has dined at my table and slept in my bed each day and night of these past three months. He would have killed me had his conscience allowed it and still he may one day, once he tires of feeding me."

That reminded Teddy. He pointed to the floor of the cell. "Could you hand me that spoon?" he asked, anxious to finish the tasty rice pudding. Ulrik seemed annoyed but fetched the spoon and handed it to Teddy, who wiped it on his sleeping gown and resumed feeding his face.

"Wait a minute," said Penny. "Did you say Wenzel was your step-twin?"

"My *evil* step-twin."

"I'm sorry, but what the heck is a step-twin?"

"He is my twin by marriage only. You see, my father died when I was young and my mother was remarried."

"To someone with a kid who looked exactly like you?"

"Yes," said Ulrik, as if such a thing were an everyday occurrence. "Except for that eyebrow of his."

"Of kin but not of blood," said Penny. "So that's what the ghost meant."

"Ghost?" said Ulrik. "You mean Penfold? Is he still stealing lines from Shakespeare?"

"Afraid so," said Penny. "Listen, my family and I have traveled a great distance. We came here to return the White Gold Chalice to its rightful owner, but . . ."

Ulrik became suddenly very excited. His perfectly matched eyebrows danced about and he pressed his jowly face to the iron bars. "You have the White Gold Chalice?"

"Well, not anymore," said Penny. "We thought Wenzel was the cup's rightful owner, so we gave it to him."

Ulrik threw up his hands, beside himself. "Ugh! Will my torment never cease?"

"It will," said Penny. "Now that we're here. Somehow, we'll get the chalice and bring it to you."

"Well, that will certainly solve all my problems," said Ulrik. "Being locked up in a dungeon will be far more tolerable with a fancy chalice from which to drink."

"It's a basement," said Teddy with his mouth full of pudding. "Not a dungeon."

"Is there a key?" asked Penny.

"There is but one, so far as I know," said Ulrik. "Yannick keeps it on a string about his neck."

"Don't worry," said Penny. "We'll get you out of here. We'll come back. Is tomorrow night okay?"

"Well, let me check my availability . . ."

"There's no need to be sarcastic," said Penny. "We are trying to help you, you know."

"Sorry," said Ulrik. "I'm just a bit cranky after being holed up in here for so long."

"I understand," said Penny. She and Teddy bid Ulrik good night and promised to return the following evening with the White Gold Chalice and the key to his basement cell.

They carefully placed the rug over the hatch door and hurried stealthily down the hallway to the room Teddy shared with his father, his brother, Pinky, and Digs. Penny followed and immediately woke Mr. Cheeseman, thankfully without having to hit him on the head with a spoon.

Though he was quite exhausted, Mr. Cheeseman did not mind being woken up because he just happened to be right in the middle of a terrible nightmare that involved being buried alive under millions of noodles. "What?" he said, shaking the sleep and the noodly horror from his head. "What is it, Penny?" He whispered so as not to wake up Chip, sleeping peacefully across the room, but it was no use.

"What's going on?" Chip groaned. He sat up and rubbed his eyes.

Penny told Chip and Ethan about the ghost and how she had run into Teddy in the hallway. She described how Teddy, anxious for another helping of rice pudding, had stumbled upon the real Duke of Jutland, locked away in a basement cell by Wenzel, his evil step-twin.

"I think you mean doppelgänger," said Mr. Cheeseman.

"No, it was definitely rice pudding," said Teddy. "Very tasty."

"No, no," said Mr. Cheeseman. "A doppelgänger is a person's exact double. And that would certainly explain why the curse persists, if indeed it exists at all."

"Either way," said Chip, "it seems we may have given the chalice to the wrong guy."

"Exactly," said Penny. "And that's why I promised Ulrik we'd go back tomorrow night and get him out of there." Mr. Cheeseman agreed. The following night, with the help of Jibby and his crew, they would return the White Gold Chalice to its rightful owner . . . and its rightful owner to his rightful position as the Duke of Jutland.

CHAPTER 19

Professor Boxley and Gateman Nametag spent another day waiting in the shadow of the great castle, hoping to see the great Ethan Cheeseman emerge from within. But on this day Ethan was busy with other matters. He and Captain Jibby stood atop the northwest tower where Penny had encountered Penfold the plagiarist ghost the night before. The two men looked down upon the beach below where the *Sea Urchin* still sat, half buried in the sand, its black and silver flag flapping in the ocean breeze.

Away from the watchful eye of Yannick, the two men secretly formulated their plan to rescue Ulrik and take possession of the White Gold Chalice from Wenzel, who, at this early stage in the day, had already smacked his funny bone on a tabletop, cut himself shaving six times, pulled not one but two groin muscles, and picked up something rather unsavory off the couryard lawn that he had mistaken for sausage. This is why animals were not allowed in the castle.

Though Wenzel didn't realize it at the time, his honored guests would actually be doing him a favor by relieving him of the White Gold Chalice and its vicious curse. Ethan had only one requirement for the plan: that it be executed with absolutely no violence.

"Come now," said Jibby. "A little violence never hurt anyone. Besides, without it I don't know how we're gonna get that chalice back. Wenzel hasn't put it down since dinner last night. He even took it to bed with him. Not sure if you've noticed, but the door to his room is pretty fiercely guarded—and it's the only way in."

"It's the only way in?" said Ethan. "What about the window?" Jibby and Ethan leaned out as far as they could, trying to get a glimpse of Wenzel's chamber window some thirty feet below.

"It's an awfully tiny window," said Jibby.

"Sure is," Ethan agreed. "It would take a very small person to squeeze through it."

"Yes," said Jibby. "And it's a good thing we just happen to have such a person."

The castle courtyard was awash in the soft sunlight of early November. Chip, Penny, and Big took advantage of the unseasonably warm weather, chasing Pinky and Digs around the impeccably manicured grounds, which featured two spectacular fountains and hedges so sharp and tidy that they appeared to have been trimmed with a laser. Teddy sat on a marble bench, watching the fun and feasting on an apple Danish that was nearly the size of his head. Ethan slid in next to him and scruffed up his hair.

"Don't eat too many of those." He spoke without looking at Teddy, instead keeping his eyes focused on Yannick, who was standing across the way and looking back at him. It was obvious that the duke's personal valet was very anxious to see the castle visitors visit someplace else. He had already asked Ethan no fewer than a dozen times when they planned to be on their way.

"But Yannick said I could have as many Danishes as I want," said Teddy. He waved to Yannick enthusiastically and Yannick returned a wave with considerably less passion.

"Yes," said Mr. Cheeseman. "But we can't have you gaining any weight. Right now you're the only one small enough to sneak in through the duke's window and take back the White Gold Chalice."

That's what Mr. Cheeseman said, but what Teddy heard was, "You're the only one who can save us, Captain Fabulous. Without you and your gravy-stained sidekick, we don't stand a chance." This was the first time in his life that being small didn't seem like such a bad idea after all. He squared up his jaw and threw back his shoulders. "You can count on me," he said.

"I know," said Mr. Cheeseman, scruffing up Teddy's already scruffed-up hair.

The next order of business was to get ahold of the key to Ulrik's cell. This would be no simple task as Yannick wore it around his neck and, as far as anyone knew, never took it off. Jibby thought he had the perfect way to abscond with the key until Mr. Cheeseman reminded him that hitting a person in the head with a wooden mallet until he loses consciousness would be considered a form of violence.

"It's a bit of a gray area," said Jibby. "But let's not be picky."

"Wait a minute," said Ethan, eyeing Jibby's Swiss Army hand. "Didn't you say you could pick any lock with that hole punch of yours?"

"Oh yeah," said Jibby. "I did say that, didn't I?"

That night, as the castle slept, Big and Penny removed the floor-to-ceiling curtains from their window and Big used her knife to slice them into long strips. These strips would make the harness by which Captain Fabulous would be lowered over the wall to Wenzel's chamber window.

When they finished, they sneaked down the hall to the room shared by Dizzy and Aristotle and let themselves in. As seafaring men, they were well accomplished in the way of knot tying. So proficient were they that the construction of the harness took no more than twenty minutes. Digs followed closely behind as Big took the harness to the rooftop, where Sammy, Chip, Teddy, and Mr. Cheeseman were waiting. Penny, meanwhile, set out to retrieve Jibby and his lock-picking right hand.

"Are you sure this thing is safe?" asked Mr. Cheeseman, giving the harness a good tug to test its viability.

"If Dizzy and Ari made it, I'd bet my life on it," said Sammy.

"Okay," said Mr. Cheeseman. He was more than a little nervous about the idea of dangling his youngest child over the edge of a fifty-foot wall. "Ready?" Teddy nodded and climbed into the harness.

"Just don't look down," said Chip.

"Just don't drop me," said Teddy.

"Or me," said Gravy-Face Roy.

Sammy wrapped the ends of the curtain strands around his wrist and gave Mr. Cheeseman a nod.

"Remember," said Mr. Cheeseman to Teddy, "when you're even with the window, give us a thumbs-up." Teddy smiled and displayed a practice thumb. "Good. And if you get in any trouble just give two sharp tugs on the harness and we'll get you out of there."

Over the wall he went and Sammy lowered him slowly until Teddy displayed the agreed-upon signal. He was at window level, looking in at the sleeping impostor and the White Gold Chalice resting on a stand next to the bed. Gently and slowly, Teddy pushed the window inward.

Sammy continued to let out slack on the harness as Teddy squeezed through the tiny window and dropped quietly to the floor. He slinked across the room toward his polished prize while Wenzel mumbled and chuckled in his sleep. Perhaps, thought Teddy, he was dreaming about someone else being buried beneath millions of noodles.

Teddy gently lifted the White Gold Chalice from its perch and started back the way he came. As he began to squeeze through the window, the mumbling and chuckling abruptly stopped. Slowly, Teddy turned to see two eyes, one with a giant bushy eyebrow above it, staring straight at him.

In the dark, Wenzel could only make out the silhouette of a small, elflike figure. He sat up quickly. "Who are ja and vut dar ja vantun?" he demanded.

"Uh . . . Sandman," said Teddy. "Gotta go now. Pleasant dreams." Teddy gave two quick tugs on the harness and Wenzel watched as the Sandman flew away into the night. He prepared to go back to sleep when suddenly it occurred to him that there was no such thing as the Sandman. He scrambled from his bed and hobbled across the room on his broken foot. He stuck his big round head through the small square window and, looking up, saw Teddy being hoisted back toward the castle roof.

The moonlight struck the polished cup in Teddy's hand and made its way back to Wenzel's disbelieving eyes. He pulled his head back into the room and turned to find the White Gold Chalice gone. The guards outside the chamber door were snapped out of their bored stupor by Wenzel's scream and rushed into the room just as Teddy was pulled onto the roof. He displayed the cup proudly.

"I got it," he said as Sammy relieved him of the harness. "I got the White Gold Chalice."

"Nice," said Chip, offering Teddy a high five.

"Good work," said Mr. Cheeseman.

"Yes," said Teddy. "But Wenzel saw me. I told him I was the Sandman but I'm not sure if he believed me."

257

"The Sandman?" said Mr. Cheeseman. "We'd better get out of here."

While Dizzy and Aristotle stood watch at the trapdoor, Penny led the way down the dim corridor with Jibby, Jake, and Juanita right behind.

When they approached the cell, Ulrik had his puffy cheeks pressed to the bars as if he'd been standing there for hours, awaiting their arrival. "You came back," he said with surprise and relief.

"Of course I did," said Penny. "I told you I would. These are my friends Jibby, Juanita, and Jake."

"Yes, yes," said Ulrik impatiently. "That's all very nice. Now get me out of here. You did get the key, didn't you?"

"No need," said Jibby. He snapped out the hole punch on his Swiss Army hand. "I can pick any lock with this right here."

"So you didn't get the key then," said Ulrik. He threw up his hands and sighed. "Unbelievable."

Jibby looked at Penny and shook his head. "Is this guy for real?"

"Sorry," said Ulrik. "Just anxious to get out of here, that's all. I'm sure you understand."

Jibby knelt in front of the lock and went to work. Tension mounted as he probed, poked, and prodded its inner workings. A bead of sweat formed on his forehead and trickled down, making room for a fresh bead.

"I thought you said you could pick any lock with that thing," scoffed Ulrik.

Jibby stopped what he was doing and looked at Penny again. "You know, I think maybe I prefer the fake duke to this one."

"Wenzel is quite the host," said Penny.

"He sure knows how to throw a wingding," Jake agreed.

"All right, all right," said Ulrik. "I apologize. Now please continue."

Wenzel ordered the guards to search the castle, find the chalice, and place his once-honored guests under arrest. "Ja, Hertugen," they said.

They burst from the room and hurried down the hallway with Wenzel and his damaged foot struggling to keep up. They turned the corner and ran into Yannick, hurrying toward them in his nightgown. "What's going on?" he demanded in Danish.

When he heard the news he immediately uttered the Danish phrase for "I told you so." As it turns out, every language has one. He called for more guards and soon another dozen heavily armed men joined them. Yannick led them to the great hall, where they were shocked to see, standing at the far end, Penny, Jibby, Juanita, Three-Eyed Jake, Dizzy, Aristotle, and an exact replica of the Duke of Jutland. The guards looked at Ulrik, then back to Wenzel. "Hertugen?"

"How did you get out?" Yannick demanded. "I have the only key and it's right here." He displayed the key and Jibby countered by displaying his right hand, the hole punch still snapped in position.

"I can pick any lock with this thing," said Jibby. He turned and spoke directly and deliberately to Ulrik. "Any lock."

"Devious," said Yannick, his lips squeezed so tightly together they turned white.

"Isn't it, though," said Penny. "Using a phony version of the real thing. Something with which you should be very familiar."

Yannick turned to the guards and ordered them to arrest the impostor. The guards appeared confused, so he clarified his statement by pointing to Ulrik.

"This isn't the impostor," said Penny. She leveled a finger at Wenzel. "There. There's your impostor."

Now the guards were really at a loss. Except for the eyebrow, the two men looked identical and, no matter how much Yannick insisted that they arrest Ulrik, they could only stand there, dumbfounded.

"It should be quite an easy matter to resolve," said Ulrik. "For instance, everyone knows the real Duke of Jutland speaks perfect English."

"Ja," Wenzel agreed. "Der Hertugen shpekken prefect Engelsk."

And because the guards spoke limited English themselves, both renditions sounded acceptable to them. Again Yannick demanded they take Ulrik into custody. They moved his way but Ulrik raised his palm as if it were a powerful force field.

"Wait!" he said. "It is also a well-known fact that the real Duke of Jutland has a birthmark on his chest shaped like Portugal." Ulrik tore open his shirt, sending buttons bouncing off the stone floor and revealing a small birthmark on the left side of his blubbery chest that was indeed shaped like Portugal.

"I told you he was the real duke," said Penny.

"Arrest that man," shouted Ulrik with a sharp jab of his finger in Wenzel's direction.

The guards moved toward Wenzel and were about to seize him when he reached up and tore open his shirt. The guards stopped and gawked at the Portugal-shaped birthmark on Wenzel's chest, identical in shape, size, and location to Ulrik's. Even Yannick was surprised to see this.

"What?" said Ulrik, his frustration level reaching its limit. "All right, this is ridiculous."

"Ja," said Wenzel. "Das en ridunkulassen."

"Okay," said Ulrik. "It is also a well-known fact that the real Duke of Jutland is an excellent yodeler." He placed his hands on his hips and launched into a demonstration of some of the finest yodeling human ears had ever heard. When he was finished, he pointed sharply at Wenzel once again. "Seize this impostor!"

The guards moved in but Wenzel interrupted their advance with his own display of yodeling, some of the worst that two vocal cords had ever produced. This should have resulted in his immediate arrest except for one problem.

Everyone knows that it is virtually impossible to tell good yodeling from bad yodeling and so the guards just stood there, drowning in a sea of confusion.

"Enough!" shouted Yannick in Danish. "Listen, you idiots. If anyone would know the real duke it would be me, his personal valet, right? And that is the not the duke!"

The befuddled guards moved toward Ulrik when a powerful voice froze them in their tracks.

"Hold on here!" said Ethan Cheeseman, bursting into the room. Following him in and taking position at his side were Chip, Teddy, Sammy, and Big. Because Teddy had risked his life to retrieve the White Gold Chalice, he was allowed to hold it and was promised the chance to deliver it to the real Duke of Jutland. "We have traveled a great distance to return this cup to its rightful owner."

Teddy held up the shiny goblet for all to see.

"We all know it belongs to the Duke of Jutland," Mr. Cheeseman continued, pacing back and forth like a courtroom lawyer. "But there seems to be some confusion as to which of these two gentlemen fits that description. However, I believe there's a very simple way to settle this once and for all. Everyone knows that the real Duke of Jutland is named Ulrik. Isn't that right, Wenzel?"

"Ja," said Wenzel, with a big stupid grin, completely unaware that he had just given himself away. "Det er rite."

With a mere nod from Ulrik, the guards descended upon Wenzel and Yannick. "You're making a big mistake," shouted Yannick.

"Ja," said Wenzel. "You aven milk un baag mushtaken."

"I believe there's enough room in the cell for both of them," said Ulrik in Danish. "You'll find the key around his neck."

"No," said Yannick as the guards dragged him and his cousin away. "You can't put me in the dungeon."

"It's not a dungeon," Ulrik called out. "It's a basement." He turned his attention to Mr. Cheeseman. "Now, I believe you have something that belongs to me."

"I do," said Mr. Cheeseman. "Teddy? Would you like to present the duke with the chalice?"

"Okay," said Teddy. He raised the cup high above his head and threw it toward the duke. It spiraled through the air like a football. The group held its collective breath as the chalice seemed to hang in the air forever. This was it. The second the chalice reached the duke's outstretched hands, the curse would be over. For real this time. That is, if Ulrik truly was the cup's rightful owner as Jibby insisted. The duke smiled in anticipation and reached for the flying goblet, which passed right between his hands and clobbered him mercilessly on the forehead. He staggered back and the White Gold Chalice bounced across the marble floor with a heart-sickening *clang*.

"Don't worry," said Ulrik, nervously gathering himself. He scurried over to the chalice and picked it up. "I'm not cursed, I promise. Just clumsy, that's all."

"Are you sure about that?" said Jibby. "Because if it turns out you're not the real duke, I'll break your arm." Jibby caught Mr. Cheeseman's eye. "In a very nonviolent way, of course."

"I am the real duke, I swear it," said Ulrik.

"There's one way to find out," said Dizzy. Slowly and hesitantly, he slid the earmuffs off his head. He waited for the vertigo from which he had suffered for years to overtake him but it never came. He took a few steps and still felt nothing but perfect balance. He spun around twice, then performed a very impressive backflip, landing with the authority and equilibrium of a ballet dancer.

Cheers of triumph, joy, and relief rose up and filled the room. The pain in Sammy's back faded instantly and Aristotle found he could immediately answer the question "Why did I come in here?" Of course, some of their maladies were irreversible. Jibby was still missing his right hand and Three-Eyed Jake still had only one eye, but the important thing was that after years of pain and suffering the curse of the White Gold Chalice had finally been lifted.

Jibby called for his fiddle and an impromptu celebration broke out and lasted for several minutes—until the revelry abruptly stopped when Teddy said, "Hey, where's Pinky?"

It was true that Pinky was nowhere to be found. In fact, no one could remember having seen her for quite some time, and in all the excitement they had failed to take notice of her absence.

Mr. Cheeseman and the children ran to the courtyard but did not find her. From there they searched every room in the massive castle, including the basement, but failed to find any sign of their psychic hairless dog. Chip wondered if she had run away, her feelings hurt by being shushed so many times when all she was trying to do was warn her family of the many dangers that surrounded them.

Some might argue that Lassie was the biggest canine hero of all time but, while Lassie would run and get help after little Timmy had fallen down a well, Pinky would have warned little Timmy of the danger beforehand, thus averting the need for all those firefighters, paramedics, and network news helicopters.

Yes, Pinky was the world's most heroic dog, and they would not stop searching until they found her.

While Gateman snored peacefully just a few feet away, Professor Boxley could not persuade his brain to shut down. He'd been lying awake for hours in his bed at the inn, wondering. He wondered whether he'd be stuck here forever, a castaway in time. If so, he imagined what he might do to survive. Perhaps he would discover electricity, he thought. That should pay pretty well. After that, he would invent the lightbulb, the electric fan, radio, television, and the waffle iron. His thoughts then turned to waffles, slathered in melted butter and rich maple syrup. His stomach began to growl but was soon interrupted by a commotion out in the street. He rushed to the window and saw, beneath the full moon's glow, a large group of people walking about, all shouting the same thing. It was a name they were shouting and the name was Pinky. "Pinky! Pinky, where are you?" the people hollered into the night. A closer look confirmed it. One of the shouting people was Ethan Cheeseman.

"It's him," the professor said to his sleeping roommate. "Come on, let's go!" The professor jumped into his pants, stepped into his shoes, and ran out the door by the time Gateman could lift his groggy head from the cornhusk-filled pillow.

"Wait up," said Gateman.

While the people in the street continued their calls for Pinky, another name rang out in the cool night air.

"Ethan! Ethan Cheeseman!"

At first, Mr. Cheeseman wasn't sure if he should believe his own ears. His name was being shouted by an unfamiliar voice in Jutland, Denmark, in the year 1668. He spun toward the strange voice to find a pudgy man in a white wig rushing his way with something that appeared to be the barrel of a gun pointed toward him.

"Dad, look out!" cried Penny.

The man closed in and Mr. Cheeseman, without thinking, drew his fist back and punched him squarely in the chin, knocking him to the cobblestone street and sending his wig flying. The man also dropped what he was holding, which turned out to be not a gun but a rolled-up magazine featuring a photo of a young Ethan Cheeseman accepting his prestigious Scientist of Tomorrow award.

Jibby and his crew quickly appeared at Mr. Cheeseman's side. "Nice punch," said Jibby with an atta-boy pat on the back. "For a pacifist."

"Ahhh," screamed Mr. Cheeseman, who had just discovered another good reason not to punch people. It really hurts.

"Who are you?" Chip demanded of the man. "What do you want?"

"This is your friend," said Big. "The one I told you about." She picked up the magazine and handed it to Chip. "And here is the painting."

"Yes," said the professor, rubbing his jaw. "I'm an old friend of your father's. Or at least I thought I was."

The voice was now familiar to Mr. Cheeseman, and when the pain in his hand subsided to the point that he could open his eyes, he was shocked at what he saw. "Professor Boxley?"

"In the flesh," said the professor, pushing himself to a sitting position. "I'm flattered you still recognize me. After all, it's been over thirty years."

"I'm sorry," said Mr. Cheeseman. "I'm sorry I hit you. I thought you were attacking me." He extended his non-punching hand and helped the professor to his feet. "I don't understand. What are you doing here?"

"What am I doing here?" said the professor. "Why, I came here to rescue you, of course."

The professor dusted himself off while Digs took to attacking his defenseless wig. "Let me get a good look at you, Ethan my boy. Best student I ever had, right here. Absolutely remarkable. It was with your theories and formulas that I was able to build a time machine nearly identical to yours and travel here from the future. I trust you'll find my LVR-ZX quite impressive. It's only a couple of miles from here."

If there had been any doubt in Big's mind that her new friends were from the future, it was laid to rest with all this talk of time machines and rescue missions from the land of tomorrow. "So then, it is true," she said.

"It is," said Chip.

"Wait a minute," said Teddy. "If you came here from the future, how did you know we needed to be rescued?"

Professor Boxley spoke as if the answer was quite obvious. "Because you never came back."

"But that's not logical," said Chip. "I mean, it makes no sense at all."

"I agree that it makes no sense," said the professor. "But I assure you, it's perfectly logical." Chip and Penny looked to their father.

"Professor Boxley is right," said Mr. Cheeseman. "Logic and sense are two different things."

"I don't get it," said Chip.

"Well," said Mr. Cheeseman. "If you've never played the piano before, it will make no sense to you whatsoever. But it's still absolutely logical."

"Please stop, you're hurting my brain," came a voice from the shadows. All eyes turned to see a slim silhouette of a man stepping out of the shadows and into the moonlight. Gateman's toupee and graying goatee served their purpose. Mr. Cheeseman and his children had no idea who this person was or why he was pointing a gun in their direction.

"Gateman!" said Professor Boxley. "What are you doing? Put that thing down this instant!"

"You know this man?" asked Mr. Cheeseman.

"His name is Gateman Nametag. He's my assistant."

"*Was* your assistant," said Gateman, eyeing up his future victims. "I've decided to take a little leave of absence to do some things I've always wanted to do. Like take a pottery class, record a Christmas album, and . . . get revenge." With his free hand, he reached up and peeled back his toupee. In doing so, his sleeve slid back just far enough to reveal that awful tattoo, the one that read *3VAW1X319* and, when viewed in a mirror, read Plexiwave, the evil corporation that manufactured weapons and microwave ovens and would do anything to get its hands on the LVR.

"It's Mr. 5," said Chip.

"No longer with the company," said Gateman, tossing the toupee aside. "But you may call me Mr. 5 if you like. Anything to make the last moments of your miserable lives more enjoyable."

"You killed our mother," snapped Teddy. "You should be in jail."

"That's right," echoed Gravy-Face Roy.

"Oh, I was in jail," said Gateman calmly. "Didn't like it very much. Did you know they make you share a cell with someone? Absolutely barbaric."

"I knew it," said Professor Boxley. "I knew you were no good."

Gateman responded by pointing the gun in Professor Boxley's direction. "You really should be nicer to me," he said. "After all, you're the only one here who will leave this place alive. You see, I'm currently in need of your services. But once I've done away with everyone else and once you've shown me how to work that little time machine of yours, you're fired. And make no mistake. It had better work this time. Or else." He made a gunshot sound with his mouth.

"You're makin' a big mistake here, lad," said Jibby, inching closer to Gateman. Like a boxer throwing a sharp left jab, Gateman's arm shot straight out until the gun was level with Jibby's head. Jibby raised his hands and inched backward. "Take it easy there. I'm sure we can work this out to everyone's satisfaction."

"I've no doubt of that," said Gateman, his finger tightening around the trigger that he was just about to pull when he heard a growl most vicious. He spun in its direction to see a very hairless and very angry dog charging toward him with ears back and teeth glistening in the moonlight. Pinky took to the air, leaping five times her height, flinging herself with enough force that when her paws collided with Gateman's chest, he stumbled backward and fell to the ground.

"Get him, Pinky!" Teddy shouted and watched as Pinky and Gateman rolled and tumbled in a great snarly mess toward the edge of the cliff until both man and beast fell off its edge, leaving behind an eerie stillness and a cloud of dust, the kind of which Gateman had been so fond.

For a moment, no one dared to move or to speak. "Pinky!" yelled Penny, dashing to the dropoff. She peered over into the darkness below. There was no sign of either Gateman or their beloved pet.

"She's gone," said Penny. The others rushed to her side and joined her in staring at the nothingness beneath them.

"No, she can't be gone," sniffed Teddy.

Digs sniffed too. Then sniffed again. It seemed as though he smelled something. Something that human nostrils could not.

Mr. Cheeseman dropped to his belly and hung his head over the edge of the cliff, squinting into the blackness. "It's too dark," he said. "I can't see a thing."

"Try this," said Teddy, handing the cell phone to his father.

"Yes," said Mr. Cheeseman. "Excellent idea." He popped it open and lowered his arm as far as he could over the cliff's edge. Back and forth, he scanned the area where Pinky and Gateman had gone over the edge. Finally, he saw something. It was a tiny ledge, far too small to hold a murderous corporate villain but just large enough to accommodate a hairless fox terrier. The light from the phone hit Pinky's eyes and they reflected back an eerie blue glow.

"Grab my feet," said Mr. Cheeseman. "And lower me down."

Dutifully, Dizzy and Jake each took an ankle and Sammy and Aristotle held on to them for added support. Together, the four men carefully lowered Mr. Cheeseman over the edge of the cliff. A moment later, he shouted out an okay and Jibby's men pulled him back up, dragging him a few extra feet away from the side of the cliff for safety. Mr. Cheeseman sat up. Cradled in his arms was Pinky, unharmed and happily licking his face.

The children ran to her to deliver hugs of joy and due praise for saving the family once again. Digs gave Pinky a look that seemed to say, "Not bad. Not bad at all."

271

"Well, I'm certainly glad your dog's okay," said Professor Boxley. "But I feel absolutely terrible about my assistant. Terrible, that is, that I brought him to you, the very man who killed your mother."

"It's okay," said Penny. "You didn't know."

"But I should have," said Professor Boxley. "I was so sad when I learned of your mother's passing. She was a good woman. Beautiful and smart as a whip."

"Thanks," said Chip. "It'll be all right. We're going to go back to just before she was poisoned to save her life."

The professor sighed and looked to the ground. He shuffled his feet and appeared generally uncomfortable.

"What? What is it?" asked Penny.

"There's . . . a problem, I'm afraid," said the professor. "A problem with the science."

"What kind of problem?" asked Mr. Cheeseman, though he was not sure he really wanted to know the answer.

"I'm not certain," said Professor Boxley, "but it appears that the Time Arc may be a one-way street."

CHAPTER 20

By daybreak, a thick layer of clouds had rolled in and the low gray ceiling was a perfect match for the mood of the group that, only hours before, had been in such a celebratory frame of mind. So much had changed since that moment when the curse was ended, when, for once, the tide seemed to be turning their way. Now Mr. Cheeseman and his children had been advised by Professor Boxley that their plan to move forward along the Time Arc might very well be a mathematical impossibility, leaving them stranded forever in the late seventeenth century.

They gathered in the great hall of the castle where Ulrik had summoned them, not for a wingding but for a simple thank you before they set out. For their role in ending the curse and restoring him to his throne, Ulrik determined that each of them was worthy of a handsome reward. And though he may have been the rightful owner of the White Gold Chalice and the true Duke of Jutland, this did not preclude him from being incredibly cheap, as the reward amounted to nothing more than a few measly coins each.

"Good luck to you all," he said with a regal wave of his hand. "I remain forever in your debt."

"You sure do," mumbled Aristotle at the sight of his paltry prize.

"All right," said Jibby. "Let's move out now."

And so off they went, Jibby and his crew, Mr. Cheeseman and his family, Big, Digs, and Professor Boxley, marching out of town and toward the forest, to the resting place of the one-way time machine known as the LVR-ZX.

For Chip, the situation seemed especially dire. Under the worst-case scenario he and his family would be forever stuck in the past and would never again see their mother alive. However, if his genius father could somehow outsmart science itself, it very well could mean saying good-bye to Big forever. Unless he could convince her to come along. After all, she did say she would like to see the future, but did she really mean it? And even if she really wanted to go, would his father allow her to join them?

Chip stole a glance at Big and wondered if she was entertaining the very same thoughts. But like the rest of the group, neither of them said a word as they ventured deeper and deeper into the increasingly dense forest.

Nearly invisible with its reflective outer shell, Professor Boxley's time machine sat right where he had left it, and this time he was lucky not to have parked it on a giant anthill.

"Wow," said Mr. Cheeseman at the sight of her. "She's a beauty all right."

"I like the LVR better," Teddy huffed.

"That's rude," said Penny.

"It's also true," said Gravy-Face Roy, preparing for a flick on the head that never came.

"The two machines are identical, technologically speaking," said the professor. He gave it an affectionate pat, as if the LVR-ZX were a golden retriever. "I've just added a few upgrades here and there for speed and comfort. And if you think it looks good from here, come check out the inside." The professor keyed in the code and opened the pod door. "After you," he said to Mr. Cheeseman.

The interior of the LVR-ZX was a luxury version of the LVR, with reclining leather seats and a faux walnut control panel, which Mr. Cheeseman scrutinized carefully, finding that the professor was right. Technologically speaking, the LVR and the LVR-ZX were identical. It therefore stood to reason that if the LVR-ZX could not be made to go forward in time, then neither could his prototype, the LVR.

"Okay," said Mr. Cheeseman. "Let's give it a try."

He and the professor agreed to a test run. While the others waited outside, the two scientists would set the controls for five minutes into the future and hope for the best.

"Stand back, everybody," said Mr. Cheeseman. "And face the other way. The light can be pretty intense and we certainly don't want to blind anyone."

Mr. Cheeseman waited until everyone was facing in the opposite direction. The last to turn was Chip. "You can do it, Dad."

"Thanks, Chip."

Mr. Cheeseman closed the door and the professor lit up the engines, which lit up the surrounding forest with a bright turquoise light. Mr. Cheeseman entered the necessary coordinates, factoring in things like gravitational pull and the Earth's rotation. He threw the switch and the engines whirred and whined but the chronometer failed to budge. He took a deep breath and tried again with the exact same disappointing result.

Mr. Cheeseman leaned on the control panel, his chin to his chest. He knew exactly what he wanted to say but it took a moment for the words to find their way through his tightly clamped lips. "Well, it looks as though you were right, Professor," he said. "And now that I think about it, it makes perfect sense."

The pod door opened and out stepped the professor and his one-time student. Teddy was the first to turn around. "Well? Did it work?" he asked excitedly. "Is it five minutes from now?"

"I'm afraid not," said Mr. Cheeseman. "It appears the professor was right. The Time Arc is a one-way street."

So devastating was this news to the children that they felt as though they might pass out at the sound of it. "I don't understand it," said Penny, her voice cracking with frustration. "Jibby and his crew traveled forward through time."

"That's right," Jibby offered.

"Not along the Time Arc, they didn't," said Mr. Cheeseman, barely hiding his irritation. "Electromagnetic kinesis is unpredictable and entirely uncontrollable. A lightning strike is far more likely to kill you than to transport you through time." Mr. Cheeseman then decided he was not irritated. He was angry. Angry with himself. He threw a frustrated punch at the air, which he found to be a lot less painful than throwing one at someone's chin. "Stupid!" he said. "I should have considered this before I put you all at risk."

"It's okay, Dad," said Penny. "It was worth the risk."

"It's not okay," said Mr. Cheeseman. "To overlook something like this is entirely unacceptable. I'm a scientist and I ignored basic science."

"So then . . . we are stuck here forever," said Teddy.

"Probably," said Mr. Cheeseman. The children just stared at their father. Never before had they seen him so defeated, so utterly at a loss for an answer. Then he got that look. It was immediately recognizable. It was the look that came over him whenever he was about to announce an ingenious new plan. "Probably," he repeated, "but not necessarily."

If this statement was meant to cause widespread confusion throughout the group, mission accomplished. "I don't get it," said Penny. "You said Professor Boxley was right. The Time Arc is a one-way street."

"Exactly," said Mr. Cheeseman. "It may be a one-way street but perhaps not a dead-end street. I once knew a brilliant scientist who proposed a very interesting theory about time. This scientist suggested that time is an ever-expanding circle, and if you were to travel into the past, eventually you would reach the Great Sync, the place where the beginning of time meets the end of time." Mr. Cheeseman demonstrated by making a circle with his hands. "And if you managed to get past this connector of *then* and *when* without being burned alive, you would find yourself in the future, traveling backward through time."

"Incredible," said Professor Boxley. "And which scientist is the author of this fascinating theory?"

"I know who it is," said Penny, the words fighting their way around the lump in her throat. "It's Olivia Cheeseman."

"That's right," said Mr. Cheeseman. "Your mother is the brilliant scientist who came up with that theory."

"That's what she meant," said Penny. "That's what she meant when she said 'Round and round it never ends, north is south then north again.'"

"I think you're right," said Mr. Cheeseman. "The Earth was once thought to be flat and sailors feared that if they ventured too far, they would fall off its edge."

"The world's not flat?" said Dizzy. This earned him one of Captain Jibby's patented slaps across the back of his head.

"It's quite round," said Mr. Cheeseman. "Therefore if you travel due north long enough, eventually you'll find yourself at the North Pole. From there, any step you take is south. The Great Sync could be thought of as the North Pole of time travel."

"Will Santa be at the big sink?" asked Teddy.

"Perhaps," said Mr. Cheeseman. "No one's ever been there, so there's no telling what it's like."

"Let me get this straight," said Chip. "Are you saying we can still get home?"

"I don't know," said Mr. Cheeseman. "It's a very good theory, but a theory is all it is. If we try it, there's the very real possibility that we could find ourselves falling off the edge of time. And that's just one of the many dangers. In fact, the risks are so great and so numerous that I'm going to leave the decision to you kids. With my knowledge of science, we could probably make a pretty good life for ourselves right here in 1668."

"We could invent television," the professor chimed in. "And the waffle iron."

"But we'd never see Mom again," said Chip.

"Yes," said Mr. Cheeseman. "That's right. We would never see your mother again."

"Then the decision is easy," said Penny. "We go."

"Yes," agreed Chip. "We have to go."

"Let's do it," said Teddy.

"*Vámonos*," said Gravy-Face Roy.

And so it was decided. Ethan Cheeseman, along with his three smart, polite, attractive, and relatively odor-free children, their hairless psychic dog Pinky, a sock puppet named Gravy-Face Roy, and a scientist from the future named Professor Acorn Boxley would attempt to do what no one ever had before. They would sail backward through time until they found themselves in the future once again. Or at least they would try.

But before they could do that, there was some business to take care of. You might think with the number of times they'd had to say good-bye to Jibby and his crew that it would get easier, but this was the toughest one yet, especially for Jibby and Juanita, who secretly feared their direct descendants may be on their way to an untimely death.

"Don't you worry," said Jibby to Mr. Cheeseman. "If my great-great-great-great-granddaughter Olivia said it's so, I believe it."

Mr. Cheeseman nodded, not entirely sure. Aristotle stepped forward, a new clarity in his eyes. "The end of the curse has restored my psychic abilities," he said. "I see good things for you, Ethan. Very good things."

"Thanks, Aristotle."

Though he had the strength of two and a half men, Sammy hugged Penny with the strength of only one. Three-Eyed Jake knelt down and scruffed up Teddy's hair and Teddy scruffed up Jake's in return. Big and Digs took turns chasing each other around the LVR-ZX. Chip turned to Big, who had said nothing for a very long time.

"So," he began. And that's as far as he got.

"I've decided," said Big. "I've decided that I would like to go with you. I would like to see the future."

Chip sighed heavily. "I would love for you to come with us," he said. "But I can't let you."

"I don't understand," said Big.

"I'm sorry, but it's just too dangerous. You heard what my dad said. There's a very good chance we won't make it, that we'll fall off the edge of time and be burned to a crisp. But we have to try, because it's the only way to save our mother's life."

Big wasn't quite sure whether she felt hurt or angry. She decided that what she felt was a combination of both. "I see," she said.

"But listen," said Chip. "If we do make it . . . if everything works out, I'll come back for you, I promise."

Big shook her head, flinging tears from her eyes. "No."

"No?"

"No. Because if you don't come back, I'll know that something horrible happened to you. So tell me right now that you'll never come back. That way I can imagine the best for you, as I've been able to with my father these past three years. Tell me, Chip. Tell me you'll never come back."

Chip looked at the ground, then back at Big.

"Tell me."

"I'll never . . ." Chip's throat constricted and choked off the flow of words. He took a deep breath and tried again. A whisper was all he could manage. "I'll never come back," he lied.

Big pulled the baseball cap from her head and handed it to Chip. "Here. You'll need this when you pitch in the World Serious."

Chip took the hat, inscribed with a white letter *P* for Pals, and placed it back on Big's head. "I'll get a new one. Besides, it looks a lot better on you."

Big threw her arms around Chip and squeezed tightly. Chip squeezed back. He knew this could very well be the last time he would ever see Big. Slowly, he moved his face closer to hers and kissed her lightly on the lips. She pulled away and, for a brief moment, Chip's fiercely beating heart sank like a stone. But the moment was brief indeed as Big set her own fears aside and kissed Chip back.

Mr. Cheeseman watched and smiled and remembered the first time he had kissed Olivia. He felt both happy and sad for his eldest child. Teddy and Gravy-Face Roy pushed their way between Chip and Big and hugged her around the waist. After all, she wasn't just Chip's pal, she was theirs too. Penny hugged Big from the side and Mr. Cheeseman wrapped his arms around the whole group.

"Okay," he said finally. "If we're going to do this, we should probably do it now. Before we change our minds."

Chip took a deep breath and, with one final kiss, separated himself from Big, which, if you can imagine, felt a bit like separating himself from his right arm.

Pinky gave Digs one last affectionate nudge and Mr. Cheeseman reminded Big and the others to make sure they kept their backs to the LVR-ZX once the engines kicked in. Then he guided Pinky and his children toward the time machine, allowing them each one last wave, or, in Chip's case, one last sad smile. "I'll never forget you, Big."

Big said nothing. She bit her lower lip and watched through watery eyes as the boy she knew as Chip Krypton walked out of her life and into the LVR-ZX.

Inside the time machine, Mr. Cheeseman made sure that Chip, Penny, Teddy, and Pinky were firmly buckled. Then he told his children he loved them, hoping it would not be the last time. He took the pilot's chair and Professor Boxley took the copilot's. He plugged some numbers into the machine's computer, setting their destination for two days before Olivia had been murdered. He took a deep breath and then another.

Penny took hold of her little brother's hand and squeezed. "Are we going to die?" he asked.

"Round and round, it never ends," said Penny with a soft smile. "No, Teddy. We're not going to die."

"I believe you," said Teddy.

"Me too," said Chip.

Gravy-Face Roy said nothing.

"Hold tight, everyone," said Mr. Cheeseman. "Here we go." He placed his hands on the controls and hit the ignition switch. The engines fired, coating the trees outside in a blue-green glow.

Captain Jibby and his crew turned and covered their eyes. Big did not turn. She just stood, staring at the device that was about to take Chip away from her forever.

283

Juanita draped a friendly arm across her shoulders and turned her away from the hypnotic glow of the time machine.

A second later, with a *whoosh* and a flash of brilliant white light, the LVR-ZX was gone.

CHAPTER 21

If you can imagine traveling at several times the speed of light in a train with no windows, never knowing if, at any moment, you might plow into the side of a mountain and burst into flames, then you have some idea as to how Mr. Cheeseman and his passengers felt as they raced along, farther and farther into the past, closer and closer to the beginning of time and, perhaps, to the end of their lives.

The numbers of the chronometer changed so rapidly, it was nearly impossible for Professor Boxley to make out any specific dates as the speedy LVR-ZX covered thousands of years in mere seconds and millions in minutes. "Six hundred thousand BCE," he announced. Then a few moments later, "Eighty million."

As quickly as they moved along the Time Arc, Mr. Cheeseman knew it could be hours before they reached the Great Sync, if such a thing even existed. After all, the Earth was generally thought to be over four billion years old, so they would have to travel at least that far.

Of course, if Olivia's theory proved to be wrong, they

might find themselves tumbling off the edge of time into a fiery abyss, or simply gliding along indefinitely until their oxygen supply ran out. The whole thing reminded Chip of a story he had once read about a mountain climber who fell into a crevasse a hundred feet below, breaking his leg in the process. With no chance of climbing up and out of the icy chasm, the man decided his only chance of survival was to climb down, farther and farther into the pitch black, in hopes that he might find another way out. That the man survived to tell his story gave Chip hope that they, too, would end up where they wanted to be by defying logic and traveling in the completely opposite direction.

Nearly an hour had passed since takeoff and nearly all the blood had been squeezed from Penny's hand by Teddy's forceful grip when the professor shouted, "Three-point-five billion BCE."

In the next few moments, the smooth, quiet ride became both less smooth and less quiet. The walls began to rattle, lightly at first, then increasing in intensity, growing more and more violent with the passing of each minute and with every millennium.

"Four billion BCE."

The noise reached a thunderous volume and sounded as though a hundred cave cops were outside, pounding on the LVR-ZX with billy clubs.

"Four-point-five billion."

With the sudden screeching of a freight train locking up its brakes, the time machine rotated sharply to the left, then back to the right, then to the left once more. Finally, Mr. Cheeseman could control its movements no longer and the LVR-ZX went into a barrel roll, spinning at a dizzying rate.

The professor was the first to lose consciousness and the others soon joined him in passing out from the centrifugal force that threatened to scramble the very brains in their skulls. None of them would see what happened next. Up to that point, the numbers on the chronometer had come in logical succession. But suddenly, they made no sense whatsoever. Four-point-five billion was followed by 1779, which was followed by 164 million BCE. From there the date jumped to 1207, then to 3518, then back to 4207 BCE, and so on. Date after date popped up in random order until finally the readout went completely blank as the LVR-ZX came to an abrupt and silent halt.

Mr. Cheeseman had been the last to black out and was now the first to come to. Slowly, the others' brains began settling back into place, and they opened their eyes to find the LVR-ZX motionless, leaning slightly to one side.

"Is everyone okay back there?" asked Mr. Cheeseman, turning in his seat to check on his children.

"I'm dizzy," said Teddy.

"What happened?" asked Chip, using a couple of hard blinks to refocus his eyes. "Where are we?"

"And when are we?" asked Gravy-Face Roy.

Professor Boxley leaned forward and checked the chronometer. "I don't know," he said. "The entire control panel's gone out. Not only do I not know where or when we are, I've no way to check the atmospheric conditions outside. Opening the pod door could be suicide."

"It's not as though we have a choice," said Mr. Cheeseman. He unbuckled his safety belt, and the children did likewise. He moved to the door and slowly gripped the handle. "Okay." He took in a deep breath and expelled it forcefully, like a child blowing out birthday candles. "Everybody ready?"

"Like you said," Penny remarked. "We don't have much of a choice."

Mr. Cheeseman looked to Pinky. "Well?" But Pinky did not growl. Just because she sensed no danger, however, didn't necessarily mean that none existed. Mr. Cheeseman pushed the handle down and took one last pause before pulling the door inward. Light, oxygen, and the smells of dry grass and wildflowers poured in.

Mr. Cheeseman and his passengers stepped out of the LVR-ZX to find that the highly reflective, oblong time machine sat in the middle of a large, empty field, bathed in a soothing, midday sun. They turned and looked in every direction, hoping for some sign of where and when they might be.

"I don't see anything," said Teddy. "No buildings. No people. No anything." Teddy was right. There was nothing they could see to suggest where they might be and there was certainly nothing to indicate they had made it back to the twenty-first century.

"What do you think, Dad?" asked Chip. "Is this the beginning of time?"

"Or the end," said Professor Boxley.

"Or somewhere in between," said Penny.

Before Mr. Cheeseman could venture a guess, a faint noise rose up in the distance.

"Wait," said Teddy. "Listen. Thunder."

"No," said Chip, certain it was not thunder and just as certain that it was a sound he had heard before. "It's not thunder. It's . . ."

"Look!" shouted Penny, jabbing her finger toward the sky, sending all eyes upward. "It's an airplane!"

"It's a 737," said Chip. "That can only mean one thing. We made it! We're back!"

For reasons he could not explain, the sight of the plane made Mr. Cheeseman laugh. He laughed and laughed and could not stop as the tension poured from his body with every giggle and guffaw. His joy and relief were contagious and soon the entire group was laughing hysterically at the sight of that beautiful metal bird rumbling across the sky.

"She was right," said Penny when the laughter finally tapered off.

"Yes," said Ethan, fighting to catch his breath. "She was right."

"So what do we do now?" asked Chip.

"We find her and tell her," said Mr. Cheeseman with another hearty laugh. Professor Boxley watched with joy and envy as Mr. Cheeseman's children practically knocked him over with the force of their hugs.

"Which way do we go?" asked Teddy.

"I don't know," said Mr. Cheeseman. "But whichever way we decide, I feel like running."

"Me too," said Penny.

"Yeah," said Chip.

"Let's do it," said Teddy.

"Professor?" asked Mr. Cheeseman.

"Sounds good to me," said Professor Boxley with a smile.

And with that, Mr. Cheeseman bolted across the field with his children close behind, and his one-time mentor slightly farther behind, on their way to save the life of the brilliant scientist known as Olivia Cheeseman.

But that, my friends, is a whole nother story.